FORBIDDEN LOVE

She glanced at the window and then at Nicholas. Startled, she found his face close to hers. She was aware of the heavy, betraying pulse beat in her throat and then of nothing but the shadow of his face, his mouth upon hers. His lips were hard, ruthless, like no other touch she had known in her protected life. A man who would have his way, and whose strength she had always sought without being aware of it.

Her recent fright accentuated the excitement of this moment. When he let her go, they were both breathless, and for an instant she was dazed. He caught her arms, saying huskily, "How I hated you once!"

Careen

VIRGINIA COFFMAN

A DELL BOOK

Published by
Dell Publishing Co., Inc.
1 Dag Hammarskjold Plaza
New York, New York 10017

Dell ® TM 681510, Dell Publishing Co., Inc.

ISBN: 0-440-18110-0

Printed in the United States of America
First printing—November 1977

For Robin Daniel Skynner,
friend and future great

CHAPTER ONE

The rain stopped briefly in the afternoon, just before Beth Milford reached the Galway coast in her hired pony cart. Although she had a passionate aversion to showing the white feather, she found the view at this point more scenic than safe.

If I had this animal's good sense, I should be the better for it, she thought as the cart came to a halt and the skittish animal began backing away along the sheep track which crowned the coastal cliffs.

"Here, boy! These are your cliffs. You know them better than I. Do get on."

Much good her coaxing accomplished! She decided she simply didn't know ponies, and stood up in the cart to get a better look at this forbidding path bounded by the cliff's edge on the left and a pretty green bog on the right, spreading its tentacles inland to the eastern hills.

Actually, the wild Atlantic cliffs appeared very like the Cornish coast which she often visited in order to appreciate more fully the return to Milford Hall, her own spacious home in Somerset.

At the age of twenty-seven she considered herself unlikely ever to marry, since her admirers, many of them just back from Brussels and Waterloo, must be motivated at least in part by her comfortable inheritance. Now that neither parent nor a companion with the vapors was present to remind her of propriety, she could afford to indulge a few odd humors. Among her current humors was the visit, entirely unescorted, to her Cousin Arabella's orphaned daughter in the west of Ireland.

"The only unselfish thing I have done in years," she had admitted to Cousin Arabella's solicitor, Aeneas Murgatroyd, Junior, in Bristol.

"I am persuaded you are wrong, Miss Beth. Anyone as lovely as you, if I may say so, could never be other than generous."

She had dismissed this tribute with her charming smile and the cynical thought that any presentable female was lovely when she had an income of eight thousand pounds a year.

"Careen is my heiress. Her mother, my Cousin Arabella, and I spent several years growing up at a young ladies' academy near Bath."

He murmured, "But this child's mother was your senior, of course. Anyone would guess by the look of you."

She had been annoyed at the deliberate effort to flatter her. "My Cousin Arabella had been at the academy three years before I came, but somehow she always seemed younger. Now, her daughter Careen is of an age when I think we should become acquainted before we decide on the school for her."

"You see, Miss Beth, you cannot conceal your tender heart. I am persuaded you loved your Cousin Arabella as a sister."

She had wrinkled her nose at that. "Very often I detested her! But we had our good times together, I confess." She hated having noble motives assigned to an act of penance. Her addled, empty-headed Cousin Arabella had thought of nothing but her own comfort and pleasure and would go to shocking lengths to gain anything she wanted, including the attentions of the young gentlemen at the elegant Pump Room in Bath, or during the infrequent dancing at the Assembly Rooms which the girls had attended properly chaperoned.

When, after returning to Ireland reluctantly, Arabella surprised everyone by marrying a respectable young Irish landowner named Faversham, Beth had sent an expensive present and trusted the newly knighted bridegroom would keep his volatile Arabella happy. Careen was born within the year and it seemed to all who had known Arabella that she must be content. As Lady Faversham, she now carried a title which delighted her on those rare occasions when she and Beth met. To this was later added her husband's governorship, but always these joys carried her farther from the child, Careen, almost forgotten in her grandmother's gloomy house on the west coast of Ireland.

Beth had thought very little about the child growing into girlhood without her parents. Then came the trip to Australia, the governor's death, and Arabella's startling remarriage in the Antipodes. In a shockingly short time her death occurred.

Murgatroyd, Junior, shook a bony finger at Beth coyly.

"Now, Miss Beth, if you detested the late Lady Faversham, why would you have made her child your heir?"

"That was my father's last request to me. He was quite taken with her on one occasion when he visited our school. If I did not marry, he said . . . Well, at all events, young Careen is now my only relative, and her grandmother is dying." She shrugged, rushed on in the effort to avoid sentiment. "I must go to her. There is no one else."

"You may deny, young lady, but we know your good—"

She laughed. "Think what you like." She extended her hand, and when he had bowed over it, she put up her vivid blue parasol and left, stepping briskly as usual. She was amused to hear Murgatroyd, Senior, who was hard of hearing, remark to Junior:

"Demmed fine gel there, for a daughter of Old Milford. Never thought that leggy little redheaded creature would turn out so well."

So here she was, asking considerably more sense of a hired pony than she had used herself in making the last leg of her journey alone in a country of which she knew nothing. The animal appeared to know quite well what he was about. He had decided to retreat. He began to circle, dragging the cart and nearly pitching her out over the abrupt edge into space. She caught a glimpse of wild Atlantic combers roaring against the cliff a great distance below. Then she recovered her balance, caught the lines again, and shouted her father's favorite oath, "Gad's life! Forward, boy!"

General Milford himself could not have done better. The pony leaped to order, trotted around facing the north again, and started off. Pebbles rattled under his hooves, spun over the cliff's edge. She wondered how long it would take for the pebbles to reach the waves far below. There were pools of water in the rocky ground of the trail ahead, and the pony managed to wade through each of them, sending little showers up in Beth Milford's face.

She had just brushed vagrant drops off her travel

cloak and her practical green bonnet when the sea wind swept across the path and began to lash at her with stinging force.

What a miserable climate Arabella had chosen in which to settle her daughter! It was more like incarceration.

In one of those dazzling surprises of which primitive landscapes are capable, the cliffs ended abruptly. Looking over the edge as the sheep trail turned and began to descend, Beth saw a stream far below, meandering toward a narrow beach of shingle from across boggy lowlands and the distant hills.

At the far side of the stream, almost encroaching on the beach, were a dozen whitewashed coteens. The local village of Saltbridge, obviously. It looked desolate on this November day, but she imagined the place might have its own charm in summer, when there was some human activity in the muddy path outside the cottages. Still, it seemed a ghastly place for a genteel young lady like Careen Faversham.

"It is time someone looked out after the girl," Beth reminded herself.

The trail slanted steeply down the cliff's face and the pony obeyed her hand on the lines, but he was clearly-reluctant, and it took all her persuasion to get him down to the oceanside and the stone bridge that arched over the stream. It was a small, sturdy bridge of considerable age, and undoubtedly gave its name to the village.

Beth reached for the letter in her reticule and consulted her instructions from the girl's grandmother, Lady Hagar Faversham:

I assume your coachman will cross the bridge at the village. As a local man, and I strongly advise you to employ one of the local lads from Ballyglen, he will be familiar with the bridge. You will then cross our tiny Saltbridge Vale, and continue north along the shore. Almost immediately, you will see on the near horizon the remains of Faversham Tower, built to defend the family against the Ferocious Natives. From what I have heard of you, I don't suppose they will intimidate you.

I do not often plead my condition, but I want to see my Careen cared for before I go. Her mother was always a flibbertigibbety. And never more so than when she married that frightful convict in the Antipodes an indecently short time after the death of my son.

I trust I do not ruffle your sensibilities when I tell you she deserved to die in that lamentable shipwreck. A pity the convict did not drown with her.

Your obedient servant,

Hagar Faversham

A woman of spirit, Beth decided, and could not dislike her for her frankness. Apparently, Hagar Faversham expected Beth to know that the "remains of Faversham Tower" was the residence of the lady and her granddaughter.

She had signaled the pony to enter upon the bridge when she heard a horse's hooves picking their way down the cliffside behind her. The rider was moving at a steady, moderate pace, but the bridge seemed narrow and the pony too skittish, so she pulled back on the lines and waited for the rider to pass her.

Meanwhile, a woman in black homespun, with a red

shawl over her head, came out of one of the white-washed coteens, threw a tub of slop out to a couple of pigs who grunted contentedly at their meal in the middle of the muddy path. Seeing both Beth and the rider behind her, the woman stared at them briefly, then dragged the empty tub back inside and slammed the door.

A specimen of Ferocious Native? Beth laughed silently and glanced back, half-expecting the same cold, incurious look from the rider. He was a big, ruddy man. She decided some would have called him handsome, especially as now, when he gave her the first friendly grin she had seen since leaving Ballyglen several hours earlier.

He leaned toward her from the lofty height of his white stallion. "Good evening, ma'am. I'll lay fifty guineas you are the long-awaited Miss Milford. May I presume to welcome you to Saltbridge? Not but what the native population has already showed you a warm face."

Warm face indeed! She was amused, thanked him for his graciousness, and admitted her identity. He seemed to be English to judge from his accent and his imperious references to the "native population." Small wonder the Irish locals slammed their doors when they saw him. She gave him her hand. He took it gallantly, brought it to his lips.

"I must tell you straightway, ma'am, that I was a great admirer of your late lamented father, General Milford. His heroic death at Corunna was a sad blow to us. A sad blow."

She felt it unnecessary to remind him that General Milford, ever pigheaded, had died as the result of a collision between his carriage and an Iberian mule. She loved her father, and often saw in herself certain

resemblances to him, but she was not blind to his
character. How many soldiers had gone to their
deaths due to his same pigheadedness, she hated to
speculate. Since this nice soldier seemed sincere, she
thanked him and was informed that he was Major
Kevin Wells.

"Now resident in a fairish country house inland a
trifling distance along that carriage road."

Just beyond the bridge was an ill-kept road which
ended here at the village, having paralleled the stream
through that broad, green, boggy region below the
eastern hills. She wondered what this very English
soldier was doing in such an alien countryside.

"Have you lived here long, sir?"

" 'Fraid there was no choice. My wife had inherited
property here. I was invalided home last year after
Waterloo, and we came to this ghastly place. My poor
Molly died rather unexpectedly, and I? Well, I—" He
shrugged and pulled up his collar against the wind. "I
go off to Dublin now and again, even to London.
Serves to give me my bearings once more, you might
say. Pity the wind has set in. Yesterday was quite tol-
erable. Regrettably, we part company there beyond
the bridge. My way is east on the road. Unless, of
course, you would care for an escort. Faversham is
less than a league north along the sheep track after
you leave the coteens. The path is a trifle wider. Matter of fact, carriages have formerly used the path. You
are close to the sea at all times."

"Thank you. I can do very well," she lied cheerfully.

"My respects to Lady Hagar. And Miss Careen."

"Then you are acquainted with my young cousin?"

He said briefly, "Not well. Molly knew the child
rather better at one time, I believe. Over that hill you

will get a view of Saltbridge Tower. Or what is left of it."

She caught his brisk change of subject when she had asked him about Careen. Or was it Saltbridge Tower he disliked?

He waited until she had crossed the bridge and waved back at him. Then his big stallion galloped over the bridge, turned abruptly to the right, and went east on the carriage road, spattering clods of mud in all directions.

The low, windswept hill north of the village provided a barrier against northerly gales, and before the pony cart started past the coteens, Beth caught at her bonnet and retied its ribbons, preparing for the onslaught of salty mist off the Atlantic when she reached the crown of the hill.

The slope was gradual, and being prepared for the shock of the blast, Beth had been able to withstand it indifferently well. From the top of Saltbridge Hill the view unfolded northward of foam-covered strand that sloped inland toward a higher, darkly wooded area. It must be beautiful when the sunset glowed upon that beach which looked so desolate under these gray, mizzly skies.

On the horizon, built at the edge of the wooded area, was a huddle of ancient, lichen-covered stones dominated by the so-called tower, a square that looked like nothing in the world but a swollen, three-story chimney. There were even crenellated battlements, but the whole of it could not have impressed the Ferocious Natives. The tower was set inside a walled quadrangle about two stories high, with low, heavy doors opening inward from one branch of the sheep track. The track itself seemed to have been en-

larged to accommodate grander vehicles since it had
passed the major's carriage road at Saltbridge.

On a sunny afternoon there would be another couple of hours before dusk, but the leaden gray atmosphere already melted the real into the fantasy, and
she wondered if she had imagined movement and
lamplight in the woods about halfway between her
pony cart and that absurd Saltbridge Tower.

The light flashed again, then dark, then light, and
she realized it must be a lamp swaying on a wagon
that was being drawn through the woods, probably to
remain for the night. It seemed a furtive business and
she wondered why the travelers did not make their
camp on the beach, above the high-water mark. A
tinker's wagon. She could see it now as it passed
through low, prickly shrubs long punished by the salt
winds. Knives and shears and calico, numerous bottles, elixirs, and potions, almost anything a peddler
could sell, dangled along the side of the wagon. Then
she saw a brightly clad female leap off the wagon and
go to the old nag's head to lead on the reluctant animal.

By the lamplight it was clear that the tinkers were
gypsies. The agile, middle-aged female who had
leaped to the ground wore large earrings that looked
like loops of coins and glittered in the light. Her full
skirt was green and the blouse a faded pink that
gleamed like satin and very possibly was. Her hair
was only half confined by the red kerchief. There
were at least two other gypsies with her. The one who
seemed to be an elderly male saw Beth on the path
between woods and ocean. He pointed. Then he and
the female started over the shrubs and shingle toward
Beth.

Beth did not know how many more there might be
in the band and was furious at her own discomfort.

She wanted very much to give the pony a signal to hurry but this seemed the depth of cowardice, not the act of General Milford's daughter, so she sat straight-backed and calm to all outward appearances as the two gypsies came loping over the ground to head her off.

"Sweet, noble benefactress!" called the agile woman she had first seen, her big teeth all agleam with the attempt to be ingratiating. "Do come and see our wares. Only five minutes. . . . One minute. Home-spun of superb quality. A shawl of such threads as you would not see in heaven. Scissors sharp as daggers, mistress. *Daggers!*"

As a matter of interest, the strapping gypsy woman herself wore a shawl woven of cashmere pastels and worth many guineas. Beth wondered by what means she had obtained it.

"Another time. I am late now."

She caught a flash of still another gypsy approaching and this time signaled the pony on. He lurched forward, only to be stopped by the old male gypsy who seized his light, delicate harness. The gypsy running to join them was likewise male, not much over twenty. Unlike the silent old man who was tougher than he had at first appeared, the good-looking, black-eyed young male looked anxious, and protested in what Beth assumed to be the Romany dialect.

What puzzled Beth was the attitude of the young woman who was bound that Beth should leave her cart, wander off into the woods with them, and doubtless get her throat cut. The gypsy seemed to be teasing, having a ghastly joke at her expense, as if the game might be more important than the robbery.

"Very well," Beth said when the woman ignored the pleas of the young male. "I'll drive the pony up to the gates of the tower. That wall ahead of us." And much closer now, she thought. She expected the gypsies to turn and look in that direction, which would give her a chance to take up the light buggy whip as a stinging weapon if they tried force.

But only the two males were distracted. The overpowering female kept her full attention upon Beth who had to grope for the switch furtively while the gypsy put more persuasion into her request.

"Mistress, come now and see the beautiful things we offer. And so cheap! You will pay mere farthings."

Beth's fingers closed about the whip handle while she said pleasantly, with a very firm note, "They are watching for me at those gates, and I will deal with you and your merchandise afterward. Good day to you."

The mud-colored pupils in the woman's eyes seemed to contract. For an instant Beth steeled herself to fight off an attack. She found herself cold with such a rage that it conquered her fear. She raised the whip and a shaft of light cut across the cart, between the gypsy and Beth. This time the woman swung around with all the coins in her looped earrings sending out flashes of gold. The heavy, iron-studded gates in the Faversham wall had opened and the light came from a strong lamp hung just inside the quadrangle.

Whatever had been the gypsies' real purpose, and it might be no more than they claimed it to be, Beth had no intention of finding out. She brought the whip smartly over the woman's knuckles, shouted, "Quick, lad!" to the pony. In his dash forward, he knocked off both the woman at Beth's side and the old man whose grip had loosened on the pony's lines. They seemed mesmerized by the light, or its source.

The path took a slight upward turn and Beth was

sure her pursuers might have reached the jolting little cart if they had exerted themselves, but she was intensely relieved when they didn't. The pony did not stop at the open doors but trotted inside the quadrangle where, by exerting considerable strength, Beth managed to pull him up.

"Welcome, Cousin Beth." The silvery voice came to her out of the twilight darkness.

Beth stepped down. She managed to say calmly,
"That was quite a welcome!"

CHAPTER TWO

"Cousin Careen?" Beth asked, scowling into the vague shadows that surrounded her. "Where are you? This place is infernally dark."

The tinkling, musical voice ran on. "How good of you to come! I am persuaded Mama would never have expected it of you. We being so poor, and you so very rich, dear Cousin!"

While Beth digested the shadings in this charming voice, with their several layers of meaning, she tried at the same time to identify her surroundings. A heavy man of middle age closed the gates, one at a time. Beth glanced out, but could not see the gypsies. They had vanished with surprising speed. The trail back to Saltbridge Hill and the tiny village beyond was beginning to drift into sea fog.

As the Irishman at the gates raised the big storm lamp off a hook, Cousin Careen took form beside the cart, mischievously smiling. She was a slight girl close to womanhood, and remarkably pretty, with dusky hair framing a vixen's face and eyes of an oblique shape very like a fox. Before Beth could quite accustom herself to the sight of an almost adult Careen, the girl embraced her.

"Dear Cuz, come in and eat your supper porridge and tell us all about your journey. You've no notion how tiresome it is here in winter with no visitors from outside. Come!"

Beth was not immune to the girl's friendliness, whether it was genuine or not. Seeing that the gateman had taken the pony in charge and would doubtless collect her bandbox and portmanteaux, Beth let herself be led by her young cousin. A girl this pretty should certainly be brought to England to prepare for her coming out before she became a complete urchin, or got into a more adult form of trouble.

"Your mother's death was a sad business indeed, Careen," she began, "but I should imagine the—ah—person your mother had married would make no claim to your guardianship. I am told by your mother's solicitors that this leaves your care to Lady Hagar and me."

Careen said, "Through this door. It opens directly into what we call the great hall. No. I shouldn't think that vile convict would want me. A pity, too."

Beth thought she could not have heard correctly. "You would prefer his guardianship?"

"Lord love you, no! But he's said to be rich as Midas. He's an Ex, you know."

"X?"

"Not a real convict. An ex-convict. Shipped to Botany Bay or whatever, long ago, and made good in Australia. Why else do you think Mama would have married him, poor, little penniless governor's widow that she was!" There could be no doubt of the ridicule in the girl's voice when she spoke of her mother. "I fancy I see Mama now, dabbing a tiny lace handkerchief at her big eyes and telling this convict how cruel it was of—of her husband, forcing her to make the long voyage to the Antipodes and then having the bad taste to die practically on Australia's doorstep."

"Careen!"

"Well, I believe in facing the fact." This was so like something Beth might have said that she could not feel in honor bound to stop the girl. "Mama wanted my— She wanted Papa to take the post so she could be governor's lady of Australia. He died, poor man, and she instantly set her cap at a rich ex-convict. It served her proper when she died so soon after."

"How is your grandmother's health? Much improved, I trust."

"Crabbed as usual, but that's Grandmama's way." Her lively eyes sparkled as she changed the subject. "Dear Cuz, I hope the tinker's wagon didn't alarm you. Tzigana and the others mean no harm. Tzigana is the—the one who stopped your pony cart. They come through this district very often, and we thank heaven for it. They just have a strain of humor you English may find a bit—lively."

Beth said, "All of that."

"I like Tzigana. She is often here gathering kelp or anything else that may bring a few farthings. You musn't mind her."

Beth let the matter go.

She did not see much of Faversham Tower on the way up to what proved to be the bedchamber assigned to her one flight above the long main room on the ground floor.

"We put you here, so you might be close to dear Grandmama, but I must say, I thought you would be older," Careen explained. She added that hot bricks would be placed in her bed at once. "You probably don't have our Irish fortitude, so there'll be a warming pan as well, after supper."

In that moment Beth decided that she would turn

into a block of pond ice before she would accept a warming pan.

"Quite unnecessary, I assure you, my child. When may I see Lady Hagar? And perhaps, in the meantime, you had best tell me what is the nature of her illness."

"Her stomach. An ulcerated stomach, the surgeon in Dublin calls it. But I intend that she shall live forever." Then Careen's sloe eyes crinkled in amusement, and Beth was certain that the male population of the British Isles would find that laugh enchanting. In a great many ways, there was something of the enchantress about her, and Beth, shocked at her own thoughts, did not altogether trust the girl.

"How funny to hear you call me *my child!*" Careen said. "For you see, I am quite well grown. Mama was no taller than me when she met dear old Papa. What a lamb he must have been! A lamb to the slaughter in dear Mama's hands. And then it turned out that he had no money. Only this musty old dungeon we live in."

"Who told you all those nasty things about your mother?"

She said airily, "Oh, Grandmama!"

Beth decided Lady Hagar was not the best guardian for the girl during these present years. She looked around the austere, monastic bedchamber with its ancient bed curtained in a velvet so old and so infrequently shaken that it was difficult to guess the original color. The coverlet and linen seemed newly laundered, but the carpet must have been laid at least a score of years ago, during the last few of which it had not even been cleaned.

There was an exquisite French reading stand near the window. The inlaid top of the stand was of porcelain so perfect it might have been a Sevres design. A small but useful dressing glass had been set on the porcelain top. Beth ran one finger over the design.

"How lovely! I understand a few of these were brought to England during the French Revolution to be sold by the émigrés, but nothing more beautiful than this."

She became aware that Careen had been watching her, even waiting for this reaction. The girl said with a casually modest gesture, "I—we thought you might like it in your room. It is the only nice piece we have, but we wanted to make you feel at home."

Beth studied the stand, wondering what to say that would tell the girl she read between the lines very well. She said after a little pause, "Of course, it came from your room?"

Careen colored. "How did you ever guess?"

"Never mind. Let me wash off some of this mud and dirt, and then I want to meet your grandmama."

The girl stood there looking awkward for the first time. She glanced around the room, gave a forced little smile, and then said, "I'll leave you here for a few minutes. Then I'll come back." When she reached the door she seemed compelled to turn briefly. "You are not quite what I expected, Cousin."

"Nor are you."

The girl went out, looking a trifle chagrined.

Cold as the room was, and its bitter damp oozed out of every crevice, it had an intriguing view of the sea from its single window. Beth opened the window and then the shutters and was nearly blown over by the first gust of wind. Once she had withstood this, she guessed that on a clear or a sunny day the expanse of Atlantic, like the long strand of beach beyond the little northbound sheep track, would be well worth studying.

Meanwhile, it was freezing and she closed shutters and window in a hurry. Her luggage had not yet arrived, but she found that the carafe on the heavy, badly made old commode held warm water. She poured most of it into the cracked bowl beneath it and, using a neatly mended homespun towel, began to wash herself. She was ready when a young female knocked and, upon being admitted, accidentally waved her candlestick in Beth's face and in a wisp of a voice inquired if everything was satisfactory.

"I'm Dorothy, mum. Being as how I'm from over the sea, my lady thought you'd prefer me to look out for you." The girl was gentle and timid, traits carried out in a face that might have been attractive if more animated. Beth felt sorry for her and assured the girl that she needed nothing at the moment.

"Perhaps you could help me to undress later, if you would be so kind. You see, my own maid would not cross the Irish Sea for all the spice in the Indies. She tells me it sets badly on her stomach. Or vice versa, I think." She smiled but got no flicker of expression in return and gave up. It seemed a pity, though. Dorothy looked only a trifle older than Careen and might have been pretty if someone took her in hand. At Carlton House, where the Prince Regent entertained in London, blondes were said to have come into the fashion this season.

"Thank you, Dorothy. That will be all." The girl stood there awkwardly and Beth added, "You may go."

"Sorry, mum, but my lady says I am to bring you to her. Supper is served in my lady's bed-sitting room."

Really, I might almost be in one of Mrs. Radcliffe's

wild romances! she thought. Everyone was behaving so absurdly. She threw a shawl around her shoulders and started after the girl with her wavering tallow candle. Beth's sense of walking through a melodrama was heightened by her view of the pitch-black passage which the lively presence of Careen Faversham had formerly obscured. Beth had known the tower was small and she saw now that this and probably the floor above contained only three rooms, plus the staircase and landing passage. Fortunately, Dorothy's destination was only across the hall. She knocked timidly but was heard by the alert individual inside and told in the voice of a sergeant major to "Enter, girl!"

After the unsettling events of the past few hours, Beth expected to see an ancient crone, at the very least. Lady Hagar Faversham was seated among numerous pillows in a four-poster bed without tester or curtains. A peat fire blushed and glowed in the grate at the far end of the room and gave the air a curious, acrid scent that put Beth in mind of her tense ride over the cliffs and the encounter with the gypsies.

"My dear Elspeth, I do appreciate your making this unpleasant journey."

Beth came to the side of the bed and took the hand Her Ladyship extended. It was hard, dry, and bony, a little like her long, equine face. There was no elegance, but a deal of strength in the set of her head, the high-bridged, prominent nose, the jaw. She did not look in the least ill. She was remarkably ugly, yet not unattractive.

Beth said, "I came at once, ma'am. But I trust you are feeling more the thing."

Dorothy seemed destined to become part of the whitewashed walls until Lady Hagar suggested abruptly, "You, there! Don't hang about . . . hanging about. Go and see if you can make my granddaughter presentable for supper."

Dorothy bobbed a curtsy and disappeared into the unlighted passage, which smelled of mold and dampness.

"Now, my girl." Lady Hagar tapped the coverlet at her feet.

It was pleasant to be called "my girl" again, more so than the name "Elspeth" which she had always hated, and it seemed a much more genuine flattery to Beth than Careen's talk about her youthful appearance. She said quickly, "Your granddaughter must be one of the most beautiful creatures in—"

"Ireland?" As in Careen's remarks, there may have been a slight edge to that.

"Britain. But I agree it is time Careen went into a female academy. There is an excellent school near Bath, in the neighborhood of Milford Hall."

"Just so. Just so. I hoped I might count upon you. It would be a disaster if you behaved like that unspeakable creature who married my son. Not the slightest interest in the fate of her child."

Beth was very familiar with Arabella's qualities, but so many views agreed with hers that, in despite of herself, she kept remembering moments when she and Arabella had shared happy moments, dancing in the same set, gossiping after the candles were snuffed in the school, walking along the quiet, green lanes of Somerset, and describing the male they would one day wish to marry.

"Your ladyship, Arabella was my cousin and met a terrible death at sea. Since she has drowned and is gone, please, let us discuss a subject less painful."

The woman's eyes studied her. They were sharp, observant eyes, and very shrewd, without the soften-

ing influence of good manners. Beth began mentally
to revise downward Lady Hagar's goodwill.

"I am not one for mincing words, but you may be
right, Elspeth." Beth winced at the name and suspected the woman knew it. Lady Hagar, showing
signs of secret amusement, went on. "My unfortunate
granddaughter must become a lady in despite of her
own inclinations. She has run wild since my stomach
began to give me those excruciating aches and pains. I
have always eaten quite well. I now seem to be paying the price. I could drink my bottle of the good Irish
with the best of them, in former times. Now, it seems
that a mere two mugs of whiskey will put me in mis-
ery."

Beth controlled her surprise at this astonishing
piece of information. "I noticed that Careen seems to
be acquainted with those gypsy tinkers who are
camped close by in the woods between here and Saltbridge Hill."

She caught a tiny flash—of alarm?—apprehension?—
in Lady Hagar's eyes before the woman shrugged and
dismissed the matter.

"Gypsies move about very freely on these coasts.
And the tinkers are nearly always welcome. You must
count your change, of course, but they do bring pleasure into the lives of these wretches who live in the
coteens. Major Wells has driven them out countless
times. He disapproves of gypsies, tinkers, the local
peasants, and almost anyone who lives west of the
Irish Sea."

"What a pity! I met him near the village and found
him charming."

The woman leaned forward. This time there was no
mistaking her reaction. "Did he know you?"

"Instantly. There seemed to be no doubt. I suppose he heard you speak of me."

"Fumdiddle! The man's never set foot in Faversham Tower since Molly Wells died. So he was pleasant to you. Well, well. . . . I wonder if he has decided to be civil, now that we have a visitor from the Great World. No mistake. It would help matters. Did he say he would visit you here?"

"No. But he seemed friendly. I received the distinct impression—in fact, the major said his late wife and Careen had been great friends." Beth remembered suddenly that odd little hesitation, the way he said *at one time*, and the major's anxiety to change the subject. She watched Lady Hagar, who started to say something, said "hmph" instead, and then:

"Look behind you."

It was a curious remark, the words harmless, yet they conjured up chilling ideas. Beth had not completely turned before her Cousin Careen tapped her on the shoulder, laughing.

"Say no more about me. I am here now to defend myself."

Lady Hagar's horsey face broke into a fond grin.

"Little rogue! Quiet as a cat. Sneaking about everywhere. You never can hear her coming. Your Cousin Elspeth has been telling me she met Major Wells, who proved to be quite civil. What do you think of that?"

Careen shrugged. "Splendid, if one likes being bored to death. He used to be quite dashing, but now he's dreadfully—military. His wife was my dearest friend. Molly and I used to think nothing of walking three or four leagues a day. Once we walked clear to Ballyglen, Molly and Kevin and me. Grandmama, shall I order up our supper?"

Her grandmother made a sign of assent with one

hand while explaining to Beth in a vain attempt to lower her voice, "The child was to have gone walking with Molly Wells beyond Wells Hall and across the bog, the day Molly was lost. But it was misty weather. And I forbade Careen to leave the tower. The major professes to believe my grandchild could have saved a strapping lass like Molly Wells from the bogs if she had been along."

"Grandmama . . ." Careen cut in very softly and the old woman nodded.

"Promised I wouldn't discuss it. But it does infuriate me to have this poor child lose the few friends she has, all because chatterboxes will gossip."

"Here is supper, Grandmama."

Beth looked around. With an effort she managed to conceal her dismay. She had not eaten since a brief cup of tea and a meal cake at noon in Ballyglen, and the gateman, a sullen fellow with a heavy, brooding face, now brought in a tray meagerly set with what appeared to be a bowl of gruel and two bowls of porridge, a pot of smoky, peat-flavored tea, and a bottle of the powerful local poteen with one glass. The whiskey—or whatever it was—had been set for Lady Hagar who poured half a glassful and drank it down to the amazement of Beth and the amusement of Careen.

A double-leaf table in the corner and two chairs were brought out beside Her Ladyship's bed.

Beth decided there was nothing for it but to take up one of the huge spoons and plunge into the odious mess of porridge. At least it was preferable to the gruel.

Lady Hagar smacked her lips, savoring the last taste of the powerful dark liquor she had downed. "Ah! That should make the gruel bearable."

Beth could not resist asking, "But why do you eat the gruel, your ladyship?"

"For my health's sake, of course. I was told it does very nicely for the belly."

Careen grinned. "Stomach, Grandmama."

"In my day, we called things by their proper name."

Beth persisted. "Yes, but isn't that—that drink bad for your stomach?"

"Well, whyever do you think I eat the gruel?"

Beth laughed and gave up.

When they had made an end of the nauseous mess, Lady Hagar sent Careen away with the tray, though the bottle of poteen remained near her hand.

"As a tonic in the night," she explained.

Beth said gravely, "I understand, ma'am." She had already wished the robustious invalid good night when Her Ladyship called to her:

"Elspeth!" There was an immediacy in that call. When Beth looked at her, the older woman said anxiously, "You will take her away soon. Will you not?"

"If you wish, ma'am. We'll talk more tomorrow." She took up one of the candleholders and went across the passage to her room.

She found herself yawning prodigiously, which was unusual. At home, and particularly when at the routs or concerts in Bath, she was awake and often dancing until all hours. Perhaps the clammy weather affected her in this odd way.

One would think this bitter cold would keep me awake, at least until I have prepared for bed, she thought as she fastened the ribbons of her nightgown and then her all-too-thin robe, and began to brush her hair before the looking glass. But every stroke was an effort. Belatedly, she remembered the long ride from Ballyglen and the several occasions when it had been necessary to rein in the pony, times when she exerted every muscle. Small wonder she was tired now.

"Not tired. Sleepy," she contradicted her reflection in the mirror. "Now you are being silly. It is the same thing, after all."

It was pleasant in some ways to feel drowsy the first night in an unfamiliar old house. Neither the damp nor the crackling, rustling sounds typical of such a place would annoy her. She could scarcely lift her arm for another stroke and gave up. The brush fell to the floor and she reached for it, almost losing her balance.

"It's sleep for you, my girl," and she climbed into the bed, pulled blankets and sheets around all but the top of her head, and went off to sleep in no time.

She was roused by shouts, calls, and groans somewhere nearby. It seemed to take her forever to come out of a dream-filled sleep, and even after she opened her eyes to find that she had forgotten to snuff the bed candle, she still found herself dazed. Her dreams had been singularly unpleasant, too. Full of gypsies capering around her while she appeared to be bound to a maypole and unable to breathe freely. Or was the maypole a small stake for burning witches? A horrid business, at all events.

She sat up, tried to get her bearings, and saw that the smothering sensation came from the blankets with which she had barricaded her head against the cold seeping in around the warped window frame.

Meanwhile, there was the cause of her awakening: grunts, groans, and an occasional shout. No one but Lady Hagar could make those earsplitting noises, and they were surprisingly powerful for a dying woman. She untangled herself from the bedclothing, climbed down to the worn carpet, and, shivering violently, felt her way to the travel coat and good morocco slippers laid onto the chair when no maid had appeared to help her prepare for bed. There was no lock on the door, so she pulled it open and stuck her tousled head out. A candle on the broad newel post seemed about to gutter out, but at least it gave some illumination to the hall and staircase. The sounds came from Lady Hagar's room as she had suspected. Beth crossed the hall, knocked, and receiving even louder groans, took this for an invitation to enter.

Lady Hagar was sitting up in her great bed, clutching her stomach. The light through the yellow glass chimney of a lamp accentuated the sick woman's sallow complexion. She muttered, "Damned gruel does for me every time. Fetch me that bottle."

The bottle contained the local form of alcohol, the poteen she had not finished at supper. Beth tried to point out reasonably that the alcohol and not the gruel had been the culprit, but Lady Hagar snapped her fingers. "Don't dawdle, girl! Pour into the glass."

With her fingers made unsteady by a yawn, Beth poured about two fingers of the powerful stuff, only to have the old woman call out between groans: "More, in God's name. A man's drink. That'll settle me nicely. Thank you, my dear. Now, stop running about the halls like a lost soul and go to bed where you belong." She took a long swallow. "Ah! That's better. Pleasant dreams. . . . Good God!"

That sudden cry snapped Beth's head up and very nearly shook away the cobwebs of sleep.

"Are you ill again, Lady Hagar?"

"I? No, no. The drink will put me to rights. But you look white as whey. And see how you are trembling."

Beth explained very patiently, "That is because I am cold."

The old lady studied her.

Impossible creature, thought Beth, and said aloud, "If you are well now, I'll go back to bed."

"A moment." Her Ladyship forced herself to add after a brief pause: "If you please. . . . You must be a very sound sleeper. I was calling for some time before you came."

Beth yawned, pulled her coat around her, and said with a sharp edge to the words, "I sleep like anyone else. I may have been a trifle tired tonight. I have had a long journey."

To her surprise the old lady waved this aside. "No, no, dear. I wasn't chiding you. It is only that Careen is an exceedingly sound sleeper when she is on this floor. I sometimes call for fifteen or twenty minutes before I rouse her. Does it run in your family, by any chance?"

"I'm sure I couldn't say." But Beth had her own private suspicions about Careen's heavy sleep. It would be quite natural if the girl simply covered her head with a quilt and ignored these preposterous night interruptions. As Beth was leaving, Lady Hagar called, "Good night, my child." She seemed chastened and thoughtful, very much subdued. What on earth had come over her?

Probably that last drink.

Beth returned to her room and, feeling the draft more strongly than ever, worked at pulling the window more tightly shut. Once the window tore at a shutter and she had to reach out and refasten the aged, crumbling wood. The ocean rolled in toward the path at the base of the tower but all seemed calm. Faint moonlight gave the fog a golden glow and lingered on a lone, black curragh, one of the small fishing boats in use along the coast. It seemed to be headed out to deeper waters and bobbed up and down so persistently it made Beth's head ache to watch it.

A shadow lengthened along the wet sand and she looked down, wondering what fisherman had chosen this hour and the Faversham grounds for his work. Contrary to her first notion, the shadow belonged to one of the gypsies, the woman called Tzigana. She suddenly began to gather kelp, draping it over her arm as she strode along the beach. Beth knew there were many uses for these long ropes of seaweed that looked almost translucent in the foggy light, but the hard work of kelp gathering seemed uncharacteristic of these gypsies. And had Tzigana begun to gather the kelp just as Beth looked out of the window?

If not kelp gathering, what the devil was Tzigana doing out there? She seemed harmless at the moment, however, moving on and out of sight along the beach.

Beth finished fastening the shutter, closed the window firmly, and went back to bed. It was harder to sleep this time, but eventually she dozed off after the candle smoked abruptly and died.

CHAPTER
THREE

Before she opened her eyes the next morning, Beth huddled down among the covers, sighed contentedly, and hoped the hour was early enough so she need not move until more sunlight crept through the warped and weathered shutters. She was used to the noisy entrance of her own maid, Dawlish, whose every move was calculated to rouse Beth and keep her from returning to sleep.

On this November morning she heard numerous faint, fluttery sounds, as if someone tried much too hard not to disturb her. She opened her eyes. Dorothy floated about the room with excruciating care to collect Beth's travel clothing without making a sound. She came to the window, obviously thought of opening it while her hands were full, and couldn't decide what to put down first.

Beth said, "Good morning, Dorothy. Hadn't I better help you?" She swung out of bed and was beside the girl in one swift move that so startled Dorothy she dropped shift, petticoat, and gown on the floor.

It was worth getting up in the icy cold to see the view, Beth decided when she opened the window, fastened back the shutters, and stared at the deep gray-blue of the coastal waters. The sunlight was dazzling

on the foam that gathered at the crest of the breakers
and closer in, along the shore. The night's heavy fog
had strewn driftwood and chains of kelp the length of
the beach which even the redoubtable gypsy woman,
Tzigana, had not been able to remove.

"What a beautiful day!" She closed and fastened the
window and stepped back to the middle of the room.
The day might be chilly, but the bright sunlight made
the air seem cheerful and warm. Beth washed and
dressed while Dorothy stood by silently, making Beth
nervous by her very stolidity.

It took much longer to brush and make her hair
presentable than to be fastened into one of her fashionable new emerald green gowns with its long, full
sleeves and slightly billowing skirt. The once-popular
high waistline had at last, daringly, reached the natural waist. Beth had never cared too much for style or
apppearance, but her fine auburn hair, which looked
glorious when carefully arranged with her emerald
half-tiara and long earbobs, was the bane of her life
on ordinary occasions. Today she caught up her hair
into a knot and skewered it with hair bodkins.

In the looking glass she saw Dorothy's shocked expression and hesitated. It was this unexpected animation that caught her.

"You don't like it."

"Oh, mum, it's not my place."

"Speak up. What have I done wrong?"

It was clear that, to Dorothy, everything was
wrong. The girl came to her, removed the bodkins,
and brushed out long strands and then wound them
into a soft knot, rather like the style Beth favored but
infinitely more flattering. Around her face the girl
brought forward wisps of hair that made all the difference.

"If I count upon you, Dorothy, I shall be beautiful yet!"

"Oh, mum, as if you wasn't!"

With considerable satisfaction Beth said, "Nonsense!" and Dorothy beamed, but she quickly reverted to the blank, dull-eyed automaton when Careen opened the door and looked in.

"How pretty you look, Cuz! Will you have your breakfast in here? Or down where there is more activity? Dorothy, you tiresome creature. You let Cousin Beth's tea get quite cold."

Anxious to avoid furthering Dorothy's discomfort, Beth said, "My fault. I was too busy dressing. Do come along, Cousin. I can have my morning tea elsewhere."

She was about to leave when she noticed that Dorothy, who had turned away from the looking glass and porcelain-topped stand, abruptly dropped the hairbrush as she glanced out the window. Beth said, "Go on, Careen. I'll get my shawl." She crossed the room, went around the bed, and passed within sight of the window. Two gypsies were down on the beach, either gathering kelp as usual, or examining the driftwood for something worth saving. One of them was the boyish, good-looking male gypsy who had protested when the others harrassed Beth. Tzigana, the woman Beth regarded as her bête noire, was nowhere to be seen. The old female gypsy, probably the boy's mother, was with him. The young male kept looking up at the west face of the tower. Beth wondered if he expected to see anyone in the house. Dorothy was the logical person, considering her bright, uncharacteristic interest a moment since, and her pale face was still suffused by a blush.

Beth did not pursue the matter, although she could

see that Dorothy was expecting and probably dreading her comment.

Going down the stairs with Careen, Beth asked, "Are you at all anxious to leave Ireland with me?"

Careen did not reply at once. When she did so it was after a typically sly side glance, one of the first of her unpleasant habits that Beth hoped would be rooted out by proper schooling.

"Perhaps. It would be a pity to leave while Grandmama is ill. Don't you think it might be more practical if we could make things nicer for her here at the tower? Mama never did anything for her after she married that rich convict. We hoped she would use a little of his money to give us—I mean Grandmama—some new things. Furnishings from Dublin. And repairs to the outbuildings around the courtyard. All that."

"And she did nothing?"

"In the three letters she sent us from Australia after she married that rich convict person, she kept saying Dear Nicholas wanted her to come home to meet us and was planning the voyage."

"Dear Nicholas?"

"Nicholas Cormeer, the ex-convict. But she needed ever so many gowns and pelisses and hats and whatnot before she could come home. To Grandmama and me. Imagine!" She laughed. "They all went down with the ship outside Sydney harbor. All the pretty things, including Mama. And the ugly old convict was saved."

Beth felt she should scold the girl for this unfilial talk about her mother, but regrettably, Beth was inclined to agree with Careen. Nor did she doubt the truth of Careen's story. It was so like the Arabella she had known in her girlhood. But throughout the excellent breakfast of pork, eggs, oatmeal, and tea, Careen kept returning to the subject of what a few hundred guineas could do for Saltbridge Tower, and it was necessary to suggest that Careen concern herself less with money and more with her future education.

To which Careen added the unanswerable rider: "That is all very well if one has money."

There was nothing Beth could do until she was able to discuss with Lady Hagar the possibility of removing Her Ladyship to England with Careen. Careen's mercenary feelings superseded all other emotions except one, her affection for her grandmother. Beth was happy to find this in the girl's favor.

Lady Hagar was suffering from a monumental headache which she blamed upon the too-strong tea she had been persuaded to drink at breakfast. She agreed to discuss Careen's affairs with Beth when the effects of the "wretched tea" had worn off. Meanwhile, Beth allowed herself to be escorted over the property by Careen but tried not to hear quite all of the financial complaints.

The tower itself was plain and largely unoccupied. Beth was interested in seeing Careen's room on the top floor under the small, crenellated battlements, the room of which Careen was inordinately proud. Careen, as Beth had suspected, occupied a chamber with a few charming pieces of furniture, mostly French, and delicate but well kept. There were no unshaken, undusted draperies and tabletops in here. Beth was of the opinion that Lady Hagar had encouraged Careen's very natural selfishness as a payment for the neglect of her true parents, so she said nothing except to express her admiration for the bed, commode, armoire, and little tilt-top table.

One other room in the tower interested her. It was the south room on the ground floor just back of the long main hall. A parlor of some kind, possibly once used for ladies as a withdrawing salon, it was the only room that looked as if it might be frequently used. Careen was hurrying her on to show her the portieres in the main hall which were so old they had been in existence when her grandfather was a boy, but Beth caught her shoe in the threadbare carpeting of the little salon and walked out of the shoe. As she came back to step into it, she was surprised to see a pile of what appeared to be laundry behind the heavy Jacobean sofa.

"Come along, do," Careen cried, and Beth went after her. The main hall was very much what she had expected, well worn and undusted.

It occurred to Beth after a brief tour of the disused carriage house, the kitchen, and stillroom, that the dour gateman, who answered to the name of O'Beirne, and Dorothy were the only servants in the household. Since the wages of a worker in this area of Ireland were scarcely more than food and lodgings, it seemed that Careen had not exaggerated the Faversham financial problems. She admitted as much to Careen who, for once, ignored the chance to plead poverty. They had walked out of the carriage house and onto a footpath that led through the woods back of the quadrangle.

"But, Cuz," Careen insisted, "it isn't the lack of money. It's me, of course. The villagers won't work for me." Beth looked at her. Careen smiled. "Don't you understand?"

"No. At least, I hope I do not."

"Well, we shan't go into details, but why do you think Grandma wants you to take me away?"

Beth was studying the woods. The tinkers' wagon

with Tzigana and her people had been near here last night, but there were no signs of its presence today. She was belatedly conscious of Careen's question.

"You wanted me to come here, Careen, but you didn't intend to leave with me, or to go to the female academy, did you?"

"Didn't. And don't. Cousin, you know your precious academy did nothing for Mama." Suddenly, watching her, Beth thought she saw the real Careen peeping out of the fox eyes. "I've had a far better education in life itself from . . . my gypsy friends than I could have gotten from a female academy. Tzigana and the other tinkers know the real, ugly truth of life. I'm sorry, Beth, but my life is here. Even if that fusty old Major Wells doesn't think so."

The girl had certainly come to depend far too much upon her gypsy friends, but it was not her fault. The blame lay with her parents first and then with Beth herself, the girl's only living relation after Lady Hagar. And Beth felt she must go carefully, not showing too much disapproval of the gypsies, even the somewhat overpowering Tzigana. It didn't seen to trouble Careen when they saw Major Wells on his big stallion approaching Saltbridge Tower. Careen only laughed.

"How funny! This is the first time old Kevin has come visiting in almost a year. I suppose it's you he's come to see."

Beth couldn't resist saying, "Like you, he is probably enchanted by my father's money."

"Probably." Then she winked. "But perhaps not. You are in exceptional looks today. Good fortune, Cuz. I had best vanish."

"No! We'll make an end of this nonsense. Come along."

"He won't want me." Nevertheless, the girl seemed pleased at Beth's insistence and began to smooth her wild, dark hair, and then the high-waisted muslin dress which was long out of the mode, nor did its pallid pink-flower design become her. The shawl she pulled around her thin shoulders was too old in pattern and of a very unattractive puce color. It had probably belonged to her grandmother. Beth decided in this moment to be certain that Careen was dressed becomingly, to show her incipient beauty at its best.

Major Wells dismounted, walked his horse carefully over the ground and between the prickly shrubs toward the two females. He greeted both of them politely, then handed a sealed letter to Careen.

"My estate man, Hallidie, brought this from the posting office in Ballyglen. It is addressed to Her Ladyship. I thought you might like to take it to her."

Careen raised her eyebrows, reminded Beth, "I told you as much," and went running off to the quadrangle gates. The major started after her to open one of the gates, but the girl was already inside. He looked around at Beth, shrugged, and smiled apologetically.

"Not very mannerly of me, was it?"

"Careen is still a child. She enjoys running."

She found his expression a bit odd, as if he did not quite believe her.

"Do you think so, ma'am? She seems very adult to me. . . . I suppose you know her better. Molly thought she also knew . . . But no matter. I hope the letter won't upset Lady Hagar."

"Should it?" Beth was a trifle disconcerted that this comparative stranger, and one who had not previously cared to visit Saltbridge Tower, should know so much about a letter that did not belong to him.

"Now, you are suspecting the worst. No, Miss Milford, I have not broken open and read Her Ladyship's mail, but it is superscribed from the Antipodes. From Sydney, Australia, as a matter of fact. That convict fellow's name is below the seal. Nicholas Cormeer."

"Oh, no! I thought we'd done with him. As I understand it, he made no difficulties when he announced Arabella's death." Seeing his sympathetic gaze, she confessed, "I know very little about the affair. Lady Hagar sent me the news a little over a month ago. Arabella and her second husband had sailed for Ireland two months previous. The first night out there was a fire and Arabella was put in one of the boats which capsized. Cormeer apparently swam for it. At all events, he was picked up. It was he who wrote to Lady Hagar. He said nothing of Arabella's daughter Careen, and both Her Ladyship and I assumed he had no interest in her future."

"That is the understanding in the village. A nasty beggar, I've no doubt. I wonder, Miss Milford, would you be interested in seeing something of the area? Quite colorful on a sunny day."

He was looking ruddy and masculine in the bright morning light, the sea breeze ruffling his tawny hair, and she was feminine enough to enjoy his attention. But she confessed ruefully, "To the disgrace of my father, I am not a good horsewoman."

He looked so disappointed she added after a hesitation, "Do you walk by any chance?"

His surprise softened to pleasure. "Splendid! I spend much of my time walking. I believe I walk my own estate more than Hallidie does. Let me just turn Oliver—my mount—over to the Faversham groom and I'll show you the shorter way to Wells Hall. Through those woods which end on my property. Then, if you will allow us, my housekeeper can prepare a glorious Irish tea, and I'll take you home to the tower in my gig."

"I shouldn't think Oliver would be too popular a name in these parts. That beautiful stallion isn't named for Oliver Cromwell, by any chance?"

"I'm afraid I did it in defiance." He hesitated with a likable diffidence. "I have thought about this invitation since we met yesterday. It is not a secret. My housekeeper knows. What do you say, Miss Milford?"

"I would not like to disappoint your housekeeper."

He seemed to think this witty as well as delightful, and she, on the other hand, found it very pleasant to have anyone so ruggedly male eager for her company. But if the news from the Antipodes was bad, she might be needed by Lady Hagar.

"Do come and have a glass of that frightful-looking poteen, Major, while I find out whether Her Ladyship may need me. If not, I will accept your invitation, though I very much fear my credit may sink when the village hears of my shocking conduct."

"All else I agree to, but please—not the poteen! Perhaps a little whiskey."

As he escorted her inside the gates she promised not to force Lady Hagar's favorite potion upon him. But when she suggested that she fetch down Careen to bear him company in the little parlor behind the main hall, he became surprisingly stiff. "Thank you, no. I'll keep my own company until you return. Then, perhaps, you will return the sooner."

As she was leaving him with a tray of whiskey and a glass, he started to settle himself on the sofa but looked behind it in surprise.

"Good Lord! Do your servants sleep here?"

"Certainly not. Why?"

He sat down hastily, embarrassed. "I beg your pardon. I saw what I thought were homespun sheets. And that blanket. None of my concern. None at all."

She examined the sheet and the beautiful woven green blanket. They were not even dusty. "How very odd! Perhaps O'Beirne sleeps here. Poor man! He seems to be groom, cook, butler, everything but ladies' maid. I had best inquire of Her Ladyship. Or Careen."

He looked up and said, "Undoubtedly."

She replaced the bedding and, excusing herself, hurried up the stairs. After seeing Lady Hagar she must change quickly for the walk she intended to take. She only hoped that in the meanwhile Careen would not come upon the major accidentally and be further humiliated.

She intended to have this matter settled today, along with his explanation for his extraordinary dislike of this girl.

As if Lady Hagar could see beyond the door of her room, she called out, "Enter, Elspeth, my girl," before Beth knocked. More formidable than ever, the old lady was sitting straight among her pillows, with Nicholas Cormeer's letter lying faceup on the coverlet.

"He's coming. That vile convict is coming here. He claims he is Careen's legal guardian."

"Is he?" Beth asked, trying to take the unpleasant news calmly.

Her Ladyship shrugged. "Probably. Arabella may have left some paper to that effect. Well, don't just stand there making dumb show! We must do something. Keep her out of this fiend's hands."

"We might make a beginning if you let me read the man's letter."

"Very sensible. I must be getting old. Here."
It was brief and very much to the point.

> Madam.
> It has been necessary for me to put my affairs
> in competent hands, but this being done, I now
> have time to devote to the future of my ward, Ca-
> reen Faversham. I sail immediately for Queens-
> town, Ireland, and will arrive at Saltbridge
> Tower hard upon your receipt of this epistle. At
> that time I will take upon myself the considera-
> tion of her further education and her life.
>
> Your obedient servant,
>
> Nicholas Cormeer

Beth remarked, "He is blunt enough, in all conscience. And he seems to be striking at me as well as at
you. Arabella had always, more or less, told me that I
would be responsible for Careen's education."

"I make no doubt she did. Your money, you see.
Certainly, she never loved the girl's father, my son.
And I see no evidence that she loved her second hus-
band, this convict."

Without quite believing what she said, Beth murmured, "She must have loved one of them. Marriage is
a partnership of a lifetime. Without love, I should
think it would be a hell."

Lady Hagar pursed her lips. "Very true. I will always believe there was a love. Earlier. She was in
Dublin for a time before she agreed to marry my son.
There may have been a girlhood affair—Well, no matter. This convict was old enough to know women. If
he didn't then, he does now. And he'll find me quite a

team to manage, I give you my word on that! The thing is, what shall we do next?"

"I could perhaps have my solicitors approach the Prince Regent. And Lord Wellington was fond of my father. But it would take considerable time. How long have we?"

"If this letter came on the ship with him, he may be here now, prowling around Ireland. I shouldn't be surprised if he was already at Ballyglen. And from Ballyglen to Saltbridge— Well, his letter is here. He may not be far behind it."

Beth felt a strong inclination to look over her shoulder. It was that kind of news.

CHAPTER FOUR

Beth explained that she would have to tell Major Wells she could not leave the tower. Lady Hagar snorted.

"Rubbish! I want you to pursue that fellow."

"Pursue the major? Or the convict?"

"Don't be flippant with your elders, my girl. The major, of course. Bring him back into the fold. If you can make him a friend of this family again, you will restore my poor Careen's credit in Saltbridge. Everyone will know then that it was nothing but whispers, the foulest kind of lie to fight. You must go along. For Careen. As for the convict, he must have bought his pardon, or whatever it takes to be allowed to return to Britain. Certainly, he is in the good graces of the new royal governor in Australia, and with his fortune, why not? It is always the way. I am more concerned at the moment to get Major Wells on our side."

Beth could scarcely believe in Major Wells's antipathy to a girl as pretty and as young as Careen. There was no logical reason for it. Only hints, absurd beliefs with no basis in fact. "I'll certainly try to do as you suggest, Lady Hagar. It is very strange, all the same."

"Not strange at all. Just the incomprehensible stupidity of males. Go along now."

"But wouldn't it be wiser for you to tell me exactly what were the circumstances at the time Mrs. Wells died? This convict fellow may be curious, and we want to be able to answer him. Though I believe it was the major's natural grief that caused him to behave so irrationally against Careen. Still, the circumstances should—"

"There are no circumstances. Go and tell O'Beirne to care for the major's offensive horse. I saw it from that window. Oliver Cromwell, indeed!"

The mention of O'Beirne brought a small mystery to mind. "Lady Hagar, does O'Beirne sleep here in the tower, on the ground floor?"

The old lady looked insulted. "Certainly not. He has his room off the carriage house. There are no sleeping quarters on the ground floor." Her sharp eyes stared at Beth. "Why?"

"I wondered, because we—that is, I—saw a blanket and a homespun sheet in that little back parlor."

The old lady scowled, then lowered her gaze to her fingers which clawed the coverlet nervously. Seeing that this mystery had disturbed her, Beth suggested, "Very likely it may be Dorothy. If you or Careen call for anything in the night, the kitchen and stillrooms are just beyond the north end of the dining parlor."

"Yes, but it would still be necessary to pass the main hall. Besides, there is no bellpull in the back parlor." Lady Hagar rubbed her arthritic hands together, agreed suddenly. "Just so. It is Dorothy. Now, my girl, run along. And remember. Be charming to Kevin Wells."

Beth left her. She was much more disturbed by the entire attitude of the ex-convict than by the bedclothing found in the back parlor. It seemed shocking—even indecent—that a creature of Nicholas Cormeer's antecedents should have legal custody of impressionable, young Careen Faversham.

In the circumstances Major Wells's pleasure at her return went far to raise her spirits. She had changed hastily to a black riding habit worn but twice, neither occasion shedding any glory upon her. But since black was far from her most flattering color, she took care to wear her hat with its great green feather that curved along her cheek. She was rewarded by the major's compliment as they left through the dusty, only half-furnished main hall.

"Miss Milford, you are quite the loveliest sight Saltbridge has seen since . . ." He broke off, recovered quickly. "Molly was not precisely beautiful, but she had warmth. She was very honest. That and her helpfulness made her popular among the locals."

And when Molly Wells died, thought Beth, it was undoubtedly her popularity with the local villagers that made them all look for a scapegoat. Who else but the prettiest girl in the vicinity? It still seemed absurd to hold Careen responsible merely because she had failed to accompany the woman on the walk that killed her.

She hoped this visit with Major Wells would give her the chance to find out the truth about the woman's death. She had supposed Major Wells's trail skirted the copse where the tinkers' wagon had camped the previous night, but to her surprise, he started out with her on a genuine path across the thick heart of the woods. It was damp and heavy with leaf mould underfoot, the product of a long, wet summer and autumn.

Beth had very little experience with primitive areas of nature or with primitive people. She mistrusted things and people that did not follow the rules of a civilized countryside.

"Wouldn't it be easier to go by the pony track?" she suggested. "We could make greater speed."

The major smiled. "Is that the object when one goes walking in Somerset?"

A little shamefaced she laughed and confessed that it was usually her object, though other citizens of Bristol and Bath and of the Somerset country might disagree with her.

"Mrs. Wells was fond of the out-of-doors?" she asked as he helped her over a dark, spongy mass of rotting vegetation.

They passed from this dense brushwood into a path of sunlight where the growth was parted by a low wall of rocks running diagonally through the area, cutting between bushes, helping to bank a small, weed-choked stream that ran parallel to the wall, cutting through the copse.

"Molly went everywhere," the major explained. "Like you, she loved walking. When she decided Careen needed mothering, she used to walk over to the tower by this path. She said this wall should be broken through to make it easier. Going back and forth, you see."

"What does the little wall separate?"

"Molly's property is on the east and the Faversham land lies west to the sea." He stopped, seeing her interest in the little, sunlit glade. It was even more charming because everything that surrounded it was dark, damp and—to Beth, at least—depressing.

"I'm afraid I prefer open downs. The sea. Fields of grain."

He agreed enthusiastically. "I knew you would say that. I knew it moments after I left you on the bridge yesterday." She thought he was going to touch her shoulder, which was a harmless enough gesture, but she began to be uneasy over its cause. His warm hazel eyes seemed to tell her a great deal more than their brief acquaintance warranted.

"How much farther is your estate?" she asked casually.

"We are a trifle less than halfway." He took her hand, assisted her up the two stone steps and over the wall. The steps on the other side bridged the little stream. She was caught by the charm of the place so long as the sun remained here. The turgid waters of the stream were lighted on the surface by shafts of sunlight. She remarked,

"It looks as though you might see to the bottom." He looked down. Perhaps he had never noticed it before. She added, "But you see, it isn't clear at all. Only on the surface."

He laughed. "I suppose we might make philosophy out of that observation. Most people are like this stream. But not you, I think. Nor Molly."

"Your Molly must have been a very special person. And I am afraid she was not in the least like me. Shall we go on?"

"I beg your pardon, Ma'am." She had already started into the shadowed thicket beyond, walking rapidly, and he started to join her but looked back once at the pleasant little glade above the long, low wall of stones. When she saw his expression, a kind of melancholy remembrance of the past, she was sorry she had spoken so abruptly.

He joined her afterward, explaining, "Molly loved sitting on that wall in the sun, surrounded by the shadows and what she used to call 'the sinister undergrowth.'"

Beth had glanced back as he spoke. Now, when she looked ahead, she cried out at a horrifying, flesh-colored thing that rumbled across her path and into the boggy morass beyond. Major Wells chuckled at her terror.

He said, "Listen!"

The flesh-colored creature made grunting, rutting noises, splashing leaves, roots, and muddy water.

"A pig!"

"One of Shelagh Quinn's porkers, I should think. From the coteens. My housekeeper claims Quinn's pigs live off the refuse she throws out."

"I suppose your housekeeper knew your wife even before you were married." He nodded. Beth went on: "She must have been very fond of Mrs. Wells." It had occurred to Beth in the last few minutes that the gossip against Careen might have been started by the late Mrs. Wells's housekeeper, out of some passionate sense of loyalty. This opinion was reinforced by the major's agreement.

He said suddenly, "You must be tired, Miss Milford. Is this too fast a pace for you?"

She stiffened a little. There was the emotional ring in his voice again. She said in haste, "No. I want to get there. I've—I've heard so much about your lovely home. Wells Hall, isn't it?"

"A lonely house, I'm afraid, since Molly went. She died at that sunny spot in the woods back there, by the way. It was raining. She slipped on one of those steps carved out of the bare rock."

"How terrible!" She wondered that he could still travel over this strange little woods path with the memory of the tragedy. It seemed especially poignant that Molly Wells's death should have occurred at the one place on the path which was pleasant and cheer-ful.

The clumps of scrub and brushwood began to thin out into open space. A square, white Palladian house loomed up across a knoll that was less grass than rock, sand, and shale.

"Molly's house," the major said proudly. "Not to compare with your English mansions, perhaps, but rather special to me."

She let herself be propelled across the knoll to make the expected cries of admiration for a house that turned out to be genuinely attractive. And warm, even on a bright, brisk November day. But she could not concentrate on the determined efforts of the major and his stout, sweet-faced little housekeeper to make her welcome. Beth kept thinking of the unfortunate Molly Wells, dying alone and helpless, surrounded by those grim, shadowed woods.

She was aroused to the present by the major who addressed his housekeeper as "Mrs. O'Beirne." Beth asked curiously,

"Are you related to the O'Beirne at Saltbridge Tower?"

Mrs. O'Beirne's chubby cheeks grew pink.

"Not for to take note of, ma'am. A shame and a dis-grace. After me telling him what I think of him for serving that murderess! Brother to my dead husband, as was."

"Murderess? She was nowhere near Mrs. Wells, if you are referring to my thirteen-year-old cousin—"

Mrs. O'Beirne corrected her. "Fourteen, ma'am. And she was there, right enough. She was seen running in the copse afterward."

Beth snapped indignantly, "So that is the lie they are spreading! And it is a lie. Careen was with her grandmother at the time. And then, too, what possible reason could she have for letting Mrs. Wells die? What motive?"

The housekeeper was eyeing her with a frown, yet not with disapproval. It was as if she studied Beth's face and movements.

Major Wells cut in with gentle firmness, "Mrs. O'Beirne, we are not going to discuss this with an innocent young visitor like Miss Milford. She is loyal and honorable and I am persuaded Molly would have behaved in very much the same way. Don't you remember how she defended Careen from every charge, how, whenever someone said the girl was fast, or behaved like a wild gypsy or some other heathen thing, it was Molly who defended her? Mrs. O'Beirne, doesn't Miss Milford remind you of someone?"

The little woman's blue marble eyes widened as they looked Beth over from head to foot. Beth became more and more uncomfortable over this repeated comparison.

"Ay, Major! Very like. Now, would you, by any chance, have any Hallidie relations, Ma'am? That was Miss Molly before she was wed to the major."

After that, there was a great fuss, tea and cakes fed to Beth by the suddenly loquacious little housekeeper while the major hovered about in an anxious way, trying much too hard to avoid controversial subjects and to please her.

For the third time in the last half an hour she had just suggested that Lady Hagar would be expecting her, when there was a disturbance out in the stillroom, and the cook, gaunt and wild-eyed, came rushing in to complain of "them gypsies what scares a body out of his mind, wanderin' about my kitchen."

Beth stood up. She felt around for her reticule.

Seeing her, Major Wells smiled, that understanding smile reserved for helpless females and their foibles.

"You mustn't be concerned. We won't let them harm you."

"Harm me! I'm not afraid of the wretches! It's simply that I am carrying ten guineas about with me." Her indignation spilled over into anger which only convinced the major that his first assumption was correct.

"Of course. Forgive me, my dear—" She looked at him. He added hurriedly, "—my dear Miss Milford. But they really are harmless. Would you like to meet them? I give you my word, I don't allow them to camp upon my land, but I see no harm in their selling a few of their trinkets to keep the natives happy." As she hesitated, wondering whether she should leave her reticule under the cushion in the chair or fasten it to her skirt, the major put his arm around her in a massive gesture of protection.

"Now, you must not be concerned. We'll go out and meet them together. I will be with you at all times."

She felt like setting her boot heel sharply upon his instep but fortunately realized her own absurdity and let him escort her through the servants' quarters to the kitchen.

The two male gypsies, the thin, stooped old man and the good-looking boy, stood uneasily on the wide hearth with their backs to the blackened kettles hanging over the fire. Beth sniffed potatoes on the boil, a smell she found highly appetizing. The two gypsy women were at the wide cutting table where they had put out trinkets and cloth, pots and pans, and cutlery. Beth paid little attention to the elderly female who busied herself spreading their wares to the best advantage. The other woman, Tzigana of the gold earbobs and big teeth, turned and looked at Beth. It was a bold, insolent stare, but it did not hide the woman's striking appearance, or her obvious power over the actions of her tribe.

With her too ingratiating smile she addressed Beth. "Will the pretty lady look at our wares? Finest quality. See? Feel the sharpness of the knives, the fine quality of the pans. And the weave of this cloth. By the holy nuns themselves. Or jewels. See the precious rubies."

"Do not be afraid," Kevin Wells urged Beth. "This is Tzigana. She won't hurt you."

Beth wrinkled her nose at this as at the little push he gave her. She found it demeaning to oblige the gimlet-eyed, swarthy Tzigana, who kept dangling these worthless items in her face.

"Rubies, indeed!" Beth muttered as Tzigana dropped the preposterous ring with its glass stone into her palm.

The major was amused but suggested, "No doubt your cousin would like this."

"I hope she has better taste."

The cook had been complaining wildly, but the talk of jewelry soothed her and she took up everything Beth discarded.

Because the linen did seem of excellent quality and the trinkets flashed brightly, Beth began to take a greater interest in the merchandise. Most of the jewelry was cheap and gaudy, and she reached across this pile to examine an exquisite bonbon dish with sprigs of deep blue upon the fragile china handle. Probably the last unbroken piece of a valuable set. As she put the dish down, her cuff caught on the blackened chain of a locket. She took up the locket, twisted the chain away from her white cuff, and was about to toss the locket back on the table when something about the faint scrollwork of the silver surface looked familiar. Tzigana was busy selling the cook a huge pearl ring that looked flagrantly paste. Beth showed the locket to the major.

"Badly tarnished. Looks worthless to me," the major observed casually.

"I agree." Beth hoped she revealed none of her thoughts in her face. "Still, it just might do as a little gift when it has been properly polished." She dangled it and a string of blue beads before the older gypsy woman. "What is the price?"

The woman started to haggle, but Kevin Wells put some silver coins into her hand while Beth protested, struggling to get out her own money. It was no use. Wells appeared much too anxious to please her, by doing all the wrong things.

In the end the gypsies sold a pot and two pans to Mrs. O'Beirne, and having collected from Major Wells and the cook, left in excellent humor.

"And I must go, too," Beth insisted. "It is long past the dinner hour. It will soon be sunset."

"Yes, of course, Thoughtless of me. I'll have the mare put to the gig at once."

In every way Kevin Wells had been kind and obliging. She only wished he did not have this obsession about her resemblance to his late wife. As they rode down toward Saltbridge, Beth ran the locket and its chain through her fingers. She was debating whether she should tell Major Wells of her suspicions about the locket.

He smiled at her apparent interest in what was no more than a worthless gypsy trinket.

"It may look presentable enough when it is cleaned. Not for you, naturally, but for—perhaps one of your servants. Is there anything inside the locket?"

She tried to open the locket with her fingernail.

After several failures, she got it open. The tiny oval frames were empty. The miniatures inside had been removed long ago, to judge by the thick tarnish. Kevin Wells was looking at her so intently she felt she had to make some explanation.

"It is very like a locket I exchanged with my Cousin Arabella many years ago when we were at the young ladies' academy together. I still have mine among some old jewelry at home."

"And that one? Surely, Lady Arabella Faversham would never have let that befall a present of yours, Miss Milford?"

She laughed shortly. "It is exactly what she would have done."

"But what were those gypsies doing with her jewelry?" He looked around as if he would go back and throttle the story out of them, and she was sorry she had mentioned the matter. Much better to see whether this could be the same locket. Otherwise, speculation was useless. She dropped the jewelry into her reticule and tried to change the subject. Not an easy matter with a man of dogged persistence like Kevin Wells.

The carriage road was lined on the north by a copse adjoining the woods owned by the Wells and Faversham estates, and on the south by the Saltbridge stream. From the stream's low banks the water spread out south and east into the low-lying bogs where night had already fallen.

When they came to the coteens there was considerable activity. Fishermen, out in the black curraghs, bobbed upon the waves as they came in at sunset. Women were out everywhere gathering in their children as well as an occasional pig or sheep.

One comely woman of thirty or so, in the usual

black garments brightened by a shawl of many colors,
answered Kevin Wells's salute of his whip handle to
his hat by striding over the mud to his little carriage.

"Good day to you, Major," she called and Kevin explained.

"That is Shelagh Quinn, one of the few locals who
are civil to an English outlander like me."

Beth wondered if he expected them to be civil to
outsiders whose wealth of land and house was so much
greater than their own, but she had already observed
that Major Wells, like herself and most human beings,
believed whatever served his own self-interest.

"She is very attractive," Beth murmured.

The major shrugged. "Undoubtedly," but he seemed
oblivious to the woman's fine, buxom figure and her
smile that was both warm and sensuous.

Shelagh Quinn acknowledged introductions in her
pleasant way, but it was plain to Beth that her entire
concern was Major Wells. Though Beth had never
mistaken any of her own flirtations for love, she recognized the emotion in others, and it was abundantly
clear that Shelagh Quinn was in love with her land-
owning neighbor.

"Master Kevin, my boy Paddy says one of our porkers went and lost himself in your woods again. I am
that sorry—I leave it to anyone to say how often I've
been at that boy to mind the porkers! But with his
father dead in the sea and all, it's almost more than I
can do to be both father and mother to the boy. He
needs a father. That he does. But they're not so easy
come by."

Beth heard this artful, though obviously sincere,
plea with growing interest and was not surprised
when Kevin Wells rose to the bait. She had begun to

suspect that the good major's heart went out to any female in need.

"Now, now, Shelagh, promise me you'll do nothing rash. These lads hereabouts are fine fellows, I make no doubt, but you deserve a very special husband. Someone worthy of you. Bring Paddy up to the hall one evening this week. Come to dinner. And afterward, I'll have a little talk with him. As his good father might have done."

"You were always so kind, Master Kevin! I do not know as there is a soul in all of England as would have helped a wretched Irish widow the way you have."

The major blushed. "Well, now! Well, now! You will let Mrs. O'Beirne know the day you are coming, so she can have a prime roast on the spit, and beat up a sauce for some of that trout Rory McInerny brought around this morning."

Shelagh Quinn curtsied, smiled once more at Beth, and watched as they rode away. Beth felt uncomfortably certain that she had roused the woman's jealousy— or perhaps envy—without in the least intending to.

They were barely over the crown of Saltbridge Hill, with the tower on the near horizon, when the major seemed to dismiss his neighbors in the coteens.

"A good sort of woman, that. Quite capable. For a female. Needs a male, of course, but there are many widows like her along these stormy coasts. It's a solitary life and one pities them."

"Mrs. Quinn should not have much trouble attracting the right sort," Beth said. "With her beauty."

The major seemed to consider this fact for the first time and not altogether pleasurably. "Yes. I daresay. Not my sort," he added hastily, as if fearful she would form the wrong impression. All the same, she hoped she had left him with a new and better view of Shelagh Quinn. Since he showed signs of turning again to a comparison of Beth with his late wife, she said quickly,

"How different the beach looks at sunset today! Yesterday, it was shrouded in fog."

He paid little attention to the view, although, if there were anything artistic in him, she believed he should have been moved by the golden light that glowed on the long, snakelike chains of kelp coiled upon the beach. Driftwood, too, had been deposited as the waters receded, and the sea foam collected around it to form queer shapes like human bodies only half shrouded. Beth mentioned the opaque seaweed and blackened wood from the wreck of a fisherman's curragh that had been washed up to the sheep track below the southwest corner of the Saltbridge Tower.

But the major pointed out a half dozen other piles and dismissed their strange beauty with the wisdom of a long resident there. "The kelp often takes the appearance of a sea serpent. All nonsense, you know. But when the curraghs are overturned in a storm—they are only canoes, after all—one finds a body upon occasion. Regrettable, but it's the life they choose."

And the death? Beth asked herself, but said nothing. They had reached the gates to the quadrangle which still stood open, but unlike the previous night, no lamp shone to welcome them. The last rays of sunset had sunk behind the glittering waters, but in the dusk they could see enough for the major to turn over the reins to Beth, leap out of the gig, and then cross the quadrangle to his white stallion, Oliver Cromwell. The animal, having eaten his fill in the stall, now uneasily pawed the rocky ground.

As the major approached Beth, leading Oliver, the mare harnessed to the gig began to tremble and start. Beth, damning all equines, had to stand up and devote her full strength to holding the mare. A second or two later she heard a footstep on her other side and without a by your leave was pinched in at the waist by two hands, dragged out of the gig, and her feet set on the ground. Trying to keep out of the way of the mare's nervous movements, she heard a strange male voice order Major Wells:

"If you can't control your animals, for God's sake, keep them tethered apart where they'll do less harm!"

"Sorry!" the major said stiffly. He had tethered the stallion to the back of the gig and now got up into the gig and took the reins. He peered with difficulty into the shadows. "Are you safe, Miss Milford?"

"I'll see to my Cousin Elspeth," said Beth's surly rescuer before she could speak. "You had best be on your way, Major."

Thus taunted, the major lost his temper. "Is that you, O'Beirne? Now, see here, I'll not stand for your impudence."

But Beth had already guessed the truth. Whoever is out here with us, she thought, it isn't O'Beirne at all. It must be that wretched convict!

My Cousin Elspeth, indeed!

CHAPTER FIVE

In the twilight darkness of the quadrangle, Beth looked from one to the other of the two shadowed figures. It occurred to her that she knew nothing of the crime for which ex-convict Nicholas Cormeer had been shipped off to Australia. Very likely it had been murder. Whatever the case, he could not be other than a dangerous man. For this reason, as well as a faint hope that they would settle Careen's future without coming to a vulgar court case, she decided to forget Nicholas Cormeer's too-familiar manner.

"Please thank Mrs. O'Beirne for a delightful tea, Major," she told him in dismissal. "And thank you for your escort home."

The major had not been certain whether to leap down and take that unseen, ill-mannered cur by the scruff of the neck, or to preserve his own dignity. There was a note of relief in his voice when he took Beth's lead and said good-bye. He felt that for the sake of his honor he must, at least, show his claim to the lady's friendship and added, "I will call upon you soon, Miss Milford, to—ah—find out the secret of your locket."

"Goodnight, sir. Yes, indeed. You are always welcome at the tower. Good night."

She tried not to reveal any of her relief in the quick way she dismissed her kindly friend, but she felt that the sooner he was on his way, the less likely he would be to get into a quarrel with her dangerous and self-appointed cousin.

She watched the man who shared these dark surroundings move to close the gates. From his silhouette and his movements, she decided he was taller than the average, and as vigorous as Kevin Wells. Perhaps not as heavy, but a man to be reckoned with, all the same. She cleared her throat, said in the pleasantly reserved voice she used with strangers and servants, "I imagine you must be Mr. Cormeer. May I welcome you to—" This was awkward. She did the graceful thing and admitted it. "I beg your pardon. I am only a guest here." He had said nothing to help her out, and despite all her recent good intentions, she began to lose her temper.

"Where the devil is O'Beirne? And why are there no lights? I can't see my hand before my face."

The silhouette had discovered his voice again. Her newfound cousin took her arm in another of those painful grips which she assumed must be his form of politeness, and said, "Ah! That is better. I'd begun to think you were just another of the insipid females who populate these isles."

"But I, on the contrary, would have known you anywhere. From your delightful manners." And also from his slightly provincial accent, she thought, but did not add this fuel to their brisk exchange.

Fortunately, someone had set a lamp on the heavy, Jacobean table in the main hall, and by that beam of light reaching the entry passage, Beth and Nicholas Cormeer got their first good look at each other. He was very much as she imagined he would be, with black hair going a little gray about his sallow face, and deep-set, penetrating eyes so dark as to be nearly black. She considered that these distinctions, together with a hard mouth which appeared never to have smiled, gave him an ideal criminal face. In other ways his tall, erect figure was very much as it seemed in silhouette. Dangerous.

"For family relations, we do not much resemble each other," he said, after scarcely more than a glance at Beth. It was difficult to guess what he thought of her from that remark or the indifference with which he added, "Nor are you much like my late wife. Come along. The old lady is wanting her supper."

For a widower of less than four months, he seemed to lack all the proper feelings of grief, loneliness, or even bitterness. Since he was just as surly as she had expected him to be, she, too, kept to the business at hand.

"We seem to have only O'Beirne as cook. It that why he wasn't out seeing to the major's horse?"

"I am told it was O'Beirne's afternoon to spend in the village. He hasn't returned yet."

She stopped on her way upstairs.

"Good heavens! Don't tell me Dorothy attends to the cooking! With those frail hands of hers I should think the kitchen was the last place for her."

Leaning on the newel post he looked up the stairs at her.

"Since she isn't in the kitchen, I'll not be telling you so. But I will tell you this: I am not eating porridge for my supper."

Much relieved, she said, "Thank God for that! I will be pleased to join you in eating whatever else is available."

"You may. Providing you work for your supper."

He did have a sense of humor, after all. She showed her appreciation of it by her quick, light laugh.

"Of course! Simply put a pinafore about me and I shall heat water for the tea."

"If you like. But I assure you, before the night is over, you will wish you hadn't confined your meal to tea."

She leaned over the balustrade and stared at him. Whatever he expected, it would be no joke if she helped to cook their supper.

"You meant that, didn't you? About my going to work in the kitchen." His black eyebrows raised. There seemed to be no doubt that he meant it. She refused to be shamed, however, and went on boldly, "Very well. I have never prepared a meal, and if I am to begin, I shall be happy to feed my first effort to you, Cousin."

Caught in the glow from the lamp on the floor above, his eyes glittered and she thought she had angered him. She was a good deal surprised to see him smile. Not a delightful, full-blown sign of his good humor, perhaps, but he was definitely amused. Nor did he take his attention off her until she turned the corner on the upper floor landing and went to her room.

The stars were not out yet, but the blue of evening gave the sea and shoreline a silvery look that would have drawn her to longer admiration if she hadn't been aware of the unpleasant fellow belowstairs who was trying so hard to discourage her here at the tower. No doubt he expected Beth to be shocked by her uncouth relations and rush off madly to civilized England, leaving the field, and Careen, in his hands.

"Not so, *Cousin* Nicholas!" she swore as she considered the somber beauty of the ocean scene. "You may think you know me—and I'm sure you do think so—but you haven't yet begun to do battle with General Milford's daughter, my lad."

She looked down across the sand, marveling at the eerie forms taken by the kelp as it was washed about in the tidal foam. But there was work to be done, and she wanted to be at her best. Or worst. She had recognized in the ex-convict a worthy foe.

After thoughtfully considering the tarnished locket in her reticule, she closed it and hung it on the peg behind her riding habit. It was absurd to discover that her greatest problem at the moment would be a gown suitable for kitchen wear. Dorothy knocked timidly while she was examining her clothing in the armoire, and upon being invited to help select something, suggested a lavender gown with the new broadened shoulders and large puffed sleeves that would get into every pot and pan in the kitchen. In the end, Beth chose a deep blue cotton dress with a white fichu and sash. "Detestable but useful," she had remarked to Dawlish as they packed her things for the trip to Ireland. Now it was useful.

"I suppose my cousin Careen has met Mr. Cormeer?" she asked Dorothy as the girl fastened up her gown.

"Oh, yes, mum. Met the gentleman indeed!"

It sounded as though there was more to it than simple introductions. "Did Miss Careen behave well?"

"As to that, I couldn't say."

Beth began to suspect the worst. "And they quarreled, naturally. That wretched man! Where is Miss Careen now?"

"In the stillroom when I saw her a few minutes since."

"What?"

"The—gentleman set her to fetching vegetables from the winter pantry, I believe."

"The fellow certainly won't win his ward's devotion with those tactics. Hurry, dear, I had best go down and see what can be done to settle things between them."

Dorothy said nothing, but Beth, looking up suddenly, surprised a little smirk that twisted the girl's colorless mouth.

"What is it you know, Dorothy?"

"Nothing, mum. Nothing at all, only . . . when I saw Miss Careen, she was laughing so hard she didn't look to be needing anyone at all."

Beth reddened but recovered rapidly. "Splendid. Then perhaps Miss Careen will see what can be done to make peace between Mr. Cormeer and me."

The girl tittered. "Fancy that! I mean—Miss Careen making peace for anybody. She can be a terror, can that young lady. Now, you do look charming, even for the kitchen, mum, if you'll forgive the liberty."

Beth took a long, deep breath and went rapidly down to the ground floor where she hurried through several empty rooms by mistake before remembering that the kitchen and stillrooms were on the far side of the quadrangle. She hoped no one saw her wandering about foolishly, not quite certain where to go or what she was going to do when she arrived there.

A review of her brisk morning trip through the area with Careen brought her the length of the long-unused and damp-smelling old dining hall. Opening off its east side beyond the quadrangle windows was a door into the summer parlor where Careen and Beth had eaten breakfast. The kitchen was to the north of this parlor and at long last she arrived, prepared for awkwardness and even enmity between Nicholas Cormeer and herself.

Instead, Careen looked around as she stirred the contents of a stewpot and hailed Beth. "Just in time, Cuz. Do set the silver around on the table in the summer parlor. And napkins. I am willing to eat convict food and cook peasant fashion, but my aristocrat's hands demand linen." She smiled engagingly and Beth was grateful to her for making the moment so easy.

"Where is our master chef?" she asked as she set about obeying her cousin's sensible orders.

"Fetching eggs from the stillroom and wine from the rockery." Careen's eyes crinkled with excitement. "He is too marvelous! Small wonder Mama married him! And so rich, beside all else."

The "all else" baffled Beth. She supposed it was Careen's youthful, and no doubt temporary, enthusiasm for a man who brought new discipline into her life.

"How clever of him to find the rockery, whatever that might be!" Beth remarked while paying brisk attention to her work. "Anything should be an improvement over Lady Hagar's poteen. Your stepfather seems to have found his way about the place in short order."

"He's clever, that one. Walked in here while you were away at the major's house and began to give orders as if he were Grandmama herself."

Beth came back into the kitchen from the adjoining parlor.

"He walked here? Where did he come from?"

"The village, I expect. What does it matter? It's so much nicer having a man about. There hasn't been one here—not really here, I mean, since Kevin. That is, since Molly died."

Beth was aware of several despicable emotions, dominated by shame at the fact that her own arrival had precipitated no change for the better, no particular enthusiasm from her young cousin whose future she had arrogantly assumed she could shape and form. And with shame at her own shortcomings she was aware of jealousy as well. She disliked this Nicholas Cormeer for all the wrong reasons, and knew it.

I've been spoiled, she thought. I've had my way too long, and too easily.

There were so many self-reproaches she could make that she did not consider until sometime later Careen's revealing remark about the onetime importance of Kevin Wells in this house.

Meanwhile, Beth had always supposed that when she realized her faults, she corrected them immediately. But though she knew she was being unfair to Nicholas Cormeer, she could not conquer her aversion to him.

"What does Lady Hagar think of your new father?"

"I was certain they would be like a fuse to gunpowder, but it turned out quite differently."

Beth gave up. Not staunch Hagar Faversham, too! She asked herself if she had been the only one in Saltbridge whom this fellow treated as if he were the overseer and she the convict. What was there about her that made Cormeer dislike her even before they met? Perhaps he had expected to meet a lovely, fragile, sensuous creature like Arabella, and along came Cousin Beth, quite a different English dish of tea!

Slapping the napkins on the table, Beth called out, "I daresay the man's charms are irresistible. They escape me, but no doubt my own charms are not universally felt either."

"Surely that cannot be so, Cousin Elspeth," Nicholas Cormeer's sardonic voice insisted with a gentleness that made her grit her teeth.

Careen giggled, and Beth saw them both in the kitchen, the girl having taken a dusty bottle from Cormeer and begun to wipe it off on her already stained pinafore.

Aside from a stiffening of her spine, Beth managed to present a picture of complete self-possession. "Either I must learn to lower my voice, Mr. Cormeer, or you must wear noisier boots." It took considerable effort, but she was rapidly learning to cope with Nicholas Cormeer's surprises. She placed the heavy silver epergne in the center of the table. "I see that the table is set for four. Are we to have the pleasure of Her Ladyship's company at supper?"

"Yes. Grandmama is curious about Nicholas. It must be that, don't you think so?"

"I don't doubt it." She glanced at Nicholas and was thrown off her stride by his unexpected smile. Was this a sign of amnesty?

Careen struggled to get out of her pinafore. Her stepfather reached over, untied the sash. She blushed and looked at him gratefully. "I'll go and bring Grandmama down. It is odd to be eating a genuine meal after dark, but I know it will be very special." She darted away on the run, through the unused, empty halls to the distant stairs across the quadrangle.

"She should have crossed the courtyard. It would have been quicker," Beth suggested.

Cormeer went to one of the long windows, looked out. "She has already taken up the lamp on the ground floor of the tower. At her age, they move fast." He passed Beth, went into the kitchen where delicious odors came from the stew bubbling in the black kettle on its fire hook.

Beth followed him after a dignified little pause. She had been inhaling all those delightful odors from the stewpot and found herself hungrier than she had been in months.

"Lady Faversham has what I believe surgeons would call catarrh of the stomach, sir. Does she know that you are preparing a dinner and not a supper? She is accustomed to eating gruel at this hour."

She was surprised when he agreed. "But I've known men in a condition worse than Her Ladyship's, and they were cured when they returned to a healthy diet." He waved a half-empty bottle of the powerful local potato whiskey. "Not, however, while they accompanied it with a bottle of this poteen at every meal."

"Have you tried it?"

"I couldn't resist the temptation. Rather like having the scalp removed abruptly."

They both laughed, and this unanimity seemed to promise peace, at least for the duration of the meal.

As they waited for the two women, the cold November night closed in around the stone quadrangle, and Beth went to stand on the hearth, holding her hands out to the warmth of the peat fire. However, Mr. Cormeer seemed bent upon shaming her, for he began to set out porridge bowls for the stew, to uncork the wine, and to behave in other ways that made Beth appear perfectly useless. She turned from the fire, took up the teapot, and put the tea to steep.

She was looking for a knife with which to slice off chunks of the bread remaining from the previous day. Here Mr. Cormeer came to her rescue, removed the bread from her hands, and cut off thick, fairly neat slices. She sighed and wondered how she could prove her usefulness. She had hardly been a success so far.

It struck her after a few minutes that Careen had taken a very long time in fetching down her grandmother. With a teacup in each hand she went to the uncurtained windows overlooking the quadrangle and tried to make out any activity on the ground floor of the tower. She did not like to say anything which Nicholas Cormeer was certain to interpret as the flutterings of a spinster aunt. She found it slightly unnerving when Nicholas came up behind her, looked over her head, and then said,

"My convict stew must be eaten exactly on the minute. There'll be no more delays to put on frills or curl up locks."

Still in his shirt-sleeves, with only a queer, black leather jerkin to keep out the elements, he went into the darkened dining hall, pushed open one of the long-unused doors, and crossed the courtyard to the tower. A sudden absurd thought occurred to Beth as he vanished in the lowering fog. What if neither he, nor Lady Faversham, nor Careen appeared again? She shivered. The big cups rattled in their small accompanying plates and she set them down.

The sooner this godforsaken house is renovated, the better, she reminded herself. I should have acted on Careen's hints at once. I am becoming positively hagridden. What must poor Lady Hagar and Careen have gone through during these last few years? Apparently, Arabella sent them no financial help even after her marriage to Cormeer.

Beth could not recall when she had felt so guilty. While she waited, she made mental lists of changes to be made, in the estate as well as the comfort of her young cousin and Lady Faversham. One thought gave her a new complaint against this intruder, Nicholas Cormeer. He might very well outbid her, for some perverse reason of his own, attaching a young, impressionable girl and perhaps Lady Faversham as well, although she suspected the old lady's sharp eyes would see through any falseness in the newcomer.

What ailed Her Ladyship tonight? Perhaps her poor head was still suffering from all that poteen she had drunk in the night. But this could hardly delay Careen so long. When she found her grandmother ill, she might ring for Dorothy, or return and let everyone know there would be only three for supper.

In fact, they were all taking a very long time on such a short errand.

Beth drummed her fingers on one of the leaded windowpanes, growing more and more uneasy. With a sudden end to patience she left the window, went into the dining hall, and tried the latch on the courtyard door. Behind her in the empty dark the beams overhead creaked. In some long unswept corner a large rat scrambled out of the ray of light that cut through the doorway from the summer parlor. Beth leaped out of its way, pulled the door open, and stepped onto the grass-grown cobbles.

Enclosed within the stone walls, the damp cold clung to her flesh. Hugging her forearms against the chill, she started across the courtyard, wishing some one had left the lamp to glow at the foot of the tower stairs. While she was trying to avoid the holes between broken stones, she heard voices through the window embrasure on the ground-floor passage of the tower. Seconds later, Careen appeared, running down the stairs with Nicholas behind her, holding the lamp.

Beth, too, began to run. She called, "Is she ill? Lady Hagar. Has something happened?"

Careen rushed out and across the quadrangle toward Beth. "Cousin, come and help us. Maybe you have some ideas. It's all so unlike Grandmama."

This stopped Beth in confusion. "What is it? What has happened?"

Careen was telling her tale in bits and pieces. "Dorothy and I looked in her wardobe. She isn't dressed. Still in her bedgown," when Nicholas Cormeer cut in rudely but with good sense.

"The woman seems to be gone. Not in her room, not up on the battlements, nor in any of the other chambers. She is—" He glanced around at the many rooms and single-story outbuildings facing the quadrangle courtyard. "She is apparently somewhere else."

CHAPTER SIX

Beth tried to calm the excited Careen with the reminder, "If she could walk down to dinner, she could be anywhere. Perhaps she came down early for some purpose."

"In her bedgown?"

"Undoubtedly she wore an outfit you don't recall. That is all."

Beth looked at Cormeer over the girl's head, hoping he would add to her reassurance. Unfortunately, his expression gave her little help.

"We had better go through the rest of the house. The maidservant is examining the great hall and the rest of the ground floor. I'll look through these outbuildings that open on the courtyard. I suggest you ladies eat your supper."

"Don't be ridiculous," Beth said briskly. "Careen, come with me. I'll get a light and we will look through the buildings on the north side. You, sir, will take the south side and the east end."

He looked impatient but said, "Very well. Call me at once if she has fallen down, or is otherwise injured. I think it would tax even your redoubtable powers to carry the lady, if she needs such attention."

He gave over the lamp to Beth and returned to the

kitchen where he lighted a storm lantern and was on his way to look for Lady Hagar around the carriage house and stable. Beth and Careen called the old lady's name until they were hoarse as they examined the pantry, stillroom, and an icehouse which hadn't been used in years, according to Careen.

"And this rockery Mr. Cormeer visited to find the bottle of wine, where is it?" Beth asked presently when it was clear that Lady Hagar had not wandered into any of the service areas.

Careen gave a quick, nervous little laugh. "She couldn't possibly get down there. It's only a few rocks piled against the base of the tower. We keep our wine and vegetables there in winter, instead of using the old icehouse. You—we aren't going around there alone, are we?"

Beth looked across the courtyard, saw Cormeer's light seeping around through the carriage house as he raised or lowered the lamp to illuminate dark corners. She asked Careen, "Does she often disappear like this? Where does she go?"

The girl shook her head. "She doesn't walk much now. Last year she twisted her ankle in one of those holes between the cobblestones, near the tower entrance. Well, Grandmama immediately went to bed. We waited upon her and she loved it, especially after she began to have trouble with her stomach. It was her way of gaining a little attention." She raised her small, pointed chin. "And I don't in the least blame her. The poor dear had nothing else in her life."

"I understand. But where can she have gone? Think!"

"She wouldn't have walked away. She hates walking. I know Gramdmama, I tell you!"

Beth liked the girl for her staunch loyalty and for

her anxiety. Careen seemed to be much more her father's daughter than Arabella's.

"All right, dear. Since she can't be far away, we are bound to find her. I do think, though, we should be prepared to discover that she has fallen. Or even that she is unconscious. Otherwise, she would have heard us. Come along. We'll try those medieval halls. You aren't afraid of rats, I hope."

Careen laughed. "You forget, Cousin, I live here. I know all the rats and most of the spiders by name." She took the lamp from Beth and they retraced their steps. Before they reached the dining hall door they were joined by Nicholas Cormeer who had also examined the outside of the quadrangle wall.

"There is your pony missing," he told Beth. "And the cart as well."

"The boy from the stables in Ballyglen is to collect the pony and cart within the week," Beth suggested. "Could he have done so this afternoon?"

With sudden hope Careen looked up at Nicholas.

"It would be very like Grandmama to take herself off to the village in the cart and never a word to us."

For once Beth and Nicholas were in unison. They both rolled their eyes skyward expressively.

"At all events," he said, "we should know the whole of it when this servant, this O'Beirne, returns. He must have seen her on the sheep track, or visiting at the coteens."

They had passed the dining hall, and all entered by one of the two doors opening into the main hall. Because of its long disuse, Nicholas Cormeer was forced to put his shoulder to the heavy panels, and when the warped wood finally gave away, he and the females were greeted by a shriek from Dorothy who was wandering through the long room like a wraith.

She babbled, "Forgive me, sir. Miss Careen. I keep imagining . . . things in the dark."

"No sign of her?" Nicholas asked as he passed the shivering girl and went to examine the alcoves whose windows looked down over the bench toward a wall of fog.

Beth went in one direction, toward the back parlor, while Careen wandered into the little passage with the dining hall beyond. Then Careen called, "Let me borrow your light, Nicholas."

Dorothy, the wandering spirit, hunched up closer to Beth. "Mum, might I stay close? It is such a very— empty place."

Beth gave a conspiratorial look around them. "I agree heartily. Come then. And later perhaps you can help me to make this place more livable. Then Lady Hagar won't be running away and setting the house-hold on its ears. And Careen. I must see to it that Careen has some of the things a girl her age should have."

Now that she was in stronger company, Dorothy became a little more spirited. "I shouldn't worry about Miss Careen getting nice things, mum. Master Nicholas will see to that."

Beth kept her countenance with difficulty.

"Yes. I daresay." They were passing the back parlor, once the ladies' withdrawing room. Beth glanced around and then raised the lamp and looked behind the striped satin couch. "Very tidy," she remarked, while Dorothy's big eyes gazed blankly at the empty floor and then at Beth.

"But, mum, did you expect it not to be tidy?"

"Only a little more dusty," Beth lied. Had those bedclothes belonged to O'Beirne? They were gone now. All neat and tidy. Except for Lady Hagar's idi-

otic disappearance. Truth to tell, she was much relieved to hear that the cart and pony were gone. As
Careen said, it sounded just like a trick of the wily old
woman. Thinking aloud, Beth asked herself, "But why
would she go away secretly?"

Dorothy hurried after her as she looked into the
darkness behind the tower stairs. Nothing there but
scampering mice and quantities of dust.

"Mum? You think my lady went off to the coteens?
But she wasn't that angry, surely. Besides, she laughed
after."

"What do you mean—angry? What was she angry
about?" Beth swung around to face her, completing
the job her words had started. The girl cowered away.

"It wasn't nothing, mum. Like I said, she laughed
when she talked of it. You know how she fires up
when she— But there. You don't know her like Miss
Careen."

"Dorothy, please clear your mind of everything, and
everyone else. Try and think of nothing but Lády Hagar. . . . Are you thinking?" The girl nodded, with
her unblinking stare. "Well, then, Lady Hagar was angry with someone. Today? What happened? What
made her angry?"

"I don't know what it was that made her suspicious,
mum. Honestly. She'd been joking at Mr. Nicholas
and after he left, and I was getting out and brushing
her tea gown, she began to talk to herself. Usually, it's
just mumbling a bit. You know. Complaints, and that.
But today she said quite clearly, 'Thinks he's got me
fooled, does he?' And that give me a start, I can tell
you. I dropped her best petticoat and she never even
looked my way. She just went on talking to herself.
'I'll soon settle him, by God, I will! Soon as ever I get
to someone who knows the truth.' That scared me,

mum, and I said somthing like, 'Were you speaking to me? Did Your Ladyship want me?'"

"And did she?" But the question was only asked to keep the girl talking. Beth had begun to put these scraps of information together with the missing cart and pony.

"No, no, mum. She just showed her teeth and said it was no concern of mine. She said, 'If I could walk on these limbs'—only she said legs— She said, 'If I could walk on these legs, I'd scotch that convict adder quick as a wink.' Mum, what's an adder?"

"A snake."

Dorothy actually blinked. "Her Ladyship's calling Mr. Nicholas a snake? But if he's a snake, he might be— Oh, mum! No! Are we to go to bed at night with a snake?"

"No one asks you to go to bed at night with Nicholas Cormeer." Beth set the lamp on the stair behind them and took the girl by the shoulders. "Dorothy, never in your life, I daresay, have you been asked to keep a secret that—" How could she impress this girl except by a preposterous hint of what just might be true? "—a secret involving your life."

"Oh, no, mum!"

"Yes. Your life. If you even hint at what you have told me, if you tell anyone else, in the coteens— anywhere, I wash my hands of you." It was not much of a threat, but Dorothy apparently regarded it as her death warrant.

"N-no, mum. I give you my word. I do, indeed. But when I wait upon him, he might—might do me harm. And—" She clutched Beth's sleeve. "You must take care, too, mum. He's settled himself in the other chamber on the floor with yours and Lady Hagar's. He said it was more proper to be with respectable, mature ladies than on the floor above with children like Miss Careen and me."

"*Oh, he did, did he?*" Odious, detestable man! Small wonder Lady Hagar had discovered something "wrong" about Nicholas Cormeer! He'd not been sent to Botany Bay for nothing. Beth was glad she had discovered Lady Hagar's suspicions early in her visit, before she could learn to like the man. The old lady might be wrong, but Beth preferred to save her trust for a more worthy object. . . . Respectable, mature ladies, indeed!

But what was there about Nicholas Cormeer that Lady Hagar found suspicious? And what could be his purpose? Neither Careen nor Lady Hagar possessed any money. The only fortune in the family had belonged to Beth's mother and was now in Beth's hands. Doubtless, Arabella, a notable chatterbox, had informed him of her "rich cousin." Could she be his object? But Nicholas Cormeer himself was rich.

Suppose this man, this lucky survivor of a ship sinking that killed his wife, was not really Nicholas Cormeer at all? . . .

In the middle of this sinister thought, she was startled to hear the man who called himself Nicholas Cormeer speak her name.

"Cousin Elspeth, where the devil are you?" He came striding to the foot of the stairs. "We've combed the grounds and every room in this place. I've gone out and examined that rockery. She simply isn't here."

Beth said quietly, "I am inclined to agree with you." She looked at Dorothy who ducked away from him and scuttled up the stairs. Beth saw his astonished expression and was amused in spite of herself.

"Extraordinary! Is she afraid of me, by any chance? Come along. My mutton stew has probably become gruel by now. A pity the old lady isn't here to eat it."

As it turned out, he was wrong about the mutton gruel. The stew itself remained as delicious to taste as it had been to smell an hour or so earlier. None of the diners said much during the meal. Beth didn't know what Nicholas was thinking, but Careen certainly seemed worried about her grandmother's disappearance. She kept looking up and listening in a way that spread its contagion to Beth. Oddly enough, Nicholas did not seem to read the proper concern in Beth's face.

While she and Careen finished a syllabub which was left over from dinner, he asked Beth suddenly, "You feel that all is well with Lady Faversham?"

Surprised, and seeing Careen's head rise hopefully, she said, "I have no more knowledge of the matter than you, sir. Though it does seem that she must have taken the pony cart."

"And why would she do that, do you think, Cousin?"

She decided his manner had changed, not quite so much that of the pretended gentleman. Was there a hint of threat in his voice, or just sarcasm? She, too, could play games. She tried to look like Dorothy, opening her eyes wide and saying innocently, "To visit old friends, I imagine. Either that or she was running away from the tower. But that is nonsense, of course."

"Of course."

When they had finished Cousin Nicholas' supper, he went out once more to look around the area beyond the tower and the quadrangle walls. Careen and Beth repeated their earlier search of the household and found nothing, but this gave Beth a chance to agree that some of Careen's suggestions should be carried out.

Careen said blithely, "Nicholas—he said I might call him Nicholas—tells me he discussed my needs with Mama, and we are to have servants and repairs and visitors. New furniture and hangings. Maybe a birthday ball for my fifteenth birthday."

"Good heavens! Are you fifteen? I thought you were under fourteen."

She grinned, her vixen eyes gleaming. "Nicholas guessed at once, but I suppose, being a female, you wouldn't notice how well grown I am. Mama tried to pretend I was younger for ages."

How like Arabella's vanity! But Beth admitted to herself that Nicholas Cormeer, or whoever he was, had certainly accomplished a great deal in one afternoon.

"Then, Careen, you shall have the best birthday gown in Galway. What do I say? In all of Ireland! And it's time we had a cook and an abigail—a genuine lady's maid for you."

By the door to Lady Hagar's empty room which they both looked into, Careen impulsively threw her arms around her.

"You are a love, so you are! But truly, you need do nothing. Nicholas insists he must do it. I am to look upon him as my father, he says. Isn't that a silly thing to say?"

"Not at all, dear. Very sensible. Good night." She kissed Careen on her bright, windburned forehead, and went into her room. Nothing had been done to make the drafty bedchamber any more habitable, and she could imagine how cold and damp the bedsheets would be. For the first time in her life she realized all the tiny marks of comfort provided by her money. With fellow landowners of the wealthy middle class, she always acted generously toward the poor and the orphaned and others in need, but had largely taken for granted such things as abigails to put up her hair or undress her, beds with the coverlets turned down, and sheets through which a warming pan had been passed. Not to mention the mysterious business of preparing a full and complicated meal.

And a fine display of uselessness I made there tonight, she thought. I might as well have been an infant in arms for all the good I accomplished.

While she undressed and turned down the bed, she kept to the series of complaints against herself, and only acknowledged when she went to close the window drapes partway that she was actually avoiding the two real problems: the inexplicable absence of Lady Hagar which threatened to last the night, and its corollary, Her Ladyship's sudden suspicion of Nicholas Cormeer. The two facts must be connected, and since Her Ladyship and the pony cart had not yet returned, she must have stayed the night with villagers.

"There is no other place where she could spend the night, having left so late in the day."

And then she remembered Wells Hall. The very thing! Where else would Lady Hagar go to discuss her suspicions but to the only other landowner in the neighborhood, Major Wells? She would instinctively turn to him for help.

The thick, low fog crawled up the beach toward the walls of Saltbridge Tower. There were footprints on the wet sand between the stretches of kelp and shingle. More gypsy kelp gatherers? A door slammed somewhere. She looked down and made out Nicholas Cormeer's straight, dark figure. He had just gotten to his feet after kneeling to examine the foundations of the tower. He went on, kicked apart a coil of seaweed, looked out to the sea.

Beth wondered if she was suddenly growing weak and susceptible. She found herself reasoning that he really was mystified by the disappearance of Lady Hagar. If he feared the truth, that she had betrayed her suspicions of him, why was he still searching the area outside the walls? What was he looking for, if not Lady Hagar?

He walked down to the surf's edge. At moments he nearly vanished in the fog. The waves rolled up, the foam clinging to his boots. What was he thinking as he gazed out over those endless waves to some far place like the Antipodes? Was he thinking of the first voyage over those waters, the dreadful time when he must have been chained in the hold with other convicts?

Whatever his thoughts, he did not step backward to escape the rising tide. It was as if what he had once faced made him oblivious to lesser things, like the cold Atlantic waters. In the midst of her maudlin attempt at sympathy, it occurred to her that a man who had undergone such a past could be ruthless in the present. She remained at the window, watching from behind the drapes, until Nicholas Cormeer walked south along the shore, then up on the sheep track toward Saltbridge Village.

When she could no longer see him, she finally went and lay down upon the bed without undressing. Whether Lady Hagar had gone off in the pony cart or not, she might very well have met with an accident, in which case Beth would be needed. She might be useless in the kitchen but she certainly knew how to bind up an injury and had once set a broken limb for her father.

She awoke in the middle of the night, heard the breakers roaring up the beach, and felt for the candle which had burned out. Luckily, she had not closed the drapes, and the white glow of the fog at the window gave some light to the room. She undressed and got into bed. She slept until awakened by the morning sunlight on the water, and by voices that rose and fell as if one of the parties to the argument were trying to silence the other.

Beth wrapped herself in the warm if unglamorous dressing sacque across the foot of the bed, and went to the door. It creaked open in time for her to see a shaken, cowering Dorothy halfway down the stairs to the ground floor. At the foot of the stairs stood the gypsy Tzigana, with hands on her trim hips and earrings rattling. Beth slipped quickly back into her own doorway, trying to hear without being seen.

The gypsy's wheedling voice was clearly audible. "You think I go without my pay, Miss Whey Face? All these pots and pans, you think we tinkers give them to you in Christian charity? We are not Christians. We are Romany-born. I will see your mistress. She must pay!"

"No, no! You are not permitted abovestairs." Dorothy's voice went absurdly off pitch, the voice of pure panic. "Oh, do go away. Lady Hagar can't see you. And Miss Careen has such a temper! If I let you up here, she'll have me turned off without a credit, like as not!"

Beth stepped out behind her, saying with just a touch of asperity, "You, there. You will be paid later in the day. Come back then. You may leave now."

Hearing her voice, Dorothy had jumped as if doused with cold water. To Beth she made an effort at a curtsy, and pulling her skirts close around her figure, rustled away without a backward look at the gypsy woman who stood there insolently on the floor below, trying to stare down Beth Milford.

It was a study in futility. Beth had practiced the art too many times while following her father on campaign. During those years she was forever finding herself disguised in some peasant's long-unwashed clothing, suddenly forced to meet the wives of local Portuguese or Spanish officials.

"Mistress," the gypsy Tzigana wheedled Beth, seeing her bluster and insolence fail, "we are but poor tinkers. Miss Careen pays for our wares. I have been asked to come abovestairs before, to receive my pay."

"Later in the day," Beth repeated as if she had not heard a word of all this rambling discourse. As Tzigana retreated with a show of reluctance, stepping backward, Beth added, "And next time, do not try to come nearer these stairs than the kitchen. You understand?"

The gypsy woman shrugged.

"You understand?"

"Oh, ay. As you say, mistress." She continued to retreat, backward, until she reached the archway into the courtyard, where she whirled around, her bright skirts a rainbow of color, and flounced out.

Smugly satisfied, Beth went back to her room. She had never missed her own Dawlish so much as on these cold, wintry mornings when a tray of steaming tea and a basin of hot water to wash in would have been a blessing. She looked into the pitcher, poured out what remained of the water after last evening, and scrubbed her chilled flesh into warmth.

Because she was anxious to discover whether Lady Hagar had returned, she hurried into her clothing, grateful that Dawlish had packed so many winter garments. Although she might be ordered to prepare a regal breakfast for the prodigal Lady Hagar, she chose a coppery brown armozine gown, the corded silk lending warmth and the color a certain brightness on a chilly day.

Having done the best she could with her hair, she went at once to Lady Hagar's room and knocked. When she received no answer, she tried the latch and went in, where she was momentarily shaken to see that the entire household, Careen, Dorothy, and Nicholas Cormeer, had arrived before her. They stood in various thoughtful poses, like gloomy Cassandras, with no explanations to offer.

"Good morning, all," she greeted them with false brightness. "You are about to tell me that Lady Faversham hasn't returned."

"Not so much as a sign of her, mum," Dorothy murmured, bobbing a hurried curtsy.

Beth reminded them, "She would scarcely return this early. She would wait until the day is warmer." But she could see that Nicholas Cormeer, as usual, was going to disagree with her.

"May I ask why you think she is comfortable now?"

"Because she undoubtedly rode to Wells Hall to ask advice of the major. He is the only neighbor of her class available to her, isn't he?"

"And upon what matter would she want advice?" Nicholas asked stiffly.

Did he have any idea of how the woman mistrusted him? Either he did not, or he was an excellent actor. Meanwhile, Careen gasped and they all looked at her.

"But Kevin is not the only neighbor. Haven't you ever wondered where the sheep track went as it ran north of the tower? It passes the Hutterby place. Austin Hutterby was an old suitor of Grandmama's. He's been reduced by the hard times, and now he's turned

miserly, to boot. Grandmama must have gone to see
him. She always had a penchant for him. Said they
didn't make rakes today like those in Austin Hutterby's time. And he was always very good-looking. If
she stayed there the night, she would claim that his
housekeeper gave her countenance. Grandmama never
cares what people think about her." She wrinkled her
nose. "He talks like dripping honey when he is working upon a female's susceptibilities. And he paws females, as well. You know the sort."

Nicholas cut in: "Then I suggest you stay away
from the Hutterby house. No daughter of mine is
going to be pawed by a last-century rake. What do
you think, Cousin Beth? Can O'Beirne have driven
Her Ladyship north to this Hutterby?"

"I should think it very likely." She caught the infer-
ence. "Do you mean to tell me O'Beirne did not return
last night either?" It seemed all too obvious now.
Since they had both left about the same time, Lady
Hagar's faithful man of all work had driven her to
some friend for advice.

Everyone began to show relief. Beth suggested, "We
might divide forces. One of us to the village and Wells
Hall, the other to the Hutterby place."

Nicholas looked as though he would like to have
disagreed, but all he could think of was, "There are no
carriages that can be used, although the mare might
get you to Wells Hall. Which is closer, the Hutterby or
Wells house?"

Careen said quickly, "Cousin Beth might take the
mare and ride to Wells Hall. I could walk to the Hutterby place with you. It's closer."

"No. Please. I don't—I prefer not to ride." Beth saw
that the girl was thunderstruck at this confession. She
had no doubt they both rode like centaurs.

It meant nothing to Nicholas who said, "Well, then, Beth and I will walk to this place nearby, and if your grandmother isn't there, I'll ride over to Wells Hall."

Beth's pride was severely wrenched by the sight of Careen's disappointment. The girl protested, "But I know Grandmama must be at Hutterby's. She would never go to see Kevin Wells when he and his housekeeper were so nasty to me."

"And no one here to receive her, if she should come home from some other direction?" Nicholas asked reasonably. "I am persuaded you are not so indifferent, Careen."

He certainly had a good effect on her. The girl shrugged. "If you tell me to, I'll stay. Only, hurry back. Both of you. It is miserably quiet here when I'm by myself. Beth, you might like Mr. Hutterby. I don't think he'd dare to try his rakishness with you."

Beth wondered if there was a pinprick in the remark. She ignored it. "We will hurry back, dear. And incidentally, Hutterby may have some ideas about where to hire a cook, a couple of housemaids, and one or two others who may be useful." She caught Nicholas looking at her and was surprised by his smile.

"I'm afraid Cousin Beth is not at home in the kitchen. No matter. I agree. You need servants and you need to learn how to manage them. It isn't easy to become a woman of wealth and confidence like Cousin Beth. It takes years of training and observation." As the three females stared at him, Beth felt that he was revealing a wound never quite healed. He added with a fine edge to the words, "It even takes training to be a man of property."

Half an hour later Dorothy came trembling to Beth.

"Mum, she's here again. Over in kitchen like you said."

"Who is here, in heaven's name?"

"Two of them gypsies are back. The female they call Tzigana, and the boy. They wish their pay for the pans they left."

"Later. Later."

Careen said quickly, "Do give me some shillings, Cousin. I will settle the matter. I am not afraid of them. We are old friends."

Beth started to her room to get the money from her reticule, but Nicholas forestalled her. "The girl is my responsibility. I had best handle the matter."

Careen was impatient. "I'll do it. Let me."

Almost before she had the coins in her fist, she was speeding off to the kitchen.

Beth and Nicholas looked after her. Beth was puzzled, and though she could not read any unusual expression on her companion's grim face, she suspected he, too, had been troubled by Careen's action. Beth said, "I imagine the gypsy boy must have been a playmate of hers. She goes on extremely well with the gypsies, you know."

"I don't like it."

She was surprised, supposing that an ex-convict would not feel so superior to a band of tinkers, but he added, "There is a lack of feeling about her. I don't want her to turn out as the other one did." Beth raised her head. "Do not look at me like that. I do not apologize. It was true of Arabella."

She was not hypocritical enough to disagree, but she had hoped that Arabella's last marriage might have changed her a little, in spite of signs to the contrary. A minute later they were startled by a quick, bright laugh.

"That will be Careen," she explained unnecessarily. They were about to start toward the kitchen when the gypsy boy ran out across the courtyard, grinning but with his arms up, protecting his head as Careen ran after him, waving a soup pot.

"Robber! Thief! You won't get a farthing more."

Behind them in the kitchen doorway, the woman, Tzigana, watched, then stepped down onto the cobbles and crossed the courtyard after them.

Beth laughed. "I don't think we need worry about Careen. She does tolerably well."

Nicholas nodded, but neither he nor Beth left until they had seen the tinkers' wagon rattling south along the sheep track, and Careen had safely returned to the house. She was watching from one of the windows in the great hall as Nicholas escorted Beth northward along the sheep track. Beth looked back once, wondering if Careen's frown came from anger or from the difficulty she had in making out the foggy scene.

"So you really think this O'Beirne is with Her Ladyship?" Nicholas asked as he helped her over a pile of kelp.

"It seems too much of a coincidence that they both left at the same time."

"Probably." She thought his chief concern had been settled, but he said after a little silence, "I wonder if you will tell me the truth about my stepdaughter's relationship to the Wells family."

"I would be happy to, if I knew it. Major Wells has one story, or seems to. Lady Hagar has another. And Careen . . . I don't quite know what her version is."

"I heard about it in the village, even before I met the child. They accuse her of monstrous things."

Beth said sharply, "They are lies. Major Wells's housekeeper, who was devoted to Mrs. Wells, had some preposterous tale that Beth was seen in the woods near where Mrs. Wells died. But it is no more than stupid chatter. Besides, Careen and Mrs. Wells were great friends."

He abandoned this subject. He seemed to find her profile interesting. For the first time in several years, she felt pleasantly excited by the steady gaze of a male, and it had to be this dark-eyed stranger whose background was as mysterious as his identity.

"You are very loyal to that child," he said.

"She is my cousin, after all, and she was not well treated by her parents."

"True." He considered her. "You are quite different from the Cousin Elspeth I was led to expect."

Dear Cousin Arabella! She had never been one to flatter another female.

Beth said, "Then it occurs to me that you will rely upon your own common sense and not upon hearsay."

"Touché to that."

They said no more. The fog gradually ate away the dim sunlight and ahead of them the beach narrowed. What remained of the sand was littered with shingle, kelp, and blackened staves, clearly the remainders of a wrecked curragh.

"What a great deal of debris!" She raised a hand to shade her eyes from the white, foggy light. "I hope the fisherman was saved."

"Probably not. It is a dangerous business." They stopped as the paths diverged. A second sheep track led up to a two-story stone house that looked as buffeted by wind, fog, and salt water as Saltbridge Tower. It was surrounded by sheep wandering everywhere, in and out of the woods behind the house, and through the prickly undergrowth.

"I should think that must be the Hutterby place," Beth suggested when her companion stopped, looking along the lower path and then lower still, at the clump of driftwood and kelp washed up against an outsized rock.

"Yes, I imagine so." But he seemed fascinated by the driftwood. "Wait here. Do not go on."

She obeyed him, and watched with growing uneasiness as he cut away from the sheep track, pushed between a couple of immovable sheep, and then went down into the sand. When he reached what she supposed was the pile of driftwood and kelp, he shifted the kelp around with his boot toe. Then he knelt and began to throw aside black wooden staves. He stopped in midmotion with a piece of wood in his hand. She held her breath, stared at the thing he was examining. Belatedly, she suspected what had washed up on the beach under the driftwood and ran across the wet sand toward Nicholas.

"It's not—Lady Faversham?"

He looked up at her. "No, but I wonder if I haven't found that sterling man of all talents, O'Beirne."

CHAPTER
SEVEN

"What do you say?" Nicholas asked her, still examining the body. "Is it O'Beirne?"

She was not a stranger to death but had never seen a drowning victim and found the sight sickening. The black breeches and coat, even the homespun shirt, had been buffeted about by the currents until they were in tatters. The flesh of the hard, strong face was bloated and milk-white, but she recognized the man who had been the silent servant at the tower.

"Yes. I'm sure it is."

Hoping to blot out this too vivid memory of dissolving flesh, she turned away and in doing so caught a movement at one of the long ocean windows of the Hutterby house.

"Someone is watching us," she warned Nicholas.

He stood up and looked in the direction she pointed out. "Seems to be damnably shy, no matter who it is. What is he doing, hiding there?"

"Shall I go and fetch him down here?"

He sensed her uneasiness and offered, "I had best go with you. He sounds like an unsavory rogue at best."

On their way up to the house from whose window the watcher had quickly ducked out of sight, Beth murmured, "You don't actually expect to find Lady Faversham at the Hutterby place, do you?"

"No. It seems more likely that she went to that other neighbor. The one with the dead wife. Or even to Ballyglen."

"Without saying a word to anyone? And in her physical condition?"

"What are you implying, Cousin? Do you expect to find her washed up along the coast like this poor devil? That is highly unlikely, I should think."

She knew it, but the discovery of O'Beirne's body had shaken her, and she persisted in thinking there must be some connection, since the lady and her servant had disappeared at almost exactly the same time late the previous afternoon.

Beth was grateful for the company of her self-proclaimed Cousin Nicholas. It was good to be able to count on someone stronger than she. Her father's temper and ways had been childish in the extreme, and it was difficult to remember her mother, who had been strong-minded, wrote pamphlets for Mary Wollstonecraft and the rights of females, and who died in the overturn of a high-perch phaeton that she should never have been tooling over the badly rutted Bath Road.

Nicholas had to pound on the heavy door for several seconds before someone shuffled up to shove the bolt back and peer out. They saw one eye staring at them, birdlike, through the narrow opening.

"Well? Well?"

"We are from Saltbridge Tower, sir," Nicholas announced and then had to raise his voice and repeat this against the roar of the sea.

The eye blinked. Long, silvery snake locks framed a face that once had been sleekly handsome, but age and a natural inclination for the solitary life seemed to have dried up all the juices in that once fair face.

"Ay. You are the convict, of course. And your pretty friend? Arabella's cousin. I heard she was coming. I've ways of hearing things. What do you want of me? I warn you, there's not a drop of whiskey in the house. Nor tea. I can give you nothing."

Nicholas and Beth exchanged glances. She saw, somewhat to her surprise, that Nicholas found the miser amusing.

"May we come in long enough to discuss the body out on your beach?"

"Not mine!" Austin Hutterby cried, almost in falsetto. "I'll not pay to have it removed. Wretches who drown on my property must take themselves off as best they can."

With admirable patience Nicholas persisted. "You misunderstand. We simply want to know, in the first place, if you have entertained Lady Faversham in the last twenty-four hours, and in the second place, if any of your servants remember at what time that clump of driftwood and seaweed first appeared."

The miser considered them both. The one eye they could see kept looking them over from head to foot. Having finally decided they would present no threat to his liquor or his purse, he let them come in. He waved them to chairs in his cheerless long parlor which, like the main hall at the tower, had long since been given over to damp and mold and the ghosts of its great past. Beth sat down, feeling a need for something solid beneath her knees. She did not share Nicholas' sense of humor about this unpleasant old man.

"Mr. Hutterby, has Lady Faversham been here?"

"Not since Sunday week." Without looking at her he reached out to pat her skirts and she moved back. Instantly, he turned to Nicholas. "So you're the convict the village has been gossiping about. You've a sinister look, and that's a fact. How does Hagar take to you?"

"We go on famously."

Beth studied Nicholas without appearing to do so and was baffled by the sincerity in his remark. He seemed to believe what he said. Curiously enough, Austin Hutterby appeared to believe it as well.

"Excellent, for you must know, sir, I have long been enamored of Her Ladyship. A remarkable woman." Waving his arms for emphasis, he leaned toward Nicholas, the heel of his hand passing all too slowly across Beth's silk-covered knees. "What is this about Lady Hagar's having come to visit me? I assure you, nothing would make me happier."

Nicholas nodded, absurdly serious. He was an excellent actor, Beth decided.

"Then Lady Hagar is not here and has not been here since Sunday week." The silver-haired miser agreed with a nod. "Next, we have the body out on your beach."

"Not mine," Hutterby reminded him. "My beach, yes, but that—whatever it is out there—isn't mine. I disclaim all responsibility. Take it elsewhere."

The inhumanity of this remark was so great that Beth got up. "Cousin Nicholas, the gentleman is not going to help us. We will have to see the lord lieutenant. When I passed through Dublin, he was making a progress into Wicklow and Clare. He will be in Galway any day. I suggest we look for him at Ballyglen."

"Now, see here," Mr. Hutterby began, showing his first signs of anxiety. "Do not go running to the lord lieutenant about matters that concern none but the locals. Perhaps my people can assist you. That matter of the wretched body you found on my sands . . . Not that it is any concern of mine! . . . But still and all, I've no objection to your calling in my servants." He reached behind Beth to touch the bellpull. In doing so he managed to skim past her bosom to perform this simple function.

For some reason Nicholas, who had seen this maneuver, looked as if he would lose his temper any second. He, too, stood. "Will you come out with me and examine the body, sir?"

He managed to get Austin Hutterby away from Beth, and they were on their way to the door when a hoarse, guttural, sensual voice spoke from somewhere behind Beth, a voice she remembered.

"You ask for me, Master Hutterby?"

This proved to be the older gypsy woman from whom Beth had purchased the silver locket. She was noticeably taken aback by the sight of Beth, who smiled a greeting. Beth had nothing against the woman. All the same, it was a trifle odd to see gypsies hired as servants in the household of an Englishman in Ireland.

"Ameera, have you been out on the sands this morning?"

Beth watched the woman whose voluptuous mouth tightened suddenly. . . . She knows what is out there, Beth thought, but the woman said,

"No, sir. Not this morning. But soon I will throw out the slops, then I will go out there."

"It won't be necessary, Ameera. You may go."

The woman went away, looking puzzled. She obviously wanted to remain within hearing, and had left the door ajar, but Nicholas went over and closed the door.

Beth said, "I bought some trinkets from a gypsy

woman yesterday at Wells Hall. I thought she was your Ameera."

"Probably, ma'am. She works cheaply enough. Amazingly cheap. I hired the woman last night. The other tinkers and their wagon are to remain on my grounds if they choose, throughout the winter months. Ameera here receives her meals and thruppence a day."

"Not precisely the riches of Peru," Nicholas observed. "I wonder why she made such an arrangement."

"Perhaps in order to keep the gypsies here in the neighborhood."

Both men looked at Beth. Hutterby said, "Why should they wish to stay here? We are all poor enough, God knows."

Beth did not know why she had volunteered such an idea. As the men insisted, it was pointless for the gypsies to wish to remain here where there was little money, and nothing of consequence to steal.

"We had best be on our way, sir," she suggested. "Since Lady Hagar is not here, it is plain as a pikestaff that she went to visit the major."

"Rubbish!"

Their reluctant host's voice startled them. Nicholas asked curiously, "How so? You believe she would not have visited this Wells fellow?"

"She certainly would not. The fellow let it be known—or at all events, he never scotched the story—that young Careen Faversham fancied herself in love with him last year. She did hang about after him, making eyes and also a damned nuisance of herself, but no need for the Wells female to take offense, I say."

There was a horrid kind of plausibility about this

tale. Beth had no doubt that even a year ago the pre-
cocious and beautiful girl would try out her charms
upon the only good-looking man in her life. But had
Molly Wells actually taken her seriously? She asked
her question aloud.

"I'd say so, indeed, ma'am! A rare fine temper, had
Molly Wells. And without being a beauty like young
Careen, she could always hold her own in any male
company. What with her looks and manner, Molly put
me in mind of you, Miss Milford, in many ways." Beth
did not find this comparison pleasing. She did not like
the notion of living another woman's life, or arousing
the interest of the attractive major through that purely
fortuitous resemblance. She tried to change this talk
of similarities.

"Assuming—and I do not—but assuming that Careen
was not with Lady Hagar at the time Mrs. Wells died,
why should anyone assume Careen killed the woman?
By witchcraft? By voodoo? Mrs. Wells slipped and fell
off a series of stone steps in the copse between the
two estates. What has Careen to do with it?"

She found Austin Hutterby's sweet smile singularly
unpleasant. All his lower teeth, like tiny, crowded
seed pearls, were revealed as he reminded his audience, "Then you did not know. There was a savage
quarrel between Molly and young Careen during a so-
cial affair at Wells Hall a few nights before Molly's
death. Molly made some threat that if Careen ever set
her cap at Major Wells again it would be her last cap."

Beth said calmly, "I should imagine Careen was human enough to resent that."

"She did. For a girl of fourteen Miss Careen has a
quick tongue. Before an audience of two dozen guests
she said, 'I'll see you dead, madam, before ever I let
you dictate my life.' Or words to that effect. Two days

later Molly Wells was dead and Careen was seen running out of that copse and then lying about it."

So there it was, a concidence built into a preposterous lie! Before Beth could express herself and her indignation, Nicholas said with a decidedly menacing air, "You have made clear to me just how vicious rumor can be. My wife's daughter is quite incapable of murder. And murder is a subject on which I am accounted something of an authority. Come along, Cousin."

Beth felt like a child in the female academy, given her orders by one of the more ogreish teachers. She decided this was no time to quarrel with his manner, especially in view of his talk about convicts and murderers.

Austin Hutterby watched them leave by the door onto the beach. He made no effort to show them out, but once they had gone down to O'Beirne's body half-buried in the wet sand, Beth looked back and noted that their late host was now peering out at them in his furtive way. Beth started to call Nicholas' attention to the watcher, but he had his own more immediate problem.

"We will have to leave it here until it can be hauled away. These damned locals hold life very cheaply."

Beth straightened up, glanced again at the Hutterby place. Was that serpent-like little man beckoning to her? He was. Now what did he have in mind? Nothing pleasant, she was sure.

"Good heavens! I've forgotten my reticule. I must have left it in that odious man's house. I'll be back at once."

She went a few paces, watched him drag the body up the sand, out of reach of the high tide. Then she hurried across the ground to Hutterby's old stone house. The miser met Beth in the doorway.

She said severely, "Tell me what is the matter. Why did you motion to me?"

"Now, now, my dear, a pretty young innocent like you needs to be warned. Your old friend and mine, Lady Hagar, was well and happy. She counted on your protecting your little cousin from this creature."

"What creature?"

He raised a bony elbow in Nicholas' direction. "Does it occur to you that within an hour after that convict arrived, Lady Hagar is gone, and that thing out there—that body comes floating in next day? Mind, Miss Milford, you are dealing with a murderous convict. And you a fine, rich heiress."

She laughed harshly. "I haven't the least intention of turning my estates over to him. How is he to acquire them, pray?"

"Through his ward, ma'am."

"But that would require my death, and then . . . You are being quite ridiculous, sir. I'll thank you not to spread that kind of scurrilous lie along with the other lies this village seems to have perpetuated. Have you said all you wanted to say, Mr. Hutterby? Be certain I shall tell Lady Hagar of your warning and we will laugh together over it."

"Please convey my compliments to Lady Hagar, if and when you see my old friend."

She disliked him intensely for disturbing her, for suggesting aloud something she had struggled vainly to banish. What she very much wanted was a bland and confident assurance that all would be well, that Careen was innocent, Lady Hagar safely complaining about her gruel, and Nicholas Cormeer's appearance in Ireland coincidental with these other mysterious happenings.

She met Nicholas Cormeer almost at once. He had wrapped the body in an enormous, red-fringed cloak which the old gypsy woman, Ameera, had given to him. "A kelp-gatherer's cloak," Nicholas explained to Beth, who found another fact more interesting. Ameera had helped him with the body and given him the kelper's cloak, and she smiled and nodded as she left Nicholas. It seemed that this woman, unlike most of her tribe, had some bond with Nicholas Cormeer. Was it because they both felt like outsiders, strange ones?

"What do you think?" she asked as she and Nicholas started to retrace their steps along the sheep track to Saltbridge Tower.

"About your delightful friend, Hutterby? Or about the O'Beirne's body?"

"About anything. But especially about Lady Hagar."

She expected him to say something that would reassure her. Instead, he said, "I wish I knew what to think." He added, after an unpleasant little silence, "It seems evident she is at the major's house, or she has already reached home."

Beth agreed, and then remembered suddenly what Lady Hagar had said about this man.

"Of course. She went to Ballyglen to report her suspicions to the lord lieutenant for Ireland." The second she had finished she realized how close she had come to spelling out the woman's opinion of the ex-convict.

"Her suspicions of what?" he asked very quietly.

She was so glib she surprised herself. "Of the people who have spread those dreadful lies about Careen."

"Ah. That."

She thought she had passed the dangerous moment, but he was watching her in a way that made her exceedingly nervous. She rambled along on the subject of wicked tongues and neighborhood gossips, but during the entire walk she had the nerve-racking idea that he read her thoughts. He looked every bit the sinister convict of Austin Hutterby's warning.

CHAPTER EIGHT

Beth found it strange and not too comfortable to wander about Saltbridge Tower alone after Careen had gone into the village with her stepfather to report the finding of O'Beirne's body.

"Mark me," Dorothy said dolefully, "Miss Careen'll need that convict to look out after her in the coteens. Else they'll be laying the blame of this O'Beirne's death at her door."

"Hadn't we better refer to Mr. Nicholas as the master of the house?" Beth suggested while she changed the linen in the various bedchambers now in use. She grew a little tired of Dorothy's complaints over having to help with the bedmaking. Dorothy had repeated once too often that she was an abigail, not a chambermaid.

"Ay, mum, but all the same, it's odd seeing a lady like yourself living here as if you was a hermit, with no protection against them."

"Them?"

"Against the convict fellow and Miss Careen."

Beth smoothed the coverlet of Careen's bed and then straightened up, staring at her. "I think you would do well to explain that."

The girl twitched and twittered a bit. She had the conscience to blush at her accusation, however. "I wouldn't say anything against anybody, mum. It's only . . ." She looked behind Beth at the open doorway and then lowered her voice. "What with O'Beirne being dead and all, and now milady gone, it fair gives one the chills."

Beth said severely, "If I ever hear you talking like that again, Dorothy, I'll pack you back to England or farther."

Dorothy gasped. "Farther!"

"The Antipodes!"

"Lawks, mum! You don't mean—"

Beth waved her away impatiently. "Make yourself useful somewhere. Do!"

The girl scuttled away and Beth finished her work in the last of the tower bedchambers which happened to be Nicholas Cormeer's room on the same floor with her own and Lady Hagar's. It was a plain room. The bed had no hangings and the shaving mirror on top of a highboy was coming unsilvered. There was no armoire. He had hung his clothing on pegs in the wall, and she was surprised—though she realized she should not have been—to find he had an elegant black suit, consisting of jacket, quilted waistcoat, and small clothes which would only be worn at a ball or a royal presentation.

An old, battered sea chest caught her eye and she gazed at it, ashamed of her own curiosity, yet aware of a strong desire to open it and examine its contents. The lock was hardly adequate. She ran her fingers over it, gave it a slap, and without much effort raised the lid. It was surprising to find a number of books on top of rolls of clothing. A Bible, perhaps. She examined them. No Bibles. A copy of *Paradise Lost*, two Daniel Defoe romances: *Robinson Crusoe* and *Moll Flanders,* and *Complete Instructions for a Grand Tour of Europe.* Nothing that she might have expected. Beneath the books the clothing looked to be of cheap quality. Homespun, torn, and threadbare. She took up the breeches, then a stocking unraveled and in holes. A stain the color of chocolate circled what remained of the stocking. Blood, she thought. From a leg iron?

It seemed strange that he should have kept these souvenirs of a terrible period in his life. Unless they served to reinforce his bitterness. It was hard to guess from his manner whether he was embittered. She thought he had behaved very well toward his stepdaughter, interested in her conduct and good name, and genuinely trying to make a home for the girl, with proper servants and the rehabilitation of Saltbridge Tower.

Ashamed of her curiosity, she began to replace his articles in the old chest. The copy of *Paradise Lost* was the last to go in, and when she picked up the book with its water-stained morocco covers, a folded paper slipped out of the pages. She recognized Cousin Arabella's spidery, slanted handwriting at once.

She would not read it. Such an act must be contemptible, yet, there it was, lying open on the cold, threadbare carpet, a letter from Arabella. And typically Arabella were the phrases that leaped to the eye:

"—no fault of mine, you may be certain."

"—purest chance, I realized that we were eminently unsuited to each—"

"Although the amount you agreed to settle upon me at the time of our marriage was—"

Beth had no doubt that if she turned the sheet over, she would discover Arabella was no longer content with "the amount you agreed to settle upon me."

Beth picked up the letter, started to refold it. Another paragraph was unmistakably clear:

> Such a union, between people of our different backgrounds, was bound to fail. After you raised your voice to me last night in what I can only regard as a shocking display of temper, you can scarcely be surprised to learn that I am sailing tomorrow on the *Southern Cross*. The time of my return to civilization is long overdue. Naturally, in my anger last night, I made several statements that were not, strictly speaking, accurate, so do not imagine that you could answer me in a London court. It was very wrong of you to read my correspondence, and at all events, it has now been destroyed. Not that you would be believed, my love, with your unsavory past.

Dear Arabella! How typical!

Still, the letter left some unnerving thoughts. Nicholas Cormeer's shocking temper— Was that only expressed by "raising his voice"? And his unsavory past. What *was* his original crime?

Beth slipped the folded letter into Nicholas Cormeer's copy of Milton. *Paradise Lost,* indeed. In spite of that letter or even because of it, she could not but feel a sympathy for Nicholas. It was small wonder that his manner had less than the Carlton House polish, or that he had seemed to dislike Beth on sight. He probably thought she was a copy of her flighty cousin.

Although she left his room soon after, she found he occupied all her thoughts as she went about cleaning the ground-floor halls and the back parlor. In spite of Arabella's letter, he had been on the *Southern Cross* with his wife when the ship foundered, so it was clear that he had followed her aboard. And now he was alive and Arabella was lost in the watery deeps north of Australia. What had happened when Arabella discovered that her rich, unwanted husband was sailing with her? And what had been Nicholas Cormeer's reaction when he found his runaway bride? It must have been a singularly unpleasant meeting.

But on the other hand, the shipwreck had followed almost immediately. Several chilling ideas occurred to Beth, and she banished them quickly, but they remained somewhere back of her thoughts all afternoon, the pinpricks of anxiety.

The dinner hour passed and evening was upon the tower before anyone returned. Beth worked until it was too dark to see where she swept and dusted. She preferred to keep busy. It prevented her from thinking of all the ancient, empty rooms around her. Dorothy floated through the main hall while Beth stood looking out at the last glow of daylight with a dusting cloth still in her hand. Beth called to the girl.

"Perhaps there should be some lamps set about while I build up the fires."

"Yes, mum, but that isn't my job. Them gypsies are out gathering kelp. I could call Tzigana in and ask her to—" She saw Beth's face, added hurriedly, "However, if you wish it, I'll do it myself, mum."

"I do."

The girl set about lighting lamps and candle sconces where she could reach them while Beth brought in wood and chunks of peat and set them around in the big fireplace. It was difficult to get the firemaker to work, but by the time the room was dark and night shrouded the ocean beyond the windows, Beth stood warming her hands before a blazing fire and feeling a certain pride of accomplishment. Dorothy came in and set a candelabrum on the huge mantelpiece.

"Might I stay in sight of you, miss? It's that dark and cold outside, you've no notion. Fair chills you to the bone."

"If you like. You must be hungry. I suppose I had best find something to make a supper." But the warm glow in the heart of the fire had her mesmerized and, truth to tell, she did not like to leave it for the chill dark of the long dining hall and the summer parlor beyond.

Dorothy said airily, "Oh, no! I had myself bread and tea and some of the mutton from last night."

"I see. Then I will do the same. If the fire begins to die down, bring that peat over to the coals."

Dorothy agreed that she knew what to do. Now that she found herself near the fire in a part of the long room which glowed pleasantly, she made no objection to being alone. Beth went rapidly through the dark sector, carrying one of the candleholders Dorothy had brought in. Her shadow drifted after her, strange and attenuated in the circle of light, and she looked around several times, startled into imagining she was pursued by the wraiths of long-dead Favershams. By the time she reached the kitchen, she could smile at her own nonsensical fears. The kitchen itself was so very prosaic, so lacking in mystery.

She found several duck eggs which she did not recall seeing the previous night. Nicholas Cormeer must have gathered them this morning. It had never occurred to her to do such a thing. . . . She was beginning to find herself inadequate in a great many unexpected ways.

There were still warm coals on the hearth and she

started up the fire again, thinking to break, stir, and heat some battered eggs with a small slice of the left-over mutton. At about this time she heard a crackling noise in the cold pantry beyond the stillroom. She stopped breaking eggs into a bowl and listened. As so often happened at such a moment, the world suddenly became still. The wind had stopped. The rain had not yet blown in off the coastal waters, and even the rats must be huddling together in a harmony of silence.

She went over to the fire, stoked it, and listened again. Another crackling sound. Footsteps. She took up the black fry pan and with a firm step advanced on the stillroom door as though it were Bonaparte himself.

She gripped the heavy pan by the handle, pushed open the stillroom door, and stood aside, in case the thing beyond should decide to charge.

The stillroom was deserted. The deeply shadowed shelves were not too well stocked, but they were quite harmless at this hour. Even the rats had gone. Feeling slightly ridiculous, Beth examined the door into the pantry. The door was unbolted, and with the iron pan raised on high as a formidable weapon, she stepped into the pantry, which was apparently an outbuilding added later than the medieval halls that made up the greater part of Saltbridge Tower. The pantry floor was wooden and the wood had warped in the eternal dampness. She heard the creak of her own footsteps and recognized that the sound she had heard minutes earlier was exactly like the sound her footsteps made now.

The pantry itself was small, a mere storage area with a door opening onto the ground outside the quadrangle. The door was not quite closed. It had certainly been bolted the night before when they searched for Lady Hagar. But, of course, others had been in the kitchen since. Nicholas Cormeer, for one. Beth glanced through the deep pantry shelves, saw nothing unusual, and opened the outside door.

It was beginning to rain and the mist blew across her face. The shingle beach was in dappled shadow. She stood there, wondering if anything could have shattered that misty calm only minutes before. The wind and the mist had smudged any footprints that might remain, but there were certainly indentations around the door and they appeared to be fresh.

No one was in sight. She shut and bolted the door quickly and then returned to the kitchen. Everything seemed as she had left it. The entire business was annoying. She wondered if her own irritation of the nerves had betrayed her. She heard nothing now but the first raindrops beating against the north windows, and after a needless wait and more useless listening, she poured the beaten eggs into the iron pan. Heating it briefly over the low-burning fire, she poured this and the fried mutton slice onto a plate, got a glass of wine, and sat down to eat her long-delayed afternoon dinner.

She had not thought to close the portieres over the long quadrangle windows and could see the desolate courtyard as she ate. The courtyard was faintly illuminated by the glow from a lamp on the ground-floor newel post in the tower, a glow which came through the embrasure of the tower wall and made it possible for Beth to see anyone or anything that moved up into the tower. While she was thinking of the tower, and of Lady Hagar's mysterious disappearance—had she gone to Ballyglen to report something evil about Nicholas Cormeer?—Beth was suddenly startled to see a moving shadow cross the nearest window. Seconds later a figure peered in at her. It seemed preternaturally tall and gaunt. She dropped her spoon with a gasp and got to her feet. A hand tried the courtyard door but it was bolted. She saw the latch raised again and lowered heavily. The bolt held.

Beth sheltered the candlelight behind her palm and peered out the window. The intruder appeared to be a female of slightly above the average height. Not nearly so dangerous upon closer acquaintance.

"Who are you? What do you want?" Beth asked sharply.

"Miss Milford? It is Shelagh Quinn. I've come to help out at the tower. It is raining. Would you be letting me in, if you please?"

So this was what her nonsensical fears had led her to, Beth thought. She was even afraid of one local woman who was certainly no more than a match for her, if it came to that.

"Sorry. I had no notion," Beth called. "I was expecting my Cousin Careen and her stepfather, but no one else. Just a minute."

She went to the door, shot the bolt back, and let in the woman, who was bundled in one of the long red cloaks worn by the kelp gatherers. The cloak had gotten soaked in the rain, but she herself looked pleasant, friendly, and competent, a welcome sight to Beth.

Mrs. Quinn said, "I must not tramp in with my clogs. Let me step out of them," and did so. Then she picked them up and followed Beth into the warm room. "What a blessing a fire is these nights, ma'am! I hope I did not frighten you?"

"Not at all," Beth lied cheerfully. "Do let me take your things."

"No, ma'am. It would not be fitting. By your leave, Master Nicholas made hire of me for to keep house here. What with me at the tower there'll be others to take service as well."

"That would be a great relief. I thought there was some silly superstition against working here." Beth hardly knew where to take her. She hadn't the least notion where the housekeeper's quarters were and could only follow Mrs. Quinn, who walked into the dining hall, passed Dorothy in the main hall with a mere nod, and went on to what she announced was the housekeeper's room behind the tower stairs.

"Your English abigail, that one called Dorothy," Mrs. Quinn said as she removed the red, fringed cloak. "Will she be in my charge as well?"

"She doesn't seem to be of much use in the kitchen, that's certain," Beth admitted. "Will this room be satisfactory?" She was surprised by her own anxious, almost servile tone, but then, it had been a new experience to find herself without any more assistance than Dorothy provided.

"I'll be returning to the coteens by night, ma'am. To see after my boy who is a bit harum-scarum, since his father was taken by the sea. I only asked after that girl, Dorothy, because she is one of those I've no patience with. Aping her betters but putting up no effort to earn her way in the world."

In fairness to the English girl Beth had to explain that she was skilled as a lady's maid and this appeared to satisfy Mrs. Quinn, who explained that she would stay this night to straighten out difficulties but would hereafter leave at darkness. "Which Lady Hagar understands very well, ma'am."

"It is very strange the way she left so abruptly and without notice to anyone yesterday," Beth began. "Did anyone in the village see her go?"

"None. But I believe Mrs. O'Beirne, the housekeeper

up at Wells Hall, saw her drive by in a pony cart close on dusk yesterday. On the Ballyglen Road."

So the old lady had gone to report something about Nicholas Cormeer to the lord lieutenant after all. What secret had she discovered? What thing to his discredit? Beth wondered again what there was about the man that made Lady Hagar mistrust him. She was sorry for it. Since reading those parts of Arabella's letter, she found herself strongly sympathetic toward the ex-convict.

"I suppose Mr. Cormeer told you that our man, O'Beirne, had drowned?"

Mrs. Quinn was arranging her thick, shining hair by the little square mirror that stood on a shelf in the left side of the armoire. Her capable hands paused briefly, then went on.

"There are many drowned on these shores hereabouts. However, it does seem a puzzler, ma'am."

Beth looked at her. "In what way?"

"But how should he drown? He has no boat. He is not a fisherman. Long ago, when he lost his wife, he took to the poteen. Drank himself into a state. Lady Hagar made hire of him, saw to his health. He is passionately loyal to her. In point of fact, ma'am, it is passing strange that Her Ladyship went off to Ballyglen alone. I've never known her to go off without her loyal O'Beirne."

"Well," Beth summed it up briefly in the effort not to revert to her earlier worries, "she certainly went off without him this time."

"So it does seem."

Not the most satisfying answer. Apparently, even Shelagh Quinn thought so, for she added with reluctance, as if she did not believe it herself, "They do say in the coteens that O'Beirne must have drunk himself into a stupor at our little public house and fallen as he walked along the beach to the tower. What with being drunk and all, he drowned when the tide came in. Not but what it is most unlike him today. However—" She shrugged.

Beth watched her with interest as they returned to the summer parlor and the kitchen. Remembering the trouble that her own nervous imagination had prompted, she remarked casually, "You came around through the pantry and stillroom, I take it, before you appeared at the door in the summer parlor?"

Shelagh Quinn's fine eyes blinked. She seemed puzzled. "No, ma'am. I came up from the village. That would be on the south side of the courtyard. The gates were ajar and I crossed the courtyard. Seeing the light in this parlor, I came and looked in. Were you expecting me to use one of the north doors? It never occurred to me."

"No, no, indeed. It must have been the wind I heard." Beth laughed lightly, tossing away the problem. But it remained long after, to trouble her.

Had something—no . . . *someone*—tried to get in through the pantry and stillroom? And if so, why the stealth, and why the failure? Unless the intruder hoped to catch her unawares and, failing to do so, vanished, hoping to meet with success at a later time.

What an idiotic notion! It was worthy of one of Mrs. Radcliffe's heroines at her worst!

All the same, Beth was relieved to have the companionship of Major Wells's competent and attractive friend, Shelagh Quinn, in this great, lonely pile of stones called Saltbridge Tower. She remembered that look in Shelagh Quinn's eyes when she was in the presence of the man she obviously cared for, the major. It was odd, and rather kind of Mrs. Quinn, considering the circumstances, to offer her services here, for Beth could not forget the envy in those same eyes when Mrs. Quinn watched Beth and the major ride away that afternoon.

CHAPTER NINE

Careen and Nicholas Cormeer returned in time to share a late supper with Beth once more. Beth had lost her appetite, what with her battered eggs now congealed and her mutton slice cold, but she sat with them and drank a hot, strengthening rum fustian which Nicholas made "to put courage into all of us," as he explained it. He and Shelagh Quinn were on excellent terms, and Beth could see how he had persuaded her to come and work at the tower. He asked numerous questions, careful to find out what Mrs. Quinn would need and how many of the local people to help her.

Beth was interested and would have done something to help, had her assistance been sought, but clearly it wasn't. She had thought Nicholas was in a very good mood but discovered this was all on the surface, to satisfy Careen and keep Mrs. Quinn from guessing anything was wrong. He tried to fool Beth as well, but she would have none of that, and when she found him alone in the pantry opening a bottle of wine, she came out into the chilly little room to ask,

"How did the village take the news about O'Beirne?"

"Quietly enough, though I could see they don't believe it."

"Nor do I."

His dark eyes raised from the bottle and seemed to bore into her. "What do you mean by that?"

"Shelagh Quinn doesn't either. She said he has no boat and would not have gone into the water. How could he drown?"

"He took someone's curragh while he was drunk, perhaps."

"Was, yes. But from her tone, I think he is not considered to have been drunk recently." She lowered her voice, took a step closer to him. "Mr. Cormeer, there is something very wrong about the entire affair. Mrs. Quinn says Lady Hagar would never go anywhere without O'Beirne to guard and escort her. He was exceedingly loyal to her."

He removed the bottle's worn and crumbling cork, considered this while he asked her, "Do you believe we can accept the word of this fine, upstanding major of yours?"

"He is not my major, I assure you. In fact, I should imagine the friendship of the major and Mrs. Quinn is deeper, and of longer duration. But, yes, I would accept his word."

"I inquired of him as well as his housekeeper. They both saw Her Ladyship on the road to Ballyglen in your pony cart. The housekeeper was disturbed by O'Beirne's death. He is her brother-in-law, I take it, and she muttered something about the tower being accursed and all that dwelt in it, including her brother-in-law, but this had nothing to do with the testimony of her eyesight. She certainly saw Lady Hagar, or what appeared to be Her Ladyship, pass Wells Hall on the way to Ballyglen."

Beth found that her lips were unaccountably dry. "You say 'what appeared to be Her Ladyship.' Am I to understand—"

"A figure of speech. Please don't concern yourself." He smiled, and it was the first time she had seen that startlingly warm smile flashed for her benefit. It did wonders to brighten the somberness of his deep-set eyes and heavy eyelids. Even his thin mouth looked tender, with a sensuous and delightfully human curve. He must have been an exceedingly handsome boy before the years of servitude. She remembered again the shallow self-concern in Arabella's letter and longed to believe in him, to show herself different from Arabella. All her sympathies were with him. If only she did not remember sometimes that he had been a felon when he came to Australia and, above all, that he had been aboard the *Southern Cross* when his wife died, the wife with whom he had quarreled bitterly. Was it more than a quarrel? A matter of his masculine honor and pride that demanded her death?

In spite of the newly revealed warm and delightful side to his nature, she realized she had not received an answer to her question. Was he, or was he not certain that Lady Hagar had been seen on her way to Ballyglen?

"Please be frank with me, sir. Do you believe Lady Hagar is safe?"

After a moment's hesitation he startled her by doing exactly as she asked. "I do not know. I imagine she must have reached Ballyglen long since. Two disinterested witnesses say so. I am thinking of making a little trip to Ballyglen myself, just to make certain."

She assured him, "I wish you might do so. All the same, I won't feel we are quite safe here while you are gone."

"Thank you for your trust."

While she was recovering from this unexpected sign of his gratitude, he escorted her and the opened wine bottle back to Careen in the summer parlor. Mrs. Quinn was clearing away the table. Careen said brightly, "I'll wager you a shilling you've been asking yourselves why O'Beirne drowned himself."

Before Beth could think of anything to say to that, Nicholas ordered his stepdaughter, "Drink one glass of this and go off to bed like the good child you are."

Beth was the only one who had ended the meal with tea and her glass was now cold. She went into the kitchen, poured hot water from the kettle on the hob, and brought her tea in to drink it with Careen and Nicholas. It was bitter, doubtless having absorbed the peat flavor from the coals, but it served its purpose, heating all her cold bones and unsteady nerves.

Shelagh Quinn insisted on taking charge of the dirty dishes, pots, and pans. The ladies were being reminded by Dorothy, as she yawned in their faces, that if she was to see them ready for bed it had better be soon or she would fall asleep, she was that tired.

Careen exclaimed, "Oh, fusty work! Very well, you tiresome creature. Do come along," and the two girls went off toward the tower stairs, though Careen, seeing that her stepfather lingered to escort Beth, called out, "Nicholas, it was a divine day. I had such fun! Don't keep Cousin Beth up too long. She needs her sleep."

Nicholas looked at Beth in surprise. "What the deuce was that all about?"

Beth gave him a gamin grin that made her look much younger than her years.

"I think she is trying to hint, ever so slyly, that I am much too old to arouse your flirtatious instincts."

He shrugged his disgust. "Good God! May I not

even exchange civilities with a mature woman for fear of being thought a rake?"

Although the "mature woman" comment made her wince, she assured him gravely, "I promise not to take amiss any civilities you may pay me, sir."

He laughed at that and took her arm. "Come and enjoy that fire I saw crackling in the big hall when we came home."

Home, she thought. How good it would be if she could know for a certainty that this strangely attractive man had not destroyed his wife, if he were entirely innocent and could come to think of Saltbridge as his home, perhaps the first he had ever known! She grew sentimental just thinking about it. It was exceedingly pleasant for the independent, capable Beth Milford to find herself being more or less ordered about by this somber fellow who hadn't a single one of the graces or insipid manners of the Bath beaux with whom she was familiar. The secret was in his sincerity, she felt, but perhaps in his mystery as well. He acted as though he sought her company because he desired it, not because she was very rich and it was the fashion to seek her out.

"You are not in the least like my wife," he said suddenly as they walked into the thick shadows of the great hall.

She smiled. "I am often told that. Believe that I am no longer offended."

"Nor should you be." This was said with biting force. He glanced toward the passage leading into the tower. "I also find Careen infinitely more human than her mother. All that I expected to do for her mother I think I may be able to do for Careen now."

She reminded him as gently as possible. "I am persuaded you will not spoil the child. Perhaps if you give her things gradually, it might serve. Her grandmother has always been a good influence upon her."

He agreed. "That is what I wanted to discuss with you, Beth. You are a sensible, mature woman." She wrinkled her nose at this repeated description, but he was unconscious of having disappointed her by that flat—if honest—appraisal. "And you can advise me. I want Careen to receive everything that wealthy young ladies of good family usually have. An excellent school, a coming-out in London. Clothes and jewels. . . . She is almost a woman already, as you must have noticed. At least, that dog in the manger, Wells, thinks so."

"What on earth do you mean?"

He stirred up the coals and they both held their hands out to the blaze.

"Did you not know? This precious Major Wells made advances to Careen. At the very time his wife was befriending the girl."

"I don't believe it!"

"You don't believe it of your major friend? Or of Careen?"

"The major is scrupulously correct. He resents Careen because of just such talk. God knows how it started!" She turned her indignation upon him. "Where did you hear this tale?"

"From Careen herself. Do you think she would lie about such a thing?"

"She is Arabella's daughter. She would certainly twist a story to her own advantage."

To her surprise he seemed as angry over her defense of Major Wells as at her oblique attack upon Careen.

"I suppose your precious Wells is incapable of making love to a pretty young woman like my stepdaughter?"

"In the first place he is not *my* precious Wells. I scarcely know the man. But while I am fond of my young cousin, I think I know her better than you do. Careen has a natural interest in money because her mother has left her shockingly poor and her father was always under her mother's thumb. Careen's only trouble now is that she wants to grow up too quickly. Her mother was the same. At school Arabella was always far ahead of us in charming the male sex."

The fire lighted his face briefly, and she made out a light of amusement in his eyes.

"And were you skilled at charming the male sex, Cousin Beth?"

She felt that she should be affronted but instead laughed and confessed, "I was the repository of their love for my Cousin Arabella. Everyone told me his secrets."

"You must have known a singularly stupid group of males."

Startled, she looked at him, saw his gaze fixed upon her mouth and did not know where to look. Had she wished to discourage him, she might have risen upon her dignity and said something coolly cutting. Her common sense reminded her—the thought was always present somewhere beneath the surface—that she did not know what he was capable of, what his original crime had been, where he had been, precisely, when Arabella died. The difficulty was, her emotions got in the way of her good judgment. In her awkwardness she became fascinated by the blue heart of the flame. "At all events, I think Careen has a splendid future and a strength of character that is all her own." She recalled that she was speaking to Arabella's widower and added, "I beg your pardon. I had no right to say such a thing about Arabella's daughter."

It was not pleasant to hear him laugh at that, yet he had every reason for his reaction.

"My wife. You will scarcely credit it, Cousin Beth, but she was my wife for less than two months." He rubbed his hands briskly as though the fire were everything and his conversation mere party chat. "I have been her widower longer than that."

Caught in spite of herself by the deep note in his voice, she murmured, "I am so sorry, Cousin. So very sorry." Her hand touched his wrist, a very light, feather touch. She wanted to draw her hand back so that he would not misunderstand and suppose a "sensible, mature" woman was overstepping the bounds of propriety, but he kept her fingers briefly imprisoned, studying them.

He sat abruptly, "You need not waste your sympathy upon me. . . . Are you uncomfortable with me, Beth?"

"No." Then she decided to be frank. "It is simply that I have always conducted myself very much as I chose, and I may have behaved in an un . . . unmaidenly fashion more than once." She caught his smile and went on in a rush, "I know at my age it is quite absurd to talk of maidenly qualities, but—"

"To me, Beth, you are a maiden. I will be forty my next birthday. Now, do you see how absurd you are actually being when you hint at your advanced age? Come. You look sleepy. I'll walk with you to your room."

She agreed, stifling a yawn. "I don't understand it in the least, but this air affects me uncommonly like a dose of laudanum. It was the same the night I arrived here."

"The company you keep," he assured her as they walked up the tower stairs in a companionable way.

"No, no. You are excellent—company." She stopped to yawn. "How very odd!"

When she tripped on a step and he caught her in his arms before setting her straight on both feet, she knew something was wrong. "Please believe me, sir. I am not drunk. I am not even slightly disguised. But I have never been so sleepy."

By the time they reached her room she was in such a wretched condition it did not surprise her when he brought her into the frigid bedchamber and aimed toward the bed. This crimson horror affected him greatly.

"Good God! What were they thinking of, putting you into that ghastly thing?"

She opened her eyes long enough to explain, "Careen wanted me to—to understand how poor they were."

"Has that child been asking you for money?"

She managed to raise her head with some of her old pride and hauteur. "Careen is my sole heir. Since there is little—little likelihood of my own marriage, that girl will receive my estate. And it is only natural that she should wish to enjoy some of her good fortune before my . . . lamentable departure."

"You are quite right as always, Cousin," he said sensibly, settling her on the bed and yanking the curtains back to give her air. "It would appear that you and I are in the same unhappy state. We fear to be loved for our great fortune. We shall end by falling into each other's arms with great relief."

She grinned sleepily. "Most improper."

"Not at all. We will have the matter duly solemnized by the local vicar."

"A vicar in Galway? How silly!"

She found herself sitting on the edge of her high bed and mumbled, "—must lie down."

There was a little silence. She opened her eyes, looked around the desolate, cold room, then at Nicholas, who was bending over her with concern, chafing her hands, studying her face.

"Wh—what is . . . matter?"

He said, "How long have you been taking drugs? Tell me the truth. I have seen fellow convicts under drugs. It is a very serious matter."

Beth tried to stiffen her backbone. She cried indignantly, "I never take drugs! Whatever are you talking about? Take drugs, indeed!"

Her head lolled over. It was very heavy. She felt his palms cup her head as he held her and looked closely into her eyes.

"Then you have been drugged. Cousin, I must be rough with you. Do you understand me? Rough."

"Yes—yes. I think . . . Am I going to die?"

"I certainly hope not. On your feet now. I should think it might be laudanum drops. But you must not let yourself go off to sleep. That's my girl. Stand up . . . I've got you. Don't be afraid. Lean against me. Now . . . walk!"

It was like a nightmare remembered by day. She knew she was walking back and forth across the threadbare carpet, over to the window and returning to the door, but she did not know how. Her legs seemed to drag along beneath her full skirts. Her breathing grew difficult. Nicholas pushed open the window and held her against him while the rain beat in across her face.

"I'm drowning!"

"No, you aren't. Take a deep breath. And another."

This seemed to go on for an eternity before he was satisfied and closed the window with one hand.

"Better now?"

She mumbled something. He looked into her eyes, studying the pupils. He was so close she found herself wondering what it would be like to be kissed by those hard, firm lips. She found herself suddenly swung up into his arms with impressive ease and dropped onto the bed against the high-piled pillows. Seconds later she was wrapped in the bed coverlet and then the top blanket. It was all highly confusing.

"You are smothering me."

"Rubbish! Now, don't let yourself get cold again. I'm going to call Mrs. Quinn."

She drifted off in her warm cocoon, only to be shaken awake by Nicholas again. He called over his shoulder, "Mrs. Quinn, the tea."

"No, please." Beth tried to sit up. "I drank the tea at supper. The only one to drink it. It must have been in the tea."

Shelagh Quinn's voice behind Nicholas asked, "What does she mean? What does she say about the tea?"

Nicholas said to Mrs. Quinn, "Drink."

Beth opened her eyes to see Mrs. Quinn obediently taste the tea in the steaming mug. "I steeped it myself. None other touched it, sir."

He put the mug to Beth's dry lips and she drank thirstily. It was very strong, almost black, and made her so nervous she could scarcely hold the heated mug. Nicholas raised it to her lips again. His other arm provided strength behind her back, and for the first time in her life she felt that she was entirely under the protection of another human being.

"There's a good girl."

She beamed tiredly at his approval, heard him say, "Have you any idea who could have touched her teacup tonight?"

She tried to think of the answer and then realized he was speaking to Shelagh Quinn.

"None at all, sir. It is most mysterious. No one was near except yourself, Miss Careen, Miss Milford, and—sure, now—I forgot. Myself, it was that put the water to the boil."

Beth said, "Neither of you were here the first night. But that gypsy woman, Tzigana, was out on the beach gathering kelp. I don't trust her."

Nicholas leaned forward, raised her head to rest on his arm. "You were sick the night you arrived?"

"Terribly sleepy. I could hardly wake up when Lady Hagar screamed. She had trouble after drinking too much poteen. But no one was here that night. Neither of you."

Shelagh Quinn said, "Of course, ma'am, we were both in the village."

Beth stared at her and then at Nicholas. "*You* were here then?"

Was she mistaken or did he hesitate in some slight confusion? But when he spoke it was easily enough.

"I arrived that evening and stayed over in the little public house at the coteens. I hardly thought Her Ladyship would appreciate my arrival in the dead of night."

Beth thought over that night and the next morning. He had not made himself known then either. She had gone off to Wells Hall with the major around noon and still Nicholas Cormeer had not made himself known here at his destination. But she was too tired to think it all out and besides, she preferred not to know anything that would spoil her trust in him.

"The gypsies," she said with satisfaction. "They were around here that night," and went to sleep reassured. She had never trusted those gypsies.

CHAPTER TEN

She awoke in the night and lay there sleepily studying the room and its furnishings. Nicholas had not closed the shutters, and the rain at the window seemed to shine and glimmer as if, somewhere overhead, the moon was out. She had a headache but that was to be expected in the circumstances. Meanwhile, she looked at the various furnishings while her thoughts were upon something else altogether, the subject of her laudanum poisoning.

No one in the house could be responsible, neither Careen nor Lady Hagar—if one added that first night—nor the servants. Dorothy did not look sensible enough and O'Beirne was long dead when the drops were added to the teacup. Or to the water in the kettle? Mrs. Quinn had no reason to do such a thing. And Nicholas had done everything he could to save her.

It came back to the gypsies. They were camped on Mr. Hutterby's grounds which were within walking distance. And upon her arrival they had been hostile, to say the least. She wanted very much to believe that the gypsy tinkers, and especially the impudent Tzigana, had been responsible. They were strangers, greedy, unfriendly, perfect suspects. Almost created for the purpose of being suspected.

Something moved in the chair before the dressing

table across the room. She sat up in bed while clangors beat in her head.

"Who is there? Who are you?"

Through the silvery half-light, Nicholas' voice assured her, "Don't concern yourself. You are perfectly safe. It is nearly morning."

She found it unsettling but not distasteful to have him share her bedchamber for the night, and when she heard him cross his legs and shift his position in the creaky old chair, she murmured, "Thank you."

Just as she was closing her eyes again, his voice came to her out of the dark corner where he sat. "Beth, humor me and do not mention your illness until we have . . . explored this matter."

"Very well. Not anyone? Not even—?"

"Not anyone!"

He said it with considerable force.

She nodded in the darkness and went back to sleep.

By the time she had turned over once or twice, it seemed, the room was full of that bright light which comes out of a rain-washed, sunny sky. Someone kept tugging on the coverlet in which she was still wrapped, and she found herself looking up into Careen's laughing face.

"It's true, Cuz! Dorothy said you were mummified and you are!"

Beth unwound herself, causing further merriment in the girl.

"Cousin Beth! You still have your gown and petticoats on. And they look dreadful! So wrinkled! Didn't you ever take off your clothes last night? You really must have been disguised."

"I was not disguised. I was not in the least drunk. I happened to be excessively sleepy."

"I know," Careen said wisely, "but when you've been drinking poteen, you shouldn't take laudanum drops. That can kill you. Molly Wells's father went straight off to sleep that way and never woke again."

Beth yawned and propped herself up on her elbows. "You are a gory-minded creature, aren't you?" She considered what Careen had said. "Now, see here, Cousin, where did you get the notion that I took laudanum?"

"But everyone does. All the old people—that is, the older people do it. Grandmama does it. And they eat opium, too. I shouldn't like that. Not knowing what I am about."

Beth said, "You are very right! And let me tell you, I took no laudanum, nor opium, nor anything else. Except the tea."

Careen grinned saucily and looked over her shoulder.

"Here is your morning tea now. Here, Dorothy. Let me have the tray."

"No, please. I want to wash first."

"Let that wait. You need color in your cheeks, Cousin."

In spite of all she could do, between them they were rushing her to drink this untested tea. Beth examined the tray, made the first objection she could think of.

"It is too hot. Please, let me know. Test it. Is it too hot?"

"Bethy! What a goose you are! We always drink our tea hot. Well, let me have it. Here!" She drank, a very long swallow, and seemed to enjoy it. Beth felt guilty for her idiotic suspicions.

"Thank you. I'll take it now."

Careen set the cup down. She was just a trifle put out. "Really, Cousin, one would think it was poisoned, the way you go on."

Beth said calmly, "But it isn't, is it? You've already tested it."

Careen flipped a salute. "Enjoy yourself. But next time take care that you don't eat too many laudanum drops. Dorothy, do help her out of those horrid clothes." And she vanished.

Dorothy went to examine Beth's garments and take out a complete outfit for the morning while Beth threw off the last blanket and stood by the window, stretching her cramped muscles. She stopped when she saw the two female gypsies, Tzigana and Ameera, down on the wet sand below. Ameera, the older of the two, had a great length of kelp over her shoulder, but the other interested Beth more. She was looking up at the tower facade, perhaps at Beth's window. Beth moved closer, pushed the window open, and looked upward. Over her head, in Careen's room, the window was abruptly closed. So Tzigana had not been looking at Beth at all, but at Careen. And Beth was reminded of that first night when the gypsies annoying her had abruptly vanished when Careen opened the gates and called to her.

Beth said to the maid, "Can you see what those tinker women are doing on the Faversham beach?"

"Taking up the kelp, it does seem, mum. There's money in it, as you may know."

"Yes. Even I could see that. But why do they keep hanging about here?"

Dorothy shrugged. "Will you be wearing the barred russet silk or the green, mum?"

"The russet and my cashmere shawl. I had best hurry. I seem to have overslept this morning."

She was in the process of being fastened into a clean petticoat when Dorothy shrieked. At this point Beth expected anything and swung around, staring at the open doorway. Nicholas Cormeer raised his hands, palms up.

"I surrender. I'd no notion I would provoke such horror. Cousin, do you want to throw something about your shoulders? I'm very much afraid we are shocking your maid."

"It's all right, Dorothy," Beth told her, refusing to be ruffled by his arrival. She took up her discarded dress and threw it over her petticoat. "You came to ask if I was recovered, I daresay."

"That, too," he agreed, amused by her imperturbability. "You may go, Dorothy."

The girl's pale eyebrows went up, but she departed at his order, cowering slightly as she passed him.

He looked after her, shaking his head. "I think she expected me to strike her." He stepped inside the room and closed the door behind him. "Beth, I warned you not to mention this laudanum business, yet everyone in the household seems to have heard about your—mishap."

"Quite so. I thought you had told someone."

He said, "I don't like it. I suppose it must have been Mrs. Quinn who did the talking. By the by, you are shivering. You don't want to take a cold after last night's exertions. You had better finish dressing."

In view of his intrusion, she thought this remark the outside of enough, and was about to say so when she saw his teeth flash in a smile. Restored to a good humor she agreed. "As soon as I am permitted to do so, Cousin."

He said, "Certainly. Complete your toilette and don't stand on ceremony with me." He walked around the room, looked into every item of furniture, even looked under the bed, and spent some time at the window. She decided not to argue but at once got into her gown and laced it rapidly.

She was just tying the laces when she felt a brisk tug at the ends of her hair and cried out. Nicholas brought the smooth auburn strands around her throat and tied them ridiculously over her breast. In spite of her righteous indignation, she was aware of a sensation of delight that she would like to have prolonged. Instead, being sensible and mature, she removed his powerful hands, asked him, "Would you crush my good name forever?" and coiled her hair quickly out of his reach.

All the same, as she put the final touch to her hair and glanced into the looking glass, she caught the expression in Nicholas Cormeer's eyes and blinked self-consciously. Remembering Arabella's recent death, she found her mouth stiffening to severe lines. But she could not be too angry when she thought of that letter Arabella had written to the man who was still her bridegroom.

He did not pursue the matter. He had caught sight of the gypsy women gathering and started out of Beth's room with the warning, "Don't eat or drink anything until I am with you."

"Where are you going?"

"To find out why that tinker woman has been carrying the same dry chain of seaweed for the past two hours."

It was intriguing to Beth that he, too, found something suspicious about the gypsy tinkers, but she thought he was suspicious of the wrong gypsy. She went back to the window to watch. By now the beach was deserted. Beth gave up playing the Bow Street runner and left the tower room. On an impulse she looked in upon Lady Hagar's room but it was still deserted. The bed was fairly neat, yet she found one oddity. Lady Hagar always slept with three pillows piled behind her head. Two of them had been tossed onto the floor and jammed behind one bedpost. It seemed a very odd thing for a servant to have done, as if there had been a scramble of some sort in here. Perhaps the old lady had risen suddenly, tossing things in all directions. But the pillowcases were trimmed with the delicate Irish lace done in the convents of the country and should not be so mistreated.

Beth had heard no sound behind her but became aware of some movement and turned quickly. Shelagh Quinn stood there staring at the pillows. She seemed as surprised as Beth had been.

"Excuse me, ma'am, but did someone sleep here last night?"

"Not that I know of. It belongs to Lady Hagar."

Mrs. Quinn crossed the room with swift, economical movements and started to rescue the pillows from the dust of the floor behind the bedpost. "I know it was not like this when I retired, ma'am."

Beth found it difficult to confound this good-looking, dignified young woman, but feeling guilty at having asked the question, she blurted out, "Did you tell anyone about my attack last night?"

"Certainly not, ma'am. Mr. Nicholas particularly asked me not to mention it."

To herself Beth murmured, "Yet Careen knows."

"That she does. Miss Careen, if I may say so, knows a great deal for a well-brought-up female of fourteen."

Beth was inclined to say something sharply critical of Shelagh Quinn's interference, but in all honesty she had to admit the woman was right. She tried to solve the difficult moment by a compromise as she left the room.

"Lady Hagar takes laudanum. I suppose Careen has grown up with the notion that laudanum drops and opium are a commonplace with what she calls the old ones."

She left Mrs. Quinn beating the soiled pillows and went downstairs, surprised at a slight weakness in her knees. It was a pleasure to see the activity among all those endless rooms. Mrs. Quinn had persuaded half a dozen people either from the village or the countryside to come and help out at Saltbridge Tower. There was a man in the quadrangle, caring for the single horse, a bay mare, which remained of the Faversham stables, and a boy to help him out. Two housemaids were stirring up dust, pulling down portieres and otherwise making the ancient house presentable. And Shelagh Quinn's sister-in-law, Maureen Barnerd, a stout woman with grizzled, untidy hair, presided over the kitchen.

Careen danced through the long great hall, proclaiming, "We may have a ball, Nicholas says, to show me to the countryside. Make me eligible, you know. Oh, Nicholas is a love!" But she hugged Beth, in lieu of the lovely Nicholas.

Beth was delighted for her, though ashamed that her own generosity had been so long delayed. She responded enthusiastically to the embrace, announcing belatedly to Careen, "I had intended all this to be my contribution to your education. However—"

"But I can do very well with your fortune and Nicholas's money, Cousin! Don't trouble about my having too much. I want to go to London and take the polite world by storm, as the wealthly Mrs.—" Her eyes slanted mischievously. "Well, enough of my day-dreams."

Beth drew her away, studied her. "What is this, Careen? Are you planning for marriage without having come out properly first? How can you show off all the pretty clothes you will have? And the fine balls and routs. All that will be set at an end if you marry very young."

"But I must, Cousin. Don't you see?"

Beth began to see one thing clearly. This gaiety and excitement of Careen's was almost hysteria, an excitement that made her tremble and her eyes glitter.

"No, I don't see. What is this haste? You are only fourteen. You have years ahead of you."

"Beth, you don't really understand at all. He hasn't got years left. In a few years he will be an old man. He is almost forty already. Nicholas can't afford to wait."

Beth's smile froze in place. She felt that a long time passed before she was able to say briskly, "Yes, yes, I daresay. But meanwhile, wouldn't it be wise to dress the part? Just now, you look the child you are. Your stockings are soiled and your skirt hems are dusty. Don't you want to be at your prettiest when you see your stepfather this morning?"

Careen waved her arms airily. "Oh, no. He likes me just as I am. He said so just a little while ago."

Beth couldn't trust herself to continue this grotesque joke. She did not know whether she was more shocked over the impropriety implied in the girl's attraction to her stepfather, or whether she was simply jealous of this beautiful young creature who knew she could attract a man like Nicholas Cormeer.

She left Careen busily describing her fantasy—was

it a fantasy?—love for Nicholas to Dorothy who listened to the tale without raising a single eyebrow or flickering the tiniest smile across her colorless lips.

As for Beth's own feelings, she preferred not to meet Nicholas until she recovered her casual indifference and was able to treat the whole distasteful matter as a child's dream. But had he actually encouraged Careen? If not, was this another case of Careen's imagination which might cause endless trouble as it had nearly ruined her good name in the affair of Kevin and Molly Wells?

CHAPTER ELEVEN

It was Shelagh Quinn who apparently solved the mystery of the laudanum drops. She called Beth into the pantry where the new cook, Mrs. Barnerd, was scrubbing shelves. Shelagh pointed to a circular mark in the dust.

"Where the teakettle stood, Miss Milford. Something spilled into it and around it. Now, see the shelf above."

An overturned bottle, almost empty, lay upon the wooden shelf, its neck directly over a break in the boards. Beneath the split board was the pouring spout of the teakettle. How easily the laudanum drops had fallen into that spout and thus into the water for Beth's tea! It may have been foolish of Lady Hagar to leave her medicine among the pots and pans, but it seemed very like her.

"Thank God!" Beth found herself saying aloud and was surprised to see Mrs. Quinn's handsome eyes expressing a similar emotion. The women looked at each other. Shelagh Quinn said,

"I understand, ma'am. It is something to be grateful for."

"Grateful, is it?" asked Mrs. Barnerd, bustling to clean up the mess. "Not to my thinking. Be that as it may, it's no concern of mine."

Enormously relieved of the nervous tension that had gripped her throughout the morning hours, Beth found herself able to go about the usual activities with a heart free of some, if not all, concerns. There was still, of course, Careen's adolescent attachment to her stepfather. Or was Careen still an adolescent in her emotions?

Nicholas did not help matters when he came through the house on his way out to investigate the potato crop planted by the unfortunate O'Beirne. He asked Careen, "How goes my pretty sweetheart? Mark me, you will be the true mistress of the house before anyone knows what you are about. Mrs. Quinn will show you the way of it."

He was too busy to waste time gossiping, as he explained to Beth on the run. She gave up and set about making herself useful around the house. Having answered complaints about difficulty in conducting the work without all the equipment necessary, and complaints about Careen's unfortunate tendency to be too dictatorial, Beth found herself delighted to be free of Saltbridge Tower when Major Wells came by driving a pony cart very like the one Lady Hagar had taken to visit Ballyglen.

He passed Careen on his way to meet Beth and was noticeably aloof to her. Beth and Shelagh Quinn were shifting around the meager items of furniture in the dining hall when Major Wells came upon them. He was as booming and jovial as ever.

"Ah! I see you have chosen Shelagh to help you, Miss Milford. You couldn't do better. By the time Lady Hagar returns you should have everything running like clockwork with our good Shelagh at the helm. And speaking of Lady Hagar, one of my housemaids went off to Ballyglen to have her tooth drawn.

Bad toothache, you know. And the landlord of the Ballyglen Inn gave her this message to be delivered to the tower. Innkeeper said it was left by Lady Hagar. Addressed to you, Miss Milford."

"That is a great relief. Excuse me." The note was not sealed and was brief. She read it aloud. " 'Business at Ballyglen keeps me longer. Do not be concerned. . . . Hagar Faversham.' " Beth looked up. "That seems to settle the matter."

"Excellent. Now, then," the major took the end of the table out of Beth's hands. "Here, Shelagh. A trifle to the left. And over."

Mrs. Quinn, gazing at the floor, said without expression, "Yes, sir," and did as she was ordered.

Feeling awkward over the difference between his treatment of herself and Shelagh Quinn, Beth moved to a position beside the Irish woman, saying to her, "Let me help you."

Recalled to his best manners, Kevin Wells flushed and said gruffly, "No, no. I will do it. Ladies, please step aside."

After this unlucky beginning, things moved more smoothly. The major congratulated Shelagh Quinn upon the way she had already improved the look and situation of Saltbridge Tower. In a lower tone he added, "If that convict places difficulties in your way, you must come to me. We'll not have you working where you are not appreciated, my dear friend. And how is that fine boy of yours?"

Shelagh Quinn said her son was doing well enough, that she herself found Master Cormeer perfectly congenial, "and a gentleman in every way. Hadn't you best go along now, sir, you and Miss Milford? The day may turn dampish after noon."

"You are quite right, Shelagh. We'll be off now."

Annoyed at having her life ordered for her when she was trying to do as much work as the next person, Beth objected strongly.

"We have the great hall to make presentable."

It was Shelagh Quinn's turn to take her honest revenge. She protested, "If you please, ma'am, it might be easier if one person gave the orders. There'll be no confusion then, you understand."

So Beth went off with the major, unable to find that her presence would serve any purpose in the household. Her only consolation was the look on Nicholas Cormeer's face when they rode past him in the quadrangle and she waved and bowed to him. He, at least, found her departure inconvenient.

Or perhaps it was something else, after all. He called to her in his severe tones accentuated by the dark scowl that had once seemed fixed upon his face.

"Cousin Beth! A moment, there."

Beth looked back. Kevin Wells put out his hand, gently holding her. "That fellow makes very free with your name. I may find it necessary to school him on the proper conduct with a lady."

"No, please. I forgot to— That is, I have a message for him."

The major was not to be outdone this time. He leaped down so quickly he frightened the pony, but was too late, after all, as Beth dropped into her "cousin's" waiting arms. They stepped back out of Kevin's hearing as Nicholas asked her, "How do you feel?"

"Very well. My headache is gone and I feel very much myself." She saw his serious expression and realized this was not the disagreeable or even haughty veneer he cultivated. "Are you worried? Do you think I am in some danger?"

"Don't you?" His black eyes flicked over the stalwart figure of the major as he controlled the uneasy pony. "Can you trust that pompous idiot?"

"Sh! Not so loud. Good heavens! You can hardly believe he is responsible for drugging me. That was purely an accident. The bottle tipped over and dripped into the teakettle."

"So it seems now."

"Why do you make matters as bad as possible? At all events, Kevin was several leagues away from the tower last night. And what would his motive be?"

He laughed shortly. "I've no doubt, by the time you return, he and the village will have you convinced that I am responsible for the whole of it."

She did not insult his intelligence by pretending not to understand. "That may be. There are stupid people everywhere. But the only opinion that matters on that score is my own, isn't it? And I think you know how I regard you."

"In what light do you regard me?"

"As my noble rescuer, of course." She said it lightly, but perhaps he read something more in her eyes because he took her hand, brought it to his lips, and said without a smile,

"Thank you. I hope you mean that."

Kevin Wells called to her, "Are you ready, Miss Milford? This little creature is pleading to be on the way." He patted the pony, but his patience was wearing thin, and she said quickly to Nicholas,

"I do mean it." Then she hurried to join the major.

It was just as well. She scarcely knew this onetime convict and did not like to feel herself hurrying into some kind of relationship, even a mere flirtation. And when she dealt honestly with her own emotions, she knew that, in spite of their recent acquaintance, he aroused in her emotions she had never experienced before. She knew quite well that this was not enough to make a permanent relationship.

Now, here was Kevin Wells looking big and handsome and comfortable—no secrets in that open face with its frank hazel eyes and friendly grin.

"How comfortable you are!" she remarked as he lifted her onto the cart seat. He seemed taken aback and said nothing. He went around the cart, got in, and shook the lines over the fretting animal.

They had moved out of the courtyard and down along the shore track before he spoke.

"I'm not sure I should be flattered by that. To be comfortable is to be . . . dull, isn't it?"

"Not to me," she put in quickly to make amends. She had blurted out that truth without even thinking what he would make of it.

He said presently, "What a pleasure it is to find myself in the company of a sensible woman again!"

She said "mm" and he looked at her. "By accident, I seem to be fumbling through the entire day. When I breakfasted this morning I wished Mrs. O'Beirne a good day and offended the good lady. She is in mourning for that luckless brother-in-law of hers. I should never have wished her a good day."

"Oh, dear! That is bad." She glanced at the wide, sweeping expanse of beach and the rising ground ahead which protected the coteens of Saltbridge from the northern gales. "Then you were kind enough to come and give me a pleasant ride, and I insulted you by saying I felt comfortable with you."

"I prefer to think of that as a compliment."

She wanted to say something soothing and kind, but also she hoped he would not get the wrong impression of her friendship for him. One thing she definitely disliked and that was the repeated comparison of herself with Molly Wells, his dead wife.

"Major, I wonder if I may ask you something about my cousin."

He glanced over his shoulder. "I know very little about the fellow, except that he is a criminal. I certainly don't think you should permit him to hang about you."

"Or Careen?"

Kevin Wells hesitated. "I am quite certain Miss Careen is a match for any criminal."

She forced herself to keep an impartial view, though she resented his comment. "As a matter of fact, when I spoke of my cousin, I was referring to Careen."

He said stiffly. "I can say nothing of the girl. My acquaintance with the young lady began very pleasantly. We thought her a wild but rather endearing child. My wife had known the child from her birth and was exceedingly fond of her."

"I remember. You mentioned that. But what could have changed their relationship? You said they disliked each other at the time of Mrs. Wells's death." She knew that she was alienating him by this subject, but she felt that she had to know.

They came over the rise into the village. The entire population seemed to be outside, the men in black coming up from the curraghs drawn in along the beach beside the river mouth. The women, likewise in rusty black, were out beating clothing on the riverbank or gathering up children, or gossiping outside the local public house, probably waiting for their men who were inside.

This activity caught the major's attention and he lost the thread of Beth's question. Or perhaps he chose to forget it. Upon catching sight of the major's pony cart everyone stopped moving. It was as if all these black creatures became part of a still and silent portrait.

"Why are they watching us?" Beth asked uneasily. But she saw that Kevin Wells, too, was baffled by their behavior.

"I would hazard a guess that they are curious to see the Favershams' distinguished Cousin Beth."

"Me? They saw me the other day and I didn't produce any particular excitement."

He leaned down as they turned onto the Wells Hall Road and summoned one of the women with a wave of his hand. Although he was apparently unaware of his lord of the manor attitude, Beth suspected from the villagers' cold courtesy that they noticed it and put down one more grudge against the English landlords. The woman came obediently, but with a sullen look. She bobbed the barest curtsy. Even this gesture dipped her skirt hems in mud and Beth regretted the necessity of such gestures.

"Ay, Major?"

"Good day, Mrs. O'Faolain. I see you and the others staring at Miss Milford. I take it that you'd like to be presented to the lady."

"It'll be making no mind to me, begging your pardon, miss. But a surprising thing it was, seeing you so well and spry as it were, when gossip had you laid at death's door."

Beth leaned forward. "Please tell me, ma'am, what had you heard?"

Somewhat mollified by Beth's careful courtesy, the woman let a flicker of sympathy appear in her dour, stolid face.

"Well, now, so please you, mum, it's being said

you'd go the way of the major's wife here, and maybe O'Beirne as well. Him that stayed when he was warned of Miss Careen's evil. And there's Her Ladyship that's gone off only the good God knows where. Run away, they do say, so she'll not sleep under the roof that holds Miss Careen's black Satan of a father."

"Mr. Cormeer is not my cousin's father," Beth said. "And my cousin is a mere child."

The woman inclined her shawled head.

"That's as may be. All the same, the minute that convict arrives, off goes my lady. We saw him hanging about the public house the night he came, asking questions and all. Take care, miss. Between that convict and Miss Careen, they'll be doing you in."

The major said, "That will be enough, Mrs. O'Faolain," and set the pony trotting off.

Beth was too shaken with anger to make any comment for a few minutes. She was more keenly aware than before that everyone in the village came out to stare at her. She had the very strong sensation that they took this opportunity of seeing a woman who was doomed. She had always been healthy, uncomplicated, aware in a general way that she was fortunate to have so much, and with it the prospect of a long, reasonably contented life. It was horrible to think these strangers pictured her as dying, put upon, victimized. She had never been victimized, never "weak," pitiable.

Kevin broke the uncomfortable silence.

"You will say I am interfering."

"Are you going to say something stupid about my relations?"

"Not if you don't wish it. Miss—Beth . . . forgive me, but surely I have the right to call you that if you permit this blackguard Cormeer such liberties?"

"Now, there you go. If you insist on—"

"I apologize. But good God, Miss Milford, I hadn't heard about this business of your illness last night! What have they done to you? Was it an attempt on your life? How did it happen?"

She sighed, understanding how a friend—and she felt that he was her friend—would leap to some frightful conclusion. She put her hand out. It touched his fingers which were locked tightly around the lines. He did not try to take advantage of this indication of trust.

"Major Wells—" He looked at their hands and started to say something. She amended, "Major Kevin, you haven't given me any reason why I should mistrust my young cousin. You say she quarreled with your wife. People do quarrel. No doubt one of your servants could tell some tale about words between you and Mrs. Wells."

She had struck a nerve there. "What do you mean?" he asked her sharply, his face looking strained. "We had words, perhaps. Now and again. But I loved Molly. Everyone knew that. What have you heard? That hellcat, Careen, I daresay! She swore she would do something of the sort."

"No one has said anything. Please, be calm. I didn't mean to agitate you. But you say someone saw Careen running through the copse after your wife fell. Doesn't that sound a trifle flimsy as evidence against a child of fourteen?"

She experienced a return of his tight-lipped look that she had noticed before when she pursued the subject of Careen and her part in the mystery of his wife's death. With a sudden impatience she demanded, "How can you expect me to share your feelings when I know nothing of the real facts? You give me innuendos, disdainful glances, but nothing that can sway a woman with common sense."

He was furiously angry, she thought, but not with the dark, quick fire of Nicholas Cormeer. The major was the type who suffered inwardly with a stiff, proper front always presented to the world. Her senses might respond to Cormeer's enchantment, but something very English, very Saxon in her responded to the carefully restrained emotions of this man.

He said, "I am afraid it would be quite impossible to discuss such matters even with you."

She had suspected the problem without knowing she did so. She put in after a minute, "I am beginning to know my Cousin Careen, and I think I understand what happened and why you cannot talk about it. As a gentleman, you feel you can't accuse Careen publicly of trying to make love to you, yet that child made the advances, isn't it so?"

His face flushed darkly. He said, "Certainly not. Only a cad would—"

"Would admit it. I know. Excuse me, but I believe she misunderstood your natural kindness. And that embittered you." He said nothing. He kept studying the lines in his powerful hands, as if they would give him the answer to all of life's mysteries. She went on gently, "Kevin Wells, no one doubts your love for your wife. I only ask that you think of my cousin as a child who was trying her wings, perhaps rehearsing in her dream world for the time when a boy would come into her life and love her. This is a very lonely coast for young people."

She thought uncomfortably that he wasn't going to answer her, but just as she decided they were going to move off the Ballyglen High Road into the estate road of Wells Hall, he laughed shortly.

"You are right, of course. You said just what Molly would say if she could look back upon that . . . painful business. We took the child too seriously. That is the truth of it."

The pony started to turn, but the major pulled him up short and held him.

"Miss Beth, you believe in your cousins. I'll say nothing more of the girl. I accept your word that she has changed since she—since my wife's death. But she has someone now at Saltbridge Tower whose aim may very well be to hurry her good fortune, make her the heiress she expects to be."

"Major!"

He watched her with the keen, calculating eye that must have been his in those successful military campaigns.

"Put your belief in them to the test. Ride with me to Ballyglen. Discover just why Lady Hagar went there to see the lord lieutenant for Ireland."

Had he discovered through his household staff what the servants at the tower already knew? That Lady Hagar was suspicious of Nicholas Cormeer and intended to "unmask him" or "do something about him"? The old lady's opinion of him had not swayed Beth because she felt that she was beginning to know him. Besides, he had saved her life last night. If he had intended to kill her, it would be nonsense to have worked so hard when she might have died without his aid. And possibly, too, she was moved by the letter she had read from Arabella, and he now had all her sympathy.

"Major, you and I are friends, but even friends do not go off on jaunts through Ireland which involve hours of travel alone. You have only to wait until Lady Hagar returns, and then see what she has brought back. Surely, if she wanted the help of the authorities, someone from the lieutenant's offices would have arrived by now at Saltbridge, or perhaps be hanging about the village, asking questions, trying to discover these heinous secrets you suspect Mr. Cormeer of hiding. You don't even know what his crime was, yet you speak of him as a hardened criminal. A murderer. Even a fiend, if he did what you suspect."

"You are afraid to discover the truth. You wish to go on living in this state of ignorance. It is cowardly, and unworthy of you."

She drew herself up, her back stiff and haughty.

"I think you are either vindictive against my Cousin Nicholas for some personal reason of which I am unaware, or you are quite, quite mad!"

He, too, was stiff and angry, but he managed to say in an even tone, "Then I am to turn in here and not go on to Ballyglen?"

"You are to go to the devil, so far as I am concerned!"

Gathering up the russet folds of her skirt, she leaped to the ground. He started to get down after her but she called back, "Please do not trouble. I have had quite enough of your ghastly suspicions. Good day."

He made one more effort, though she knew from his careful enunciation that he was even more furious than she. "It is coming on for rain and you may as well remain at the hall while I have the team put to a closed carriage."

"It will not be the first time I have enjoyed a walk alone in the rain. Kindly leave me."

Even his good manners were not proof against that. She had never seen anyone so angry who still contained himself so rigidly. He signaled the pony and drove off at a spanking pace along the road to Wells Hall. As for herself, she felt well rid of him at the moment, although, in spite of her red hair, she did not enjoy quarrels. But she liked even less having her deep, well-hidden fears dragged out into the open and given a horrid kind of reality by him.

There must be nearly three leagues of walking, back to the tower. She started out at a brisk stride.

She was glad she had worn her heavy cloak rather than a fashionable pelisse. As she looked up at the sky, frowning, she realized that Kevin Wells had been right about one thing. It was going to be a much longer walk than she had remembered. She decided to use the method that always made a journey or a problem easier. She divided the trip into three parts and would worry about one sector at a time. The first would take her along the Wells Hall–Ballyglen Road back to the coteens. After that, the second part would take her over the rise. Then the longest stretch, parallel to the ocean on the west and the Wells-Faversham woods on the east.

Meanwhile, although the eastern sky toward Ballyglen was still a bright, crisp blue, the wind off the coast carried the first sprinkling of the usual late-day mist. She did not like the great, foul-smelling bog area beside the stream and moved over to the north side of the road where part of the Wells copse encroached upon the muddy tracks. She had worn strong walking shoes, knowing she might have to wade through just such muddy tracks in front of Wells Hall. But it was doubly hard work making speed while each foot felt the pull of the viscous mud.

A fisherman passed her, wading through the edge

of the bog, probably on his way to cut turf. His head was drawn down into the collar of his coat until he seemed to have no neck at all. He was prepared for the weather, and his manner reminded Beth that she would do well to hurry.

She managed to find a ridge of hard-packed earth and kept striding along this ridge until she had passed beyond the oppressive confines of the woods and the boggy ground above the bed of the stream. She began to catch glimpses of the stone bridge arching the river and was surprised by the crowd wandering over the bridge. She had not supposed there were so many people in all of the coteens. She reached the near side of the bridge and stopped to see what had attracted this excitement in the misty afternoon.

She recognized the sheep track she had taken along the cliffs the day she arrived in Saltbridge. Just where the track reached sea level after descending from the high ground, there was another track that seemed to lead off eastward, in the shadow of the cliffs toward the bog. Then she saw the rough-hewn coffin with its uneven wooden pegs. It was being borne on the shoulders of four fishermen. The village must have forgiven O'Beirne for having gone to work at the tower. Leading the mourners before the coffin was Mrs. O'Beirne, the major's housekeeper.

Although Beth had scarcely known the man, she felt that someone from Saltbridge Tower should pay Lady Hagar's respects at the man's burial. Or was Her Ladyship here? Her journey to Ballyglen had been exceedingly mysterious, not so much because of the journey itself, but the lack of any word from her was hard to understand.

Mrs. O'Beirne looked over at her suddenly. The coffin bearers stopped. It was hard to tell what she thought or felt: her heavy veil, aged and a rusty black, made it impossible to see her eyes. But when Beth stepped forward tentatively, the woman raised her hand and beckoned. Beth bowed her head, murmured "Thank you," and followed after the coffin and its bearers. It would have been extraordinary bad manners to refuse.

She felt that heads were turned but she did not look around. Since she wore no bonnet or shawl, she pulled her dark cloak up over her head to pay her respects and walked in the track of the coffin's bearers. It was not easy. They wore knee boots, and even with her heavy walking shoes, she managed to splash mud upon her stockings. There was a deal of muttering around her, but when she saw herself being stared at, she was certain she could not mistake the friendlier feeling in the eyes that studied her so furtively.

Suddenly she became aware of a hand upon her shoulder, a young male voice close by her.

"Mistress Milford, you think they will not mind if I go and pray for the man?"

She looked around, almost into the face of the gypsy boy whom she often saw with his mother and father, and with Tzigana. Seen close to he was remarkably handsome, with a swarthy complexion like brass with a greenish cast. He wore gold circlets in his ears, and these finally placed him in her mind in spite of the jerkin and jacket, and the respectable black breeches. Remembering that her acquaintance with the tinkers had always been disquieting, she glanced around and saw on the outer edge of the mourners' group the malign eyes of the gypsy woman, Tzigana, fixed upon hers with that humorous glint which not only puzzled but unnerved her. She drew away from the boy.

The boy whispered, "Mistress, no. If it please you, I wish to be your friend. You understand, please?"

His manner seemed very different from that open hostility of the others in his family. She thought he was sincere when he indicated he wished to be friends, but she did not know why he should be either sincere or her friend. She looked back again. The gypsy woman had slipped away. Tzigana was nowhere to be seen. Beth knew an instant relief and decided not to turn away the boy's young, enthusiastic offer.

"Thank you, sir. It is always a pleasure to add to one's friends." This sounded pompous, even to her own ears, but it satisfied her sense of propriety.

"You are very good, mistress. May I give you my hand?"

Feeling old and decrepit, she let him lift her over mudholes and guide her around pools of water until they were within sight of the strange little graveyard shrouded from the view of the coteens by clumps of trees and the western edge of the bog with its heavy vegetation. The place was very damp, and dark as night. The coffin was brought to a far corner and set down before an elderly priest who was unknown to Beth.

Beth and her young companion moved into the crowded little glade under the dripping branches. There was a number of Gaelic crosses over sunken graves. They still stood straight, their own lichen-covered stones looking like gray, hooded figures in the mist. Other crosses, more recent and made of wood, had already fallen over in the sunken, water-soaked ground. Beth thought this was a terrible place for a graveyard, so close to the bog, but it was not her affair. She was about eight centuries too late.

She whispered to the young gypsy tinker, "Did you know O'Beirne?"

"Not well, mistress. But he was good to the lady. If he were alive, he would not let the lady go off alone, and so far."

She stepped back into the anonymity of the thick green growth. She did not want to get too close to the bog area, but the gypsy boy moved to that side of her and looked down. He murmured,

"It is strange to bury him here. If he—or they—had destroyed him here, they need not have dropped him into the sea where— As you saw, Mistress, he washed ashore."

The priest was intoning in Latin now and Beth hoped her startled whisper would be mistaken for a prayer of her own.

"What do you know about it, boy? Did your people have something to do with his death?"

Several of the mourners looked around. The boy spoke softly, with dignity. "I am called Sylvano. No, mistress. I saw nothing, but my mother who works for Master Hutterby, she saw the body when you and the convict man found it. She says it may be O'Beirne was murdered."

"But why? Does she know why?"

He glanced at the crowd around the coffin. She was surprised to see Austin Hutterby, looking lean, fragile, and elegant in black and white, and exchanging some remark of consolation with O'Beirne's sister-in-law.

"Has Mr. Hutterby anything to do with O'Beirne's death? Does your mother know?"

"You do not understand, mistress. It is only that I knew Lady Hagar. She was kind to me. And that is

how I knew this O'Beirne. He would not let the lady
go all the way to Ballyglen alone."

Various men from the coteens splashed forward in
their black boots to murmur a prayer or a remembrance of the dour, secretive man who had—or had not—
died by drowning. Everyone began to cast glances in
Beth's direction. She was not a Catholic and knew no
appropriate Latin, but it seemed up to her to murmur
her thanks for his loyalty to the Faversham family.

Young Sylvano escorted her over the sunken ground
with its springy feel of wet turf underfoot. The mourners made way for her. They appeared to accept her
with an attitude almost friendly, not at all like the
cold-eyed indifference they had shown her the day she
arrived. She still did not understand, any more than
she understood why Sylvano was so friendly when his
mother, Ameera, and that barbaric and sinister female
named Tzigana bore her such malice.

Over the quickly made coffin she said, "Peace go
with you, Mr. O'Beirne. You deserve well of God and
of man for your loyalty and your discretion. May the
Lord bless you."

They seemed satisfied and the coffin was lowered.
Water had already seeped into the grave through the
porous ground. Suppressing a shiver, Beth stepped
back and was cut off from a further view of the coffin by O'Beirne's old neighbors who closed in around
it. She moved away, trying not to make it seem that
she fled from this unhealthy place, but it was precisely what she wanted to do.

The surge forward of the crowd, with its morbid
intention of seeing the gravediggers finish their work,
separated Beth from her too-staunch young companion. Beth's independent life had made it too difficult for
her to accept the friendship or surface emotion of

strangers like Sylvano. She might find him charming, helpful, a devastatingly attractive boy, but her nature, cool and suspicious to all but her family, made her ask herself just why the son of Ameera and the probable nephew of Tzigana should be seeking her friendship.

She managed to get out of the graveyard and reach the sheep track before Sylvano caught up with her, breathless and showing splendid teeth in a big smile. The black curls of his hair were in crisp ringlets, thanks to the mist.

"You forgot me, mistress. You are deeply thinking. Isn't it so?"

"I daresay."

He gazed into her face with a childish disappointment and anxiety that made him look younger than Careen.

"If I have offended you, please tell me the truth. What have I done? I am being on my very good behavior. I promised Tzi—"

She turned her head, her gaze meeting his. It was a stupid mistake and she knew it in an instant because he faltered, his eyes shifted. He ended on a lame and, to Beth, a false note.

"I promised myself, mistress."

"Why?"

He seemed stunned by this flat, unequivocal question.

"But because—because you are a kind lady and then this bad man comes and at once you are in danger." As her eyes sparkled angrily, he rushed on in his ingenuous way. "Everyone in the village says so. The convict comes and Lady Hagar goes off somewhere, and the O'Beirne dies, and you drink this poison. It is simple. Then I find something and I want to show it to you. I can trust you. That is all."

"You need not remain with me, Master Sylvano. I can make my way home very easily." She started off with a determined stride, feeling the lash of her damp skirts against her ankles, but it was not difficult for the long-legged boy to keep up with her pace. In desperation, for she was made uneasy by his persistence, she caught sight of the little public house at the end of the line of coteens.

"You have been most kind, Master Sylvano. But now I am to meet someone, so I must say good day to you."

She was certain by this time that he must have some ulterior motive in pursuing her. That telltale betrayal of "Tzi—" could only be Tzigana, from whom he had received his orders to conciliate Beth. To allay her suspicions? Suspicions of what? He was still protesting and apologizing when she walked past him through the muddy tracks to the long, whitewashed coteen near the shingle which dotted the narrow beach.

As the men and women with suddenly talkative children drifted back into the village, the sexes separated, the women disappearing to work in the cottages, many of the men drifting toward the public house. It took considerable courage and confidence in herself for Beth to walk into the dark interior with its makeshift tapster's bar, its peat fire glowing low and comfortably, and the smell of crackling mutton-skin on a turning spit. She was the only female inside. The tapster was male, and there appeared to be no barmaid or female cook.

Everyone stared at her blankly. Those men who had stalked over to the fire to dry breeches, shoulders, and hands made a way for her, assuming she had come here to dry herself. To the tapster, polite but wanting her elsewhere, she said, "I am anxious to avoid someone who seems determined to follow me to the tower. Please do not regard me."

"I'll be sending one of these fellows with you as escort, ma'am, if you say so."

"Thank you, no. It is quite all right."

One of the big, burly men at the fire shuffled aside to make room for her. "Ay. It's likely ye'll be worried, what with that black-hearted convict creature staying under the same roof, mum."

"No, no," she said. "It is someone else altogether. Please pay me no mind."

They tried to do so but she could tell that it was impossible. She was very much in their way, causing them to speak carefully, even to speak in English when they were able, instead of their native Gaelic which came more naturally to their tongues. They lowered their musical voices, looked over their shoulders at her. One or two tried to smile, to make her imagine they did not object to her presence, but she knew better, and unable to waste more time, she moved to the door, looked out.

"Best wait 'til it clears, ma'am," the tapster advised.

The mist slanted across a green, soggy, and deserted world. It looked as though it would not let up for many hours. With a brief thanks to the tapster, she went down into the well-worn tracks in front of the coteens and started toward the Saltbridge rise. Her heavy cloak over her head provided some protection, although the slant of the thin rain struck her across the face and made her blink repeatedly.

She watched a tall, rangy boy walking over the rise, then down toward her, but she saw soon enough that this was one of the Irish village lads. He was urging on a flock of sheep and to avoid them she took a path nearer the edge of the Wells-Faversham woods. The boy's flock shifted from side to side, hopeful of cropping their supper from the meager beach growth provided by nature. The boy smiled shyly at Beth as he passed her at a good distance.

She had already reached the Saltbridge rise and started down along the beach track with the tower on the northern horizon before her when she made out the figures of the three gypsies coming toward her on the beach track. Ashamed of her own cowardice, she was nevertheless relieved that they, following in the wake of the boy and his flock, were not upon her own path.

Considering the weather, it would be dark in an hour. The misty world was already as gray as dusk. She glanced in at the weathered shrubs acting as a kind of barrier for the western boundary of the woods. Not a place she would enter at this hour. Too many chances of breaking one's neck over an exposed root or the great piles of fallen leaves and the debris of autumn. Then, too, Beth could not forget that Molly Wells had died—or been killed?—within this forest, in a glade with the false look of peace and tranquillity.

The mist made no sound except in its light patter upon dead leaves and bare branches, but the salt wind off the sea moaned slightly as it swept over the beach, the higher ground, and through the woods beyond her. She thought at first it was this moan she heard when she became aware that someone called her name, but as she turned and looked around, she exclaimed in angry impatience.

Along came that tiresome and dogged boy, Sylvano, waving to her, calling, "Mistress! Mistress!" He seemed to have crashed out of the woods and plunged after her.

She motioned him away but he came loping on. "Mistress, come back! See? This proves. This proves."

She could not imagine what he was talking about. He looked harmless enough, and the tower was now well within sight.

"I am in a great hurry," she called to him, trying again to wave him away. But here he was before her, breathless and pointing back along the path.

"Come, mistress. The blood will wash away if it is still here."

She was both startled and revolted. Lying rapidly, she announced, "I carry a small pistol in this pocket of my cloak, if there is any difficulty."

To her surprise he did look scared as he glanced around through the mist. "I think we are safe. It is just there."

She let him go first and followed him at a little distance with her hand in the pocket of her cloak. He pulled aside the first prickly bushes, branches that might have struck her across the face, and then knelt at the tangle of roots shaded by the thicket overhead. Before joining him she looked around and into the woods beyond. The boy could not possibly be a decoy for his relations. There was nothing furtive about his attitude. He concentrated entirely upon what he had found.

It was a heavy wooden sabot, of the kind often worn about stableyards and in the courtyards. She looked at it and then at the excited boy.

"A shoe?"

"But whose shoe, mistress?"

"It might belong to anyone. What is there about such a shoe? I don't understand."

"No, no. You see, here upon the top, over the toes? There is a knife slash. O'Beirne made it by accident when he and I were throwing knives at the stable door. He dropped his knife. He was a little drunk and blamed me. I tried to rub his shoe, to hide the mark, but as you see, I failed."

She agreed to that, still not understanding. The wind had blown the shoe into the complex of spidery roots, and the sabot remained comparatively free from the rain. He wanted to put the shoe into her hand but she drew back, still suspicious that he or some hidden confederate might be about to assault her.

He smiled, shrugged, and set the shoe down on a pile of water-soaked leaves. Then he knelt, reached in among the roots, and pulled out something sodden and brown which he laid across his palm. Whatever it might be, it looked odious. She backed away, out onto the shingle of the beach.

"Look. You see? Touch it." He held out his hand. He was very proud of his cleverness.

"No. Good heavens!" Her protest was a little louder than she had intended, and as he stepped out after her, she started to apologize. She hadn't gotten the first word out of her mouth when the air around them seemed to explode. Sylvano's young, excited face crumpled into a puzzled look. In his brown eyes was the same animal hurt as in the eyes of a deer that is shot.

"It was only . . . his stocking," he insisted and fell against her quickly outstretched hands.

She cried out, tried to hold him, but went down on her knees with him. Her arms, which had gone around his thin body, came away stained with his blood. He still breathed, but he had been shot. She cried out, looked around wildly for help, and saw Major Wells

striding toward her with his rifle at the ready. All her
terror was transformed to fury.

"Kevin! Are you mad? Why did you shoot him?"

He looked grim but sounded anxious.

"Good God! The damned gypsy was about to strike
you!"

CHAPTER
THIRTEEN

"How could he hurt me? With a rain-soaked stocking? Kevin, the boy is harmless." She was tearing away Sylvano's muddy jerkin, reaching under his shirt to find the location of the wound, when Major Wells set his rifle out of their way and tried to take her place with the boy.

"You should not be doing such work, Beth. It is unseemly. I'll see to the poor creature."

She did not argue. Perhaps he knew more than she about the immediate treatment of gunshot wounds, but she doubted if his rough, soldierly ways would better serve Sylvano now.

"Can you find the wound?"

"Left side. Above the rib cage. I doubt it will be fatal. Bleeding seems no more than reasonable in the circumstances. I suppose I had best get the fellow into the village." He looked up, frowned at the thick woods growth before him. "I might get him to Wells Hall if I cut directly through the woods."

She was ashamed of her own suspicions, but he had, after all, been responsible for the boy's present state, and she didn't like to think of the major with Sylvano entirely at his mercy in that house far from the observation of outsiders.

"Major, the tower is much closer than either the coteens or the hall. I suggest you take him there, and at once."

He reddened at her implied criticism and the sharpness of her voice.

"Certainly, Miss Milford. I merely thought it improper that a household of three delicate females should be forced to care for a gypsy beggar. A male gypsy beggar."

"Three delicate females and Mr. Cormeer," she reminded him. "He can be moved?"

"Nicholas Cormeer, if I may say so, is not a fit— Never mind. Yes, I can move him. The ball seems to have gone through the body."

She tore off a sizable hem of Sylvano's shirt and pressed it onto the wound.

"Perhaps I can hold this against his body and prevent the bleeding while you carry him."

"Do not concern yourself with the fellow's bleeding, ma'am. His kind lives through anything."

Sylvano groaned as he was hoisted up into the major's arms, but his eyes opened. He saw Beth and tried to smile. It was a good effort. He murmured,

"Not so troubled, mistress. . . . It doesn't hurt. Only a very little."

She smiled and patted his limp hand. "You must be brave for just a few minutes, Sylvano. Then your wound will be cleansed and basilicum powder put upon it and you will be right as a trivet."

"You are very good."

"Major Wells is good. He is going to carry you. Come now. Grit your teeth."

The major may not have approved of his task, but he was not a man to shirk it and started out, carrying the young gypsy with a care that impressed Beth, who walked beside him carrying his rifle and now and then smiling at Sylvano. She tried to keep the rain off his face, but by the time they reached the quadrangle gates, he was soaked through and his eyes were closed. He had lost consciousness.

Beth was about to call out for help from Mrs. Quinn's new entourage inside when one of the gates was opened by Nicholas Cormeer, who must have seen them at a distance. He glanced at Beth with dark eyebrows raised in question, and it suddenly occurred to her that he must suppose she had spent the day with the major and that they had together come upon this injured boy.

"Who is it? What happened?" he asked Beth and automatically started to take the boy, but Kevin strode off toward the stable and servants' quarters.

Beth called, "No! Take him to one of the bedchambers where—Nicholas, please make him go into the tower. Temporarily, perhaps, into the little parlor behind the great hall."

The major had heard her, and before Nicholas could further humiliate him by giving him an order, he made a quick, angry turn and marched toward the tower. Nicholas started after him, saw the rifle under Beth's arm, and, astonished, asked,

"What the devil is that? Best let me have it before you blow a hole in us all."

She said shortly, "I am familiar with firearms, sir. You forget. I was a general's daughter." She did not object, though, when he took it from her and they followed the major.

"Now, what is all this? Who shot the lad? You, or our valiant hero?"

"It was an accident. The major saw us together and thought he threatened me. I must hurry. The boy needs care. Kevin won't know where to take him."

But by the time they reached the tower, the major was already settling Sylvano on the threadbare damask sofa behind which Beth had once found the curious bundle of bedclothing. The major straightened, saw his rifle in Nicholas' hand, and said with his best military manner, "My property, if you please." And to Beth, "I take it you will not require me further?"

Beth was watching Nicholas turn the boy with the brisk ease of long experience, and knelt to join him as she said over her shoulder,

"No, but I do thank you, Kevin. I understand how it happened, and I want to . . ."

The major had gone. She was sorry, but there were more important things at the moment than soothing Kevin Wells's ruffled feelings. "I'll get cloth and water, and powder."

"And a knife. There may be some flesh to be cut away."

She rushed off, dropping her rain-sodden cloak upon the floor of the great hall as she passed. She met Careen in the stillroom helping Shelagh Quinn survey the situation of both food and cooking vessels. The woman and girl seemed to be getting on very well. Beth did not know why she was surprised at this. Perhaps she had supposed Careen would be more like her mother. Shelagh Quinn was much too attractive ever to have been welcomed by Cousin Arabella as a friend. It was a hopeful sign.

"Mrs. Quinn, a young man has been injured in a hunting accident."

She was startled and regretful at her choice of words when the housekeeper dropped a basket of potatoes, crying, "Not my son!"

"A gypsy boy, Mrs. Quinn." She began to enumerate what she would need.

Careen had been picking up the potatoes. She said, "There is a young gypsy tinker who knows Grandmama. His name is Sylvano. Is he the one? Mrs. Quinn, I'll go and help my cousin. I always see to the servants when they are hurt. I'm very good at it."

Beth wondered if her cousin knew Nicholas was with the injured boy. Or could it be possible Careen was seriously interested in the health of the handsome young gypsy? And then, too, plain humanity would have been an even better reason. She told herself she should not underestimate Careen's excellent qualities.

The cousins went off together, leaving an obviously relieved Shelagh Quinn to finish itemizing with Mrs. Barnerd what was wanted when they went to shop in Ballyglen, and what was to be found yet in the still-room and pantry.

"Is he badly hurt?" Careen asked Beth.

"I'm not certain. The major thought it was not critical. I certainly hope he is right. The boy was perfectly harmless. He and I happened to see something—odd, and we were discussing it. It was all an accident. In any case, Nicholas seems to know what he is about."

Careen said, "I suppose, as a convict, he had a deal of experience with gunshot wounds."

Beth wanted to remind her, but didn't, that Nicholas Cormeer had not spent his full time in Australia as a convict. He was, after all, a very prosperous businessman and that must have taken special qualities of cleverness and determination after his wretched beginnings.

They found the boy unconscious and on his stomach, with his face turned to them. His color was bad. Beth glanced at Nicholas, who was wiping away blood.

"What do you think?"

"The wound is dirty. Where is the water?"

Careen held out a pan and clean cloth. He thanked her and she flushed in pleasure. When he took a knife to the boy's back, Beth grimly studied the wall ahead of her, until Careen, who had obviously been putting up a brave front, looked as though she might drop the water pan, which had rapidly become rust-colored. Beth took the pan, and Nicholas, who understood quite well what was going on behind him, finished his task while murmuring to the boy as though he could hear, "You will be feeling much better. Only a moment more. There it is, boy. Now, a little powder and then the wrapping. You see? You scarcely felt it."

The boy had come to consciousness, probably aroused by the pain, and gave Nicholas the merest waver of a smile. He tried to agree, to murmur, "Ummm," which made Careen and Beth exchange relieved smiles. All that remained for them to do was to make the patient more comfortable.

"He should do very well now." Nicholas collected bloodstained cloth and knife, dropped them all in the pan of dirty water, and was about to carry them off. Beth reached for them, but to everyone's surprise Careen took the pan quickly.

"I'll do it. Let me."

They looked after her openmouthed. When she was beyond hearing them, Beth said, "She has been wonderful ever since we came back. I must have been entirely wrong. I thought— God knows what I thought." Nicholas smiled.

"She is simply growing up. My daughter is going to be a splendid creature with all the virtues. Somewhat to my own surprise, I find I was born to be a father. It was, after all, the only reason I came to my . . . my late wife's homeland."

It was an interesting fact, and Beth would like to have known more about it, but the wounded boy was watching them tiredly.

"Mistress, did you bring his shoe? And his stocking?"

Nicholas looked at Beth. "What's all this?"

Ignoring him for the moment, she knelt by the sofa and felt under the edge, coming up with the still wet stocking. "I'm afraid we were too excited. We left the shoe, but we do have the stocking. It was in your hand and it caught in your boot. It fell under the sofa when Major Wells laid you down."

"Good. You see, I was right. But when you left me in the village and I started back to Master Hutterby's fields, I never dreamed I would find where it happened so soon."

"What do you mean, lad? What happened?" Nicholas was intensely interested. Beth began to wonder if he suspected O'Beirne's death was not accidental.

"I saw the shoe. It was strange. I was looking everywhere, over the sand. I kicked up a deal of rocks and shingle. But then I saw it in the roots there. Not where I thought to find it. He was murdered there."

Nicholas glanced at Beth. "Who is he talking about?"

She gave him the stocking and he examined it under Sylvano's earnest regard. "I suppose you mean O'Beirne." Without waiting for her nod, he asked Sylvano thoughtfully, running the wet stocking through his fingers, "How can you know this belonged to O'Beirne? There must be hundreds in this part of Ireland."

"Many do not wear stockings," Beth reminded him.

In his excitement the wounded boy tried to move, his body pulling against his tight bandage. "But the shoe was O'Beirne's. And the stocking—it was pulled off when his body was dragged through the mud and over those roots."

Beth explained: "Sylvano believes O'Beirne did not get drunk and drown, which seems to be the theory. He believes the man was murdered just inside those woods and thrown in the sea."

"But why?"

Beth and Sylvano looked at each other. The boy tried to shrug but winced at the effort, and Nicholas stopped any more such nonsense.

"Later, lad, when you are better. Now, you would do well to sleep. You have lost a deal of blood."

"Is it safe to leave him alone?" Beth asked when they were out in the passage.

He did not scorn her uneasiness but was curious as to its cause. "Why? From his injury? That should mend rapidly. He is healthy enough." He had been watching her and he added, "It is something else, isn't it? You are afraid of—what?"

"Why was O'Beirne murdered? That is what haunts me."

He considered the matter as they crossed the courtyard toward the nearest dining hall door. "I should think there might be a thousand local reasons why the man had to be murdered. Local feuds, hatreds. Some father of a wronged girl—"

"O'Beirne!"

"Well, then, some man to whom he owed money." He said after a little pause, "Or . . . did O'Beirne know too much about the death of the major's wife?"

She stopped in the middle of the courtyard.

"That is not humorous. There must be some other subject for you to make jokes about." All the same, while her sense of loyalty was being assaulted, some sinister thought kept rising to the surface. . . . Hadn't she always thought there was something about Molly Wells's death?

"A tender subject, this major of yours."

"Not at all. But I believe in fair play concerning Kevin Wells, just as I made him understand today that I believe in fair play concerning Nicholas Cormeer."

That hit him but he managed to grin. "Touché, Cousin. Ah! We are being watched by that charmer, Mrs. Quinn."

She thought his expression sarcastic and asked, "Don't you like her? You persuaded her to come here."

"I like her. But I don't underestimate the woman."

Beth saw Shelagh Quinn's face and figure at the long window of the summer parlor. She was lighted by the candles on the table behind her. Her strong face, with its splendid, healthy complexion, looked drawn and sad in this flickering light and shadow. She said something to the maid, Dorothy, who unlatched the door for Beth and Nicholas.

"How does the gypsy go on?" she asked them.

Nicholas said, "Tolerably well. I need a glass of wine. The poor devil has lost blood, but he may be able to sleep and recover more quickly with a little help."

Mrs. Quinn said, "Shall I take it to him, sir?"

"No. I'll stay by him for the time." He caught Beth's eye. She thought she read in his look an agreement with her that it would be well to keep the boy guarded. "Just in case his condition worsens."

He did not mean precisely that, she was sure. He followed Beth to the kitchen where he took up one of the bottles of wine intended for dinner.

"I'll take this along. Partly for the boy. Chiefly to keep me company."

"Don't you wish us to bring you some dinner?"

He raised the bottle. "I'll make do with this." He grinned. "Don't eat all Mrs. Quinn's savory fish stew. I'll have some of that for my supper."

Low-voiced, she asked, "Are you really afraid something may happen to him? Who could hurt him here? Surely, it can't be at the hands of anyone who—works here."

"We can't be certain of anything at this time. But I don't forget what happened to you last . . ." He broke off. Beth glanced around quickly and was chilled at the implication that he had been silenced by the sudden presence of his stepdaughter, Careen.

"Aren't you going to dine with us, Nicholas? I'll sit with the tinker boy as soon as we've finished. Or I can go now and eat later. I'm not too hungry."

It was sickening to think that only minutes ago Beth had been delighted and relieved over the change in Careen. Now there was this sense that no one could be trusted. Beth asked herself if her own talk of O'Beirne's stocking and shoe, the fact that she listened to the gypsy's suspicions, had brought this reversal.

"Thank you, no," Nicholas dismissed Careen pleasantly enough. "A child your age needs sustenance."

"Child! Nicholas, you promised! Girls in England are betrothed before they are my age, so don't call me a child."

"That's as may be, but you aren't in England. Now, run along. Your Cousin Beth will join you in a minute."

Careen shrugged and snatched at the teakettle on its hook over the fire, then leaped back as she almost burned herself, and felt for a piece of cloth with which to protect her hand.

"No laudanum in here tonight, I hope, Cousin Beth."

Beth laughed, a bit dryly. "Not of my doing, at all events."

"I'll test it. Or better yet, make Shelagh do it," and she left them alone.

Beth asked Nicholas, "Do you think it possible that the gypsy boy may have been wrong about the shoe and stocking? Or that he might be lying?"

"I doubt it. But after a few hours with him, I may be a better judge." He turned away with glass and bottle.

"Don't you want another glass?"

"You forget. I spent a number of years drinking any way I could get it, and anything I could get. Glasses are quite a refinement for a man in the hulks. Or a convict." He stopped momentarily. "Eat only what they eat. Nothing else."

"They?"

"I told Shelagh Quinn you expected her to dine with you tonight."

"I see." Did he actually suspect the woman? "I'll come and see how the boy is going on, later."

"Good. He may not need your company, but doubtless I will welcome it."

She felt very well set up by this and went to eat dinner in excellent spirits. Mrs. Quinn had not taken her place at the table until Beth returned and nodded to her. They sat down at the same time, one on either side of Careen who, in her grandmother's absence, sat in the hostess's chair.

It was a curious meal. All three women tried to provide a cheerful mood, but between inconsequential remarks, they must have been well aware of the sounds in the rambling buildings around them. Mrs. Quinn glanced several times at the open doors to the long dining hall. At the far end of that hall there were glimpses of the sea beyond, still carrying the faint glow of daylight. It was very late for the dinner hour, but ever since Beth's arrival the hours at Saltbridge Tower had been helter-skelter.

Perhaps Careen was thinking the same thing. She faced that view through two long rooms to the misty Atlantic. Just when everyone was obviously trying to think of a conversational subject common to them all, Careen said brightly, "We will have our dinner hours much earlier as soon as Grandmama returns. Grandmama is very particular about such little things."

"Yes, Miss Careen. That is like Her Ladyship. I am persuaded everything will be quite normal if Lady Hagar returns. I recall when she went off to Dublin for a visit and left your mother and Mr. Faversham here, there were some domestic difficulties. Miss Careen, I believe your father was not quite firm enough, but a very well liked—" Her voice trailed off. She stared at the other two. "Why do you look at me like that?"

Careen appeared paler than usual. "What did you say?"

Shelagh Quinn explained hurriedly. "Miss Careen, if you inferred that your mother was not popular, I merely meant that we did not know young Mrs. Arabella very well. When your father was knighted, just like your grandfather, we were excessively proud of him. But Mrs. Arabella—I mean to say your mother, was here such a short time."

Beth cleared her throat. "I don't think Careen is speaking of her mother, Mrs. Quinn."

Careen cut in quickly, "I don't think we had best

discuss all this now. I mean to say, so many things have happened recently. It's a little frightening." She giggled. "I shall bolt my door tonight."

Beth said, "It might be wise if we all do so. Including the servants. They certainly don't wish to prowl about the tower. I don't like the idea of your returning to the village alone every night, Mrs. Quinn. Would it be possible for you to take the chamber you have now? Just until these strange affairs pass by?"

"My sister lives in Ballyglen." Shelagh Quinn considered the idea. "She has a fondness for my boy."

Curiously, Careen looked at her. "And would you bolt your door at night, Shelagh?" The housekeeper smiled, made a faint gesture that might indicate indifference. Careen went on: "I wish you would. I think Grandmama will be terribly pleased. She will know the village no longer considers me a magdalen. A scarlet enchantress."

Beth exclaimed, "What nonsense, Careen!"

But Mrs. Quinn's somber, handsome features broke into a faint smile. "Sure, Miss Careen is quite right. There'll be those that say so. I never did. Nor will I say anything on that head now. Molly Wells trusted none that the major smiled at. But I never believed— That is, the major and I did not agree on the cause of Molly's death."

"Thank you, Shelagh. You are honest." Careen excused herself. "I'll go and see if Nicholas would like supper now, since he's missed dinner."

The older women watched her hurry away. Mrs. Quinn remarked, "If you will forgive me, ma'am, it would be small wonder if Molly Wells was jealous of her. She is remarkably pretty."

Beth watched the woman without saying anything until she was certain Careen had gone beyond hearing. Then, as Shelagh Quinn relaxed, she said abruptly, "Mrs. Quinn, you do not expect Lady Hagar to return, do you?"

"But that is absurd, ma'am. I know nothing of Lady Hagar. It's said she went to Ballyglen. Did she not go?"

"Why did you say *if* she returns?"

"No offense intended, ma'am, but I said no such thing. How could I? What would I be knowing of a great lady like that?"

There was no more to be gotten out of her on that subject, but Beth knew what she had heard. Shelagh Quinn was strongly of the opinion that Hagar Faversham would not return—alive—to Saltbridge Tower. If so, what had happened to her? This question and the constant, nagging fear that Lady Hagar might be dead haunted Beth for several hours afterward. She helped Mrs. Quinn and a new, very young girl in the kitchen, and then went through the house, noting the small but important changes made everywhere by the simple act of cleaning, scrubbing, dusting.

The evening was over in a surprisingly short time, and when she started toward the tower stairs, she saw Nicholas Cormeer finishing a late supper of what appeared to be only a cold joint of mutton and a huge mug of something dark and hot that proved to be coffee. His patient lay on the sofa, apparently asleep but shifting about now and then as if in discomfort.

Small wonder. Beth went into the room. Nicholas looked up, startled, set a lamb bone back on the tray beside him. She whispered, "Shouldn't he have a few drops of laudanum to help him through the night?"

"I've given him as much as he can safely take. I'm afraid he will simply have to get through these next hours. Hot bricks will help."

"I'll get them at once."

He took her hand, said, half serious, half lightly, "You are very good."

She pretended to be amused, though she was pleased and touched. "I'm glad I am good for something." She went along to the open areaway at the foot of the tower stairs. She had crossed the courtyard half a dozen times that day and was coming to know every corner of the long quadrangle, all the ancient, disused objects piled there, the stable and carriage house, the outside doors to the dining hall and the summer parlor, but with the rain still falling lightly on the pebbles, the earth, and the rooftops, she found the familiar courtyard full of echoes.

There were still flickering lights in the summer parlor, the weak glow from the stillroom, she thought. She threw her borrowed pinafore over her head and started to cross diagonally from the tower to the parlor door. Her imagination played numerous tricks. She had never heard so many sinister sounds in the rainy dark. Angry at her own vulnerability, she ran the last few steps, throwing herself against the door and trying the latch.

The door was bolted on the inside, which should not have surprised her. There must be someone remaining in the stillroom or the pantry. She rapped on the door, causing hundreds of footsteps to swell into an imaginary army. She called out: "Mrs. Quinn! Let me in. Mrs. Barnerd!"

In the little silence that followed, she knew suddenly that all these eerie sounds had not been imaginary. One of them was all too real. Behind her a pebble slipped as if a foot had trod upon it. The telltale sound and her edgy nerves gave her a second or two that saved her life. She moved suddenly, just as an object that appeared as light as a spiderweb was flung over her head. She thrust it away, screamed at the top of her lungs, and started to race back across the courtyard. She hadn't gotten halfway when Nicholas appeared in the tower archway with the candle that was usually set on the newel post at the foot of the tower stairs.

"Beth! What the devil! Are you all right?"

"Behind me. He is behind me."

He caught her with one arm as she reached for him. He held her in a painful, tight grip, looking over her head at the quadrangle. "Who are you? What are you doing out there?" He raised his light but made out what appeared to be an empty courtyard.

"Who is it?" She tried to twist around, to see through the slanting rain that glistened in the candlelight.

"By God! I wish I knew!"

CHAPTER FOURTEEN

Light streaked the rainy courtyard from a window over the carriage house. The tousled head of the lady's maid, Dorothy, appeared in the open window.

"I heard a lady calling, sir. Shall I come down?" Her hair was blowing around her face and she had a brush in her hand.

Furious with herself for what seemed now a ridiculous flight of fancy, Beth said, "No, Dorothy. I am sorry. It was those damnable echoes in the courtyard. Who put you up there? Are you not to sleep in the tower anymore?"

The girl called out, "Shelagh Quinn said it wasn't proper, me having a chamber near the gentry. She said the servants were to sleep outside the tower."

Beth apologized again, told her not to get wet, and the girl closed her window and a pair of ancient drapes. That brief light upon the quadrangle, however, had shown Beth as well as Nicholas that no one was hiding there after having attempted to attack her. Nor could she imagine how that threadlike thing had crossed her face and been made to seem deadly in her imagination. Could it have been a large spider on his web?

She blessed Nicholas for not using his prerogative as the wise, all-conquering male. He did not sneer at her fright but said, "Whatever it is, or whoever, he's gotten away by now. Come inside. You are soaking wet and trembling. Your would-be assassin managed to set half the household on its ear. I see the Quinn female at the window of the summer parlor. I wonder what she saw." He looked out again without letting her go. "The place is certainly empty now."

He got her into the little parlor where he made a great to-do about dusting raindrops off her shoulders and hands with the napkin from his tray. He came at last to the place where he should have started: her hair. Astonishingly enough, considering that she had only minutes before been terrified for her life, she felt like purring as his hard, calloused hands moved over her body and now her head.

She challenged him, only half believing what she said. "I daresay, you don't think there was anyone out in the courtyard."

"Obviously, he—or she—was terrified of being found out, so he can't be too dangerous. He's not going to touch you in here, by God!"

"I must have imagined the whole of it." She scarcely had time to consider this. She glanced at the window and then at Nicholas. Startled, she noticed that his face was nearer than she had expected it to be. She was aware of the heavy, betraying pulse beat in her throat and then of nothing but the shadow of his face and his flesh itself, his mouth upon hers. His kiss was as she had imagined it. His lips were hard, ruthless, unlike any touch of flesh she had known in her protected life. A man who would have his way, and whose strength and male quality she had always sought without being aware of it.

Her recent fright seemed to have accentuated the excitement of this moment. She clasped her hands behind his neck, allowed herself to be joined tightly to his body, and felt its sinuous power.

When he let her go, they were both breathless and laughed together. For an instant she was dazed. He caught her forearms, saying huskily, "How I hated you once!"

"What!"

"When I thought about Arabella's fine, rich cousin! So piously correct! I hated you through the entire voyage to Ireland."

"But why?" She laughed then. "Surely, you didn't know me well enough to hate me?"

"Arabella gave me the distinct impression that any imperfections in her character were due to the sinister influence of her older—no, her much older—Cousin Elspeth."

"That little witch!"

"So you did know my wife!" He kissed her again, this time briskly, on impulse, touching her lips with a lightness that made her wonder if she had only dreamed the touch.

On the sofa beside them young Sylvano tossed about and then tried to turn over. He groaned. Beth and Nicholas broke away quickly to attend to him. Beth held the wineglass to the boy's lips and he drank thirstily. Then he opened his eyes and asked in a puzzled way, "Why did that officer shoot at me, mistress?"

"He was mistaken. He thought—" She glanced at Nicholas who was watching her carefully. "I don't know. It was a dreadful mistake. But someone will watch you until you are well."

"You are good, mistress. And the young Mistress Careen, too. She promised to watch over me tonight, and that is very funny. Mistress Careen is so small, so young, you see."

"We understand. We will tell my Cousin Careen that you appreciate her offer."

Reassured, he closed his eyes and went off to sleep. Nicholas moved to the window and looked out on the rain-washed courtyard again. Beth stiffened with renewed fears.

"What is it?"

"Nothing. I would feel better about your safety if I could see someone. Anyone."

She would have preferred that he not specify some special danger to her. At the same time she heard footsteps grating on the tower steps and looked anxiously at Nicholas. His shake of the head and quick smile made her relax.

"That sounds like Careen's step."

Seconds later she was in the room. She wore a pinafore over an old, long-sleeved winter gown that looked as though it had been made for her when she was considerably younger and smaller. Nor did the deadly puce color flatter her dark, vibrant features.

. . . She must go with me to Ballyglen as soon as Lady Hagar returns, Beth decided once more. . . . And we must buy her all the lovely things she has been deprived of. Lengths of good materials, beautiful, flattering colors. Bonnets and the pretty sandals that are still in fashion. . . .

But where would she wear them? Across the rainy courtyard? Along the sheep track to the coteens? Careen must go to a fine young ladies' academy in Dublin. Or in England.

Careen did not seem to worry about such trivialities at the moment. She yawned but flashed her gamin grin at Nicholas, and then at Beth.

"Reporting for duty, sir. I've slept and I am ready to protect Sylvano from friends and foes. And officers who are appalling shots."

Since Nicholas was clearly not going to deny this accusation, Beth murmured without conviction, "Major Wells regretted it exceedingly. He thought he was protecting me." She saw the understanding exchange of glances between the other two, and after the excitement of the night, she hadn't enough energy or inclination to keep defending Kevin Wells. Still, she was sorry for him in some respects and felt that she had let her temper get the better of her during their quarrel early in the day.

Sylvano opened his eyes, looked up at Careen's pretty face as she bent over him. He tried to rise, groaned, and Careen said with her new note of authority, "He should have a covering. It is very damp in here."

Although some heat from the big fireplace in the adjoining great hall managed to seep into the smaller room, Nicholas started a small fire in the ladies' parlor while Careen went over to the cabinet in the corner and took out a blanket which she spread over the injured boy.

"Mrs. Barnerd will sit up with Careen," Nicholas told Beth who saw that her own surprise was no greater than Careen's. The girl wrinkled her nose.

"Not that old cormorant. She's so crabbed and irritable. Why not Shelagh Quinn if it must be someone?"

Nicholas would have none of these unfilial objections. "Mrs. Barnerd it is, girl. And I want you both to remain here together, at all times. Promise me." She nodded, but her eyes narrowed as if she were thinking over his reasons for the order.

". . . not necessary at all, mistress," the young

gypsy protested, but everyone overrode this, and when Mrs. Barnerd arrived, dour but efficient, she brought hot tea and mutton broth. Together, she and Careen fed Sylvano, who was in excellent spirits when Nicholas and Beth left him. They walked up the tower steps toward her room. They were silent until they reached the landing. He said then, "I came here to protect young Careen from your pernicious influence. Don't you find that amusing, in the circumstances?"

She looked at him. "Are you sorry you kissed me?"

"No, by God! How I could have thought you were like Arabella— Well, you aren't. You are a woman."

She laughed. "Whatever else I may be, I am certainly that."

He traced the features of her face with thumb and forefinger. "I hardly know you, but what I know of you, I love. When you return to that fine, protected class of yours in England, think of me some time. The transported thief who fell in love with you in three days."

Her expression softened, but she tried not to be too serious. He might think she regarded his past as an obstacle. Absurd thought. Since she had read snatches of Arabella's farewell letter to him, she knew her sympathies and affections were entirely with Nicholas Cormeer.

"I came here to do something about Careen's future. You came for the same purpose." She laughed. "Since we were so unselfish, surely better things are ahead for us?"

"Together? My darling child—" At her renewed laughter, he insisted, "To me, you are a child. *There is nothing ahead for us.* Do you understand me? This time, I know better than to believe, as I once did, that ladies can mate with workhouse brats."

"And if they believe it is as simple as the fact that females can mate with males?"

He smiled but not happily. Would nothing shake that cynicism of his, the cynicism he owed to Arabella and perhaps those long-ago days as a prisoner? He said with a sudden anger, "What do you know about me, my past, what happened between my wife and me? You know nothing!"

She thought of being frank, of telling him that she did know because she had read a private letter of his, but she remained discreet and said quietly, "Then tell me. What was your crime? How did you become rich, as you are said to be, and how did my cousin die? I may as well tell you, I know my cousin, so my sympathies would be with you, even if I didn't love you. Come inside and tell me."

He looked as if he might kiss her again, and she wanted to tempt him, to show him that he must have her. Perhaps he would decide that in spite of their different backgrounds he might risk their happiness. He opened the door for her and went in behind her. It was disquieting when he started around the room, which was damp and cold as usual, and examined the window, looked behind the drapes and the bed tester. He crossed to the door and bolted it, explaining with sardonic amusement,

"If it is discovered that we are locked in your bedchamber, you may be forced to marry me. Honor and all that."

"Dreadful, the choices one is forced to make in life," she remarked, playing this as lightly as he.

"Come and sit down."

She obeyed him, seated herself in the armchair and watched as he paced the worn carpet, stopped before her chair.

"I don't know where I was born, or who my parents were. I know the workhouse in Plymouth, and the docks, so I imagine I was some by-blow of a sailor and one of the females who spent her time about that district. I stole a purse when I was fourteen. . . . Careen's age. It belonged to a sailor sleeping off a colossal drunk in an alley. No doubt his bad head had made him angrier than usual. At all events, he was not quite asleep. He caught me, and feeling a proper resentment for his bad head and the hard-earned money I had stolen, he turned me in to the magistrate. I was sentenced to be transported."

She reached out her hand. He closed his fingers around hers. The hard, hurting pressure was, to her, an assurance that he needed her touch. She guessed the memories that were faintly mirrored in his deepset eyes, masked by the years that gave his face its ruthless, harsh look.

"I was not enthralled with Australia. I was put to dock work in Sydney. Several of us were hired to load one of Thad McQuade's barkentines. He had left Ireland without a farthing ten years before, and when I met him he was one of the richest men in the Antipodes. He had been a blackbirder. They carry slave cargoes."

"Yes. I know. And did you . . .?"

He shook his head. "McQuade had gone into less unsavory affairs when I came to know him. His ships carried supplies to Sydney. Anything that would fetch big sums in the Antipodes. Fashion dolls, I remember. Rich materials for the ladies' gowns only a year behind the Paris fashions. Plants. Vegetables. Oddities. And, of course, he carried sheep back to Britain, or to colonies along the way. He was a strange, clever fellow. Constantly seeking items for transport that no other shipowner would think of. Luxuries. Items that would bring a hundred times their worth. Several convicts, including myself, were leased to him for loading sheep, one of his more prosaic cargoes. One of the convicts, a vicious devil, ran mad and attacked him with a cargo hook. I got the fellow off McQuade."

"And he rewarded you. As he should have done. You were a hero."

"Not quite." He sat down on the edge of the high bed, still holding her hand in his, sometimes putting his other hand on top of it, as if he would imprison her fingers.

"McQuade put me to work, first in charge of the cargoes, later in his offices. When I was free, things happened fast. He was taken by an apoplexy, but he did not die, thank God! I was set in charge of his affairs temporarily. I tried to act as he would have done. I suppose he found it a novelty that I did not betray him, cheat him. Steal. But how could I do that? I owed everything to McQuade."

"Of course. I can understand that. And he made you rich?"

"Better. He gave me the chance to make myself rich while adding to his own success. In short, he made me his partner. He is still alive and, I am happy to say, considerably wealthier than when he placed me in control of McQuade Shipping."

She said quietly, "I begin to see why Arabella married you. She always admired success. When she married poor Mr. Faversham he was about to be knighted for betraying some French invaders here on the Galway coast to the English government. She thought he would be rich and famous. But a dozen years of marriage must have ended that hope. Then he was sent down to Australia. He couldn't understand why he should be chosen to govern a place of which he knew nothing, he told me when we met at Carlton House in London that spring. But Arabella asked everyone to refer to her as 'governor's lady.' And so it was."

"He was dying when he reached Australia. Galloping consumption, they said." He seemed to look far back into his memory, though it could not have been two years ago. "I was present at the reception for them. But it all broke up very rapidly. Poor devil could scarcely stand. And Arabella. What a lovely, sweet, helpless creature she was in her widow's weeds! Wherever I went, there she was." He laughed, but his amusement had a hard, metallic sound. "My conceit in my own charms was raised enormously, I may tell you. I had known women in my day, but I understood their interest in me. My money, of course."

Beth cut in sharply. "No!"

"Oh, yes. I had no illusions. Until Arabella. Since she was a woman of substance, I could hope she was sincere when she protested her love for me. You will say I was naive. At my age." He let her hand go, almost flung it from him. "God! What a fool! What an incredibly blind idiot! We hadn't been married a fortnight when I suspected she had never loved me—or even Faversham. There had always been someone else."

"What!" She got up abruptly. All else she had believed. She supposed Arabella incapable of love. This development was entirely new.

She moved to the window, looked out. She did not want to reveal any of her deepest emotions. But when she turned and stared at him again, she could feel the pinprick of tears and said angrily, "I have never given you any reason to insult me so."

"Insult you, Beth? Because I told you your precious

cousin had actually loved some man who was neither of her husbands?"

"Because you rate my feeling for you no higher than Arabella's."

"Beth!"

"Don't keep saying 'Beth.' You were mistaken in loving Arabella, and I don't doubt you are now mistaken in loving me."

He was shaken, and angry, and, she thought, maddeningly sincere. "Don't tell me I'm mistaken! You think I don't know the difference? Of course, I know! That is why I won't make the mistake of thinking you are my kind. I want you. I wanted the elegance and snobbery and ancient confidence of you. That was at first. But now, there is more to you. Earthy, common, my kind. And I forget who you really are. But I won't mistake again. Never again."

"You seem to fall in and out of love very easily, Mr. Cormeer. I am not quite so complicated. I love once. I never loved before, and I will not again. Unfortunately, your feelings are not so deep."

He made a motion to shake her, broke off, looking stormy and scowling. "For some reason, you want to hurt me because I will not let you throw your life away.

"You are like one of those insufferable heroes in a play, the ones who are constantly making sacrifices so they need not love the heroine. The truth is, you are afraid to take one more chance." He tried to say something but her laugh cut him short. "I quarreled with Kevin this morning over you. It is only suitable that I should quarrel tonight with you. Men can find all sorts of noble reasons for doing what they prefer. I understand about Arabella. She was unworthy of you. But I didn't give a damn about your past. I loved you almost the first time I met you. Black-hearted ex-convict that you are!"

He took her face between his hands and she touched the heel of his right hand with her lips. He said in the soft way that melted her heart but did not help matters, "I could take you now. Here in this room. I want you! You know that. But I am not going to fool myself that Nicholas Cormeer—with his made-up name—will fit into Elspeth Milford's world. Give me some credit. I won't make love to you and then leave you."

"So you leave me without making love to me!" she cried as he shot back the bolt of the door and went out into the hall. Then he stopped long enough to order her,

"Bolt the door until Dorothy comes in the morning."

"I loathe self-righteous, noble men!" She slammed the door shut and bolted it, making as much noise as possible.

She had thought it would be impossible to sleep after her quarrel with Nicholas. She kept wondering about the rest of his story. When Arabella left him, so well equipped for her future with the settlement he made on her, as was indicated in her letter that I had read, what happened then? Why were they on the same ship together? He must have gone in pursuit. And then the shipwreck.

It was small wonder that he wouldn't chance loving a comparative stranger like the cousin of a woman who had hurt him so much.

In spite of all her problems—or her consideration of Nicholas Cormeer's problems—she slept eventually, straight through the night, and upon opening her eyes to a foggy morning with the sun about to break through, she had a sudden pressing thought that was in no way connected with Nicholas Cormeer's past life. She would go down and examine that part of the courtyard where she had hammered on the door of the summer parlor, heard something behind her, and felt something spidery cross her face.

Maybe there were spiders that spun sturdy webs down from the eaves. She was not half so afraid of spiders as she was of whatever—or whoever—was responsible for these sinister happenings in the Saltbridge area.

She dressed before Dorothy arrived with tea and a calm announcement that the gypsy-tinker family had been by to take Sylvano away. Beth swung around on her anxiously.

"I hope they were not permitted to do so. They might kill the poor lad."

"Oh, no, mum. Miss Careen set down her foot. They weren't to get by her, let me tell you!"

"Well, I'm glad of that. The boy is thoroughly decent and I wish he might be gotten out of that roving gypsy life."

Dorothy's pale features broke up into a little smirk. "You do not find gypsies attractive, mum? They do have their charms when one sees them strutting about in their earbobs and their scarves and all."

"Hm," said Beth. She drank her tea and rushed out, leaving the girl with her colorless brows knit and her mouth still open.

Beth went into the ladies' parlor but found Nicholas with his dark head very close to Shelagh Quinn's attractive head. It gave her a slight shock, but they both seemed to be concerned with humanitarian matters, such as the changing of the injured boy's bandage. Everyone looked up at her. Sylvano was the first to greet Beth as if he were genuinely glad to see her. She smiled and took the hand he held out.

"Please excuse me, mistress, if I do not stand."

"You are a gallant young gentleman. Good day, Cousin Nicholas. Mrs. Quinn."

Shelagh Quinn curtsied. Nicholas finished his work efficiently, but his attention was divided. He seemed interested in Beth's every motion, yet she thought he was amused, too. He asked her, "You slept well, I trust, Cousin?"

"Divinely," she assured him with equal politeness. "I had an absurd dream. About that poor Major Wells. Dear man. I was horrid to him yesterday."

Nicholas lost his humorous look. Too late, Beth realized she had also hurt Mrs. Quinn, who said with a certain stiffness,

"If you'll be forgiving me, ma'am, and you, sir, I'll get back to the servants. They're wanting to make up the beds."

"I am leaving directly," Beth said and went out into the passage.

So Nicholas was determined not to go any further in pursuing their relationship! Her pride began to interfere with her feeling for him. She managed to live twenty-seven years without Nicholas Cormeer. She could live the rest of her life without him.

But even so, there were things about him she knew she would never forget. Even his lightest touch. His usually somber eyes, his reserve. The way he watched her, though he had made it clear there was to be nothing more between them. She wondered if anything would change his mind. Jealousy, perhaps?

That occurred to her as she saw one of Nicholas' new hired stableboys cross the courtyard toward her after returning from the gate.

"Message from Wells, mum."

Kevin's apology, of course. The major must feel ill at ease after shooting an innocent boy. She said, "Very well," and went across to the door of the summer parlor. The boy met her there, gave her the folded, sealed letter, and ran off to the stables again, with her thanks trailing after him. She broke the seal absently as she studied the pebbled ground in front of the door. She ran her free hand over cobbles and tufts of grass, but found nothing to suggest the spidery thing she had fancied in front of her eyes last night.

In the pale, foggy sunlight it was hard to think of last night's weather, but she remembered how the rain had slanted across the courtyard. It could have washed anything away, or washed it against the dining hall door, and she moved farther along under the first of the leaded windows in the dining hall. The note from Wells Hall fell open where the seal had been broken. The apology took the form of an invitation:

My dear Miss Milford,

I think you know I never meant that unfortunate young gypsy beggar should be injured. But I was quite mad with fury when I saw him apparently struggling with you. I could not see you threatened.

I have made other mistakes. Now I must make amends. Since the harm to your family came from this house originally, I ask you, and I ask Lady Faversham, if she has returned from Ballyglen, and Miss Careen and her stepfather to come to dinner Thursday evening at the hall where I trust we will set at an end the ugly rumors that have haunted us all in Saltbridge.

This will also give you a chance to meet your neighbors and to present Miss Careen to them without all the innuendo and suspicion that has surrounded her for a year.

Please come, Elspeth, for Careen's sake, if not for your own.

Your obedient servant,
and faithful admirer,

Kevin Wells

She was slightly moved by his appeal, guessing that he did feel some emotion toward her and hoped to mend matters. Since she herself apparently cared for someone who could walk away without claiming her, she understood and sympathized with Kevin Wells's feelings. But her main object in accepting his invitation would be to restore Careen's credit in her native countryside.

Meanwhile, with the invitation fluttering in her right hand, she used her left to feel over the pebbles and grass beside the dining hall door. Just when she was about to give up, her fingers, sensitive to the smoothness of the stones, rubbed against a bit of cord. Fishing line, perhaps.

She shoved Kevin's letter into the pocket of her gown and ran the light hemp cord between the fingers of both hands. There could be a hundred reasons why the line was here, but as she raised and lowered the cord before her eyes, she became convinced that it was this she had seen and felt last night before she moved suddenly and aroused Nicholas with her screams. Light as it was, this line might have strangled her. But who would believe it now, hours later, in the morning light? This was undoubtedly why her would-be attacker had not made the dangerous effort to recover it.

She got up and looked around. No one appeared to be in sight. But then, they might be at any window, servants or household, and she would never know the difference until they struck.

It was difficult after her discovery to look at the members of the household without suspicion. She excepted only one person from this: Nicholas Cormeer. Twice he had saved her. In either case it was horridly possible that she might have died without him.

Why?

What have I done to these people that they must murder me?

One answer was given to her when she discussed the prospective dinner at Wells Hall after she brought a tray of dinner in to the ladies' parlor where Careen was sitting beside Sylvano's sickbed.

"Major Wells sends his apologies."

The gypsy looked surprised and pleased but Careen, suspecting the answer, asked tartly, "Does he send them to Sylvano?"

The latter protested, "Not necessary. It was an accident, mistress. The major never gave trouble to my people."

"Don't make excuses for him, in heaven's name! Detestable man!"

"I'm sorry you think so, Careen, because he has invited you and Cousin Nicholas and me to a dinner on Thursday."

Careen gazed at her and for an instant was delighted.

"But I am not 'out.' I suppose it would matter frightfully in London. You mean Kevin wants me?"

"I think you had better read his letter and see for yourself."

The letter did not precisely soothe the girl. Her eyes narrowed as she came to the part about the "gypsy beggar," but by the time she came to the end, she tapped the letter against her teeth. "I'm to go to a fine dinner and meet the families of the district. I was only a child when they stopped calling at the tower." She looked eagerly at Beth. "It wasn't because of Molly. Not at first. It was because we had no money. We couldn't entertain. I hope Grandmama is back in time to go. But to wear new clothes, to . . ."

"Well, we must see to that at once. We had better arrange for your gowns, as long as so much is being spent on furnishings and servants for the tower. You don't think Lady Hagar will resent our choosing new lengths of material for you, new mantles and bonnets? She won't call it interference, I hope?"

"No, no. She will love you for it." Careen dropped the letter and astonished Beth by throwing her arms around her. "You made everything possible, Cuz. You are a wonderful influence on me, and on this house. Before I knew you, I thought you were just like Mama. And all I thought of was your money. Truly, I did! But now, I want you to live forever."

It came to Beth like a splash of cold water in the face that no one had a better motive than her young Cousin Careen for wanting to see her dead. No doubt, the girl was sincere in her protestations now, but Careen's present enthusiasm was based upon the offer of pretty clothes, things that cost money, and if Beth died today, Careen would have a great deal of money. She did not really believe Careen would do such a thing to her, but would someone commit such a crime on her behalf? And if so, did Careen have any suspicions?

"Thank you, Careen. But it would be well to be certain of your grandmother's opinion. I am thinking of going up to Ballyglen and perhaps returning with Lady Hagar."

"Grandmama will be happy about it." Careen took the empty dish away from Sylvano, who was now chewing meat off a mutton bone. She put the dish on the tray, took up the knife beside it, and studied the edge. But her mind was on something else. "Beth, do you know what I think?" The sudden serious note in her voice caused Beth to stare at her.

"Careen! What is it?"

"Why hasn't she come home? Whatever her reasons for going to Ballyglen, and no one seems to question them, she should have been home by this time. She often used to go off to Dublin to visit friends, and sometimes to Ballyglen, but she told us how long she would be."

Shelagh Quinn coughed. "May I collect the tray of the young man?" She became aware that both Careen and Beth were looking at her. They had not heard her footsteps and Beth wondered how long she had been listening in the doorway. Her next words would have been more satisfying if Beth could convince herself that the woman had no ulterior motive in all her obliging manners.

"I believe Miss Careen spoke of Lady Faversham. May I say that my sister who lives in Ballyglen sent a message to me this morning through Major Wells's kind assistance. My sister has taken my boy to live with her children while I am at Saltbridge Tower. She tells me Lady Faversham is said to be staying at the Ballyglen Inn. She is waiting until the lord lieutenant and his entourage arrive in Galway. I do not know why."

Beth and Careen considered this. Careen was greatly relieved, a reaction that made Beth even more uneasy. The girl had obviously been worried over Lady Hagar's long absence. Except for Careen's reaction and what it implied, Beth decided the matter was better not pursued. She knew why Lady Hagar had gone to wait for the arrival of the lord lieutenant for Ireland. She had discovered something to the discredit of Nicholas Cormeer and wanted to report her discovery to the supreme authority in Ireland. Beth wondered if she should warn Nicholas to be prepared. But surely, if they had quarreled or had some scene before her departure, he would be forewarned as to why she wished to see the lord lieutenant.

Mrs. Quinn hesitated with the tray in her hands.

"Miss Milford . . . Miss Careen, I trust there will be no difficulty. My sister and her husband are well acquainted with Master Kevin—that is, Major Wells, and he is including them in his dinner invitation."

"Splendid." Beth wondered what she was trying to say.

"And I am invited as well. Major Wells was good enough to include me."

Careen looked amused, while Beth thought it an ideal arrangement. She might flirt with Kevin Wells, as she had flirted with many other male friends in England, but Shelagh Quinn, who obviously cared for him, would be much more suited to the major as a bride if he could only see her as something other than his village friend.

"Excellent, Mrs. Quinn. Perhaps we can go in style. I believe there is a large carriage no one has used in ages. We might all ride to the hall together."

"You are too kind, ma'am, but that permission must be given me by Lady Hagar or Miss Careen."

"You have it, Shelagh. You have it," Careen put in quickly, preening herself just a little as befitted her new position.

Mrs. Quinn nodded, murmured, "Too kind" again and went off with the tray.

Careen looked after her. "Sometimes I wonder about that woman."

"What on earth do you mean?"

"I'm sure she disliked me intensely when Kevin Wells and I were friends. I just wonder if she hasn't applied those feelings to you." She laughed. "Or perhaps to both of us."

Although Beth liked and respected the young housekeeper, she saw some merit in Careen's remark, perhaps because—absurd as it might be—she still believed the cord she found in the courtyard near the dining hall door could have been used last night in an effort to strangle her.

She knew no one would believe it. There were too many normal reasons for finding a fishing line here so near the beach, but she was the one who had felt that creeping thing behind her just before the thread moved in front of her eyes, and whatever the others might say, she was convinced. The worst part of it, fully as bad as the threat against her, which made her constantly aware that she had to be prepared for attack, was the fact that her death had seemed to benefit only one person, her Cousin Careen. Now, if the suspect roll were broadened to include Shelagh Quinn, she found it much easier to protect herself against a flesh-and-blood terror which was not her own flesh and blood. The worst horror was removed, the thought that either Careen or Nicholas should logically be involved.

An hour later Nicholas himself appeared with the shoe that had belonged to O'Beirne. Now, as he explained to Sylvano and Beth, they had this evidence but could not fit it into anything except a supposition that O'Beirne had been attacked in that copse, killed there perhaps, and thrown into the water. But it did not in any way point a finger to the murderer or murderers. It seemed likely that he might have been killed for some local grievance unknown to them. Careen said, "Maybe he seduced one of the village girls," but aside from a quickly suppressed smile by every servant to whom the idea was broached, they got nowhere with that theory. Obviously, O'Beirne was not a ladies' man.

By the end of the day, however, Beth was so busy, so involved with helping to adapt one of her gowns to Careen's reedlike measurements, that there was little time to worry about fancied creatures murdering O'Beirne the Seducer, or creeping up on Beth in the dark. There had not been enough time to go to Ballyglen and buy yardage for the next evening's dinner at Wells Hall, and it was delightful to watch Careen's enthusiasm over getting a gown ready made to hand.

"Otherwise, I should have to wait forever until it was finished. And I know Ballyglen has nothing to equal this blue gauze." As Beth had expected, the blue was a marvelous contrast to Careen's ink-black hair, which she was to wear long and unconfined about her shoulders.

"If I were in Dublin—or even your precious Bath, I

would never be permitted to wear such a gown. They would say I was not 'out' yet."

"Very true," Beth mumbled with her mouth full of pins and bodkins. "And they would be right. But in the circumstances, you are the young mistress of Saltbridge Tower, and it would be a trifle absurd for you to come simpering along in white."

"I don't know how to simper."

"Excellent. Your dear grandmama would be ashamed if you ever learned."

"Why do you suppose she went off to see the lord lieutenant, Cousin? It seems very mysterious."

Beth bit off a thread. "Perhaps she knew something about . . . someone. And she thought the authorities should know."

"But who, Cuz? There is nothing she could know about you and me and Nicholas that she hadn't already known. Nicholas was once a thief, and a convict. But she knew this from Mama's letter to her, the one that told us about him when they were married. Is it someone else in Saltbridge who had secrets?"

"I don't know, Careen. I have no notion."

Careen studied her reflection in the slightly flawed looking glass of Beth's room.

"I wish Molly could see me in this splendid gown. She used to say it was a pity young females were forced to wear white. I look dreadful in white. Molly said—" She broke off.

"What a tiny waist you have! Turn about now," and when this was done: "You and Mrs. Wells were excellent friends, were you not?"

"Ever such friends. I was disgustingly young, but she liked to pretend I had quite grown up to her age. We were forever running through the woods to each other's house, over that stile made of rocks across the stream. And she said I would be a heartbreaker when I was well grown, so I wanted to see what it would be like. Not to break a man's heart at first. Only just make him want to—to take me to bed." She swung around, puzzled. "Aren't you going to say 'Careen, I'm shocked'?"

"Certainly not. I often feel very much the same way."

Careen gasped and giggled. "Oh, Cuz, at your—?"

"At my advanced age? Heavens, yes! And did you break Major Wells's heart?"

"I didn't mean to hurt Molly. And anyway, it was impossible to even crack that horrid man's heart, but I kept trying. Small chance I had! He liked 'children,' he said. To me! But he said they should not make mischief. I was so angry I kissed him and Molly saw us. I never thought she would mind. She told me to flirt with the lads when we went visiting. It was Molly who made me see what fun it was to be grown up. Nothing I could say would move her, though. She was certain I wanted to steal her silly old husband. So we quarreled and I said something hateful and so did she. And that was the end of our friendship."

Not surprisingly, Beth thought. But Molly Wells had been a trifle to blame herself, she observed as she took in a seam. "One does not teach a kitten what fun it is to catch mice and then leave one's own mouse where she can sharpen her claws on him."

Careen laughed until she choked and was sternly ordered to stand still. Beth managed to make it appear that her next question was no more than the casual result of previous conversation.

"And then she died just at that place where you had gone back and forth so many times. That stile. I saw it the other day. But how stupid of them to think a child like you was involved! It was only an accident, after all."

She felt the awkward little silence that followed. Afterward, Careen said, "I saw her lying there. I was going over to— Well, I hate to admit it, but I was going to apologize. I got to the stone steps in the woods, and there she was. I felt hideous! I touched her and shook her and I even held her in my arms, and she was dead. She had a dreadful bruise, and blood on the back of her head. I started off running, to get help, and by the time I got to the coteens, village men had found her lying there. They said things to me. Made horrible accusations. Dear God! But— you know."

Beth said guiltily, "Don't talk about it, dear. People who care for you know it was a lie. And now, they know you were innocent."

The girl blinked at her. For a few seconds she had been locked into that world of memory and regret. "There was a time, Cousin, when the only people who would speak to me, believe in me, and be kind to me, were Ameera and her husband. And Tzigana. . . . But now, all that awful period when everyone hated me will be over after I go to Kevin's dinner. They will see then that Molly's husband knows I didn't hurt her. Beth, she was my friend!"

It was very much as Beth had expected, and she believed the girl. She said brusquely, "Tomorrow night, all these people who have spread gossip and lies are going to find out just how wrong they were. And you are certainly going to be the prettiest young lady at the dinner."

"Ha!" Careen jeered. "Ameera was pretty once. And—and, of course, Tzigana. And some others. But that isn't important. A woman must have more than that."

"You see? You are an adult now. You are already wise. At fourteen."

"Fifteen." She sighed heavily. "It seems as if a person never stops learning. It is discouraging."

Beth gave her a gentle slap on the back of the blue gauze gown. "Look at yourself and your confidence will be restored. And remember. Most of the excitement and joy of life are found in learning new things. Don't give up."

Careen considered her reflection, but more critically than was her habit. It seemed to the watchful Beth that this beautiful young cousin was maturing rapidly. She turned, examined herself from all angles, and said in a thoughtful way, "Beauty means very little, after all, I suspect. I must be very grown up tomorrow night. I will act like you."

"Heaven forbid!" But it was pleasant to hear.

While Beth was about it, she got out another gown made for her trip to Ireland. It was a day dress of lilac barred silk which would suit Careen to perfection.

"Grandmama will be so happy! I hope she comes home in time to go with us tomorrow night," Careen exclaimed, her unusual enthusiasm making her suddenly look her true, childish years.

Beth wished the old lady would return, yet she was also afraid of Lady Hagar's revelations. What secret could she possibly know about Nicholas Cormeer that would interest the lord lieutenant? Had he murdered Arabella before the ship foundered?

Sometime during the afternoon she had the happy notion that this precious secret of the old lady's might concern someone else entirely. She became obsessed with this notion. She was trying to guess what it could be, or whom it involved, when a nervous Dorothy summoned her.

"Sylvano's mama is here, mum. She says he is to go away before one of us murders him."

"But that is barbaric! Surely, she doesn't think we murdered that unfortunate O'Beirne."

"I wouldn't know, mum. I only took the message-like."

Beth went down to see how serious the matter was. Nicholas had gone with the new stableboy to exercise the horses and get the old carriage out. Careen, in her new lilac silk gown, was standing in front of Sylvano's couch like a true heroine, while Ameera and her wizened mate tried to reach around her to take hold of Sylvano. The boy himself clearly wanted to remain but was torn between this desire and duty to his parents.

"They shan't take him!" Careen cried shrilly. "They will open his wound and it will kill him."

Ameera's dignity stood her in good stead now.

"Too many bad things happen here. The tower is an evil place. His father and I will take care. Do you think I do not love my own child? But he stays here and is perhaps murdered—"

"Nonsense!" said Beth.

"Tzigana says 'nonsense,' too," put in the boy's father, uttering a sound for the first time.

"Be damned to Tzigana!" Ameera cried, to Beth's surprise. "Else he learns a life that is not for him. He learns the life of the gentile. We are gypsies. Proud of our ancient line. We do not wish to be like you whey-faced ones. He must go."

Careen put in suddenly: "Tzigana wishes him to stay here?"

"It is not Tzigana's affair. Sylvano belongs to his family. Come, boy!"

Sylvano was descended from ancient tribal ways. His family loyalties must always be first. "Please, mistress, I must obey." He was on his feet now, shaky but determined. Since there was no dissuading him and he did seem able to walk, the women watched him move out to the courtyard between his mother and father. The gates had been opened and Tzigana drove the horse and brightly decorated tinker's wagon in. At the last, as Sylvano was being helped into the back of the wagon, he bent painfully, carefully, and asked if he might take the hands of Careen and Beth.

"So kind, so very kind! I will always remember what you have done for a stranger, one of our people."

Beth was amused to see that though he thanked her profusely, his dark eyes warmly regarded the pretty Careen. All the time he spoke to Beth of the discovery of the shoe and stocking, he was looking at Careen.

"Mistress, you will find the men who did that wicked thing to O'Beirne, will you not?"

"Yes, Sylvano. They will be found. Remember, we are your friends."

The gypsy Tzigana looked down at Beth, her teeth flashing. She grinned, gave the signal, and the wagon rolled out, along the sheep track toward the Hutterby grounds.

Careen was furious. "He shouldn't be let go like that. He might die."

"I'm certain he will do very well, and before you know it, he'll be marching in here to sell you some pretty trinkets." Beth took her arm and they returned across the courtyard, Careen more thoughtful than usual.

"Must he come just to sell trinkets? I mean—is he so

very different from me? Are his blood and ancestry so much inferior?"

"He and his family are probably of a purer and older blood strain than yours and mine, dear. The difference is not in his ancestry or his Romany blood. It is in his life, the pattern of his life. Could you spend years upon years wandering through Ireland, living in a tinker's wagon and depending upon the profit from the sale of knives and earbobs, and scissors?"

Careen cried passionately, "I would love it!"

Beth laughed, but she stopped laughing when Nicholas came up behind them.

"Careen, you might do well to listen when Cousin Beth warns you that the mating of people of different stations can bring disaster. Women of wealth and family—men of the people—disaster!"

Careen gave him a quick, suspicious glance, then said, "You need not concern yourself, Nicholas. I don't think you and I are suited, after all."

With Beth watching him, Nicholas reddened, utterly confounded. Beth said, "Perhaps we are all talking at cross-purposes. Have you learned anything more about O'Beirne's shoe?"

Relieved at the change of subject, Nicholas remarked, "Only that I know something of criminals and of liars. I don't believe any of the villagers know more than we do about the poor devil's death."

"And that leaves only—what?" asked Beth.

Careen said vehemently, "If you mean someone here at the tower, I don't believe it."

"Here. Or at Wells Hall. Or Hutterby House."

Beth was thoughtful. She glanced at the sheep track. "Or the gypsies."

No one said anything to that.

The evening was quiet. So much had happened on

previous nights that Beth retired early to lie awake wondering why she should have been so deeply attracted to a man who seemed to enjoy kissing her but found that beyond this he could go on very well without her.

The day of Major Wells's dinner party dawned with all omens good, one of the windswept, blue-sky mornings which made everyone say, "It should be a highly successful party." When in the afternoon Dorothy produced Careen in her full regalia, Beth was proud of her. The girl came running—almost floating—down the tower steps past Beth who had just stepped out of her room. Nicholas also had never looked handsomer to Beth. He stood at the bottom of the steps, all in black and white, even to his pale complexion and black eyes and hair.

"You look like starlight," he told Careen who laughed, consciously.

Beth came down in Careen's wake, looking very much herself in the grass-green color most obvious and most flattering to her red hair. She expected very little attention from Nicholas and was tantalized by the look in his eyes as she reached the foot of the steps and he took her hand. He brought her palm to his lips, not taking his eyes off her. She could not mistake his strong feelings for her, no matter what his protests might be about the difference in lives and backgrounds. There must be some way that she could shake him out of his absurd qualms about a difference in station or in life. He must see that they were meant for each other! At the same time she was well aware that ladies did not pursue gentlemen who had refused their clear offer of love.

They had almost forgotten Shelagh Quinn. They

heard her footsteps first and then saw her come out of her room and along the ground-floor hall toward them. She wore deep rose silk, with a natural waistline and full skirt, a simple color and style that made her excellent looks and complexion appear dazzling. Her form, too, was unexceptionable. She had, in fact, much of Careen's beauty, with Beth's grace and elegance. Simply by her presence she put both Careen and Beth quite in the shade. Beth hoped anxiously that Careen did not notice, and as a matter of fact, Careen was so excited over her own triumph, she had no fear of female competition.

Nicholas was equal to the occasion, bowed to Shelagh Quinn, and when the village lad who acted as stableboy came and stared at Careen, stammering over the sight of his childhood playmate, Nicholas offered an arm to each of the older women. Ahead of them went Careen and the stableboy, both playing roles, the boy the dashing gallant, Careen flirting, but apparently not with any intention of hurting him.

The carriage, as Nicholas announced ruefully, would be an open one, due to the fact that the rooftop had long since rotted away. Fortunately, all the women wore shawls which would serve if the wind came up. But it was an unusually warm evening for November, and even after sunset there was still a pleasant pink glow to their world. Shelagh Quinn started to take the seat facing Beth and Careen, but Careen clamored to sit beside Nicholas, so Beth and Mrs. Quinn rode side by side, and each tried hard to think up subjects for small talk.

Afterward, Beth privately thanked heaven for Careen, who chattered away to everyone. She had never been happier, or prettier. Rather embarrassingly, Nicholas kept looking at Beth. It was embarrassing because she was certain that, if she had returned that look, he would suddenly freeze into the reserved and noble fellow who talked of nothing but class differences.

Just as the last rays of the sun went down behind the distant Atlantic horizon, they reached the fork in the Ballyglen Road which led to Wells Hall. A closed coach passed them on its way to Ballyglen. The coach passed on Shelagh Quinn's side and Beth, farther away, saw only the blur of a face at the coach window.

"Can it be the Hutterby coach?" Careen asked, surprised. "He hasn't gone anywhere in a coach for ages."

Nicholas frowned into the shadow of the bogs in the easterly direction of the Ballyglen Road. "It can't have been Hutterby. He was invited to Wells Hall."

Beth said nothing. Without seeming to, she observed Shelagh Quinn, who was still staring after the vanished coach. Mrs. Quinn looked perplexed, even confused, as if she could not believe what she had seen. Nicholas, who had been so intent upon Beth a little earlier, glanced at her again and then at Shelagh Quinn.

"Mrs. Quinn, what did you see at the window?"

"Nothing, sir. Only a faint outline."

"Come now, ma'am, you did look surprised."

Mrs. Quinn gazed down at her hands which worked with the ends of her shawl.

"It was only, sir, that what I saw was—strange—the clothing, the hair, unnatural if— But I saw nothing more. I could not place it by name, yet I know I have seen the woman before. However, it is gone now. It cannot matter."

Nicholas said, "I wonder." He looked after the other coach once more.

There was no telling now who had been in the coach, or whether Shelagh Quinn had actually seen and recognized anyone. She was not a woman who talked freely.

CHAPTER
SIXTEEN

Kevin Wells was on the steps of his house, or his late wife's house, Beth remembered suddenly, to greet his guests as their carriages drove up, guests were dropped off, and drivers took the coach and team on to the stables. Stableboys obliged with the gentlemen's horses, fine, sturdy Irish horseflesh, for the most part. No one seemed to mind if these riders came in still with the signs of their long riding journeys upon them.

Kevin greeted Beth with his usual, bluff, friendly enthusiasm, but it seemed to Beth that he was watching Nicholas with more than his usual interest. She was glad to see that Nicholas noted this almost malign interest and would probably be on guard.

For her own reasons, Shelagh Quinn stepped behind Careen and behind Nicholas. The major greeted Careen with far more politeness than he had formerly shown. She responded happily, and at once was surrounded by the youngest male guests who drew her into the foyer and great hall of the house.

Nicholas lingered by Beth, but Kevin Wells reached out for her in a proprietary gesture that amused her, though she eluded his hand. And then Mrs. Quinn came forward. A coach from Ballyglen had emptied out its visitors at the same time, but it was plain to the watchful Beth that the major had been stupefied by the sight of Shelagh Quinn dressed in her best and probably least worn gown. She came forward with dignity and did not curtsy.

"Good day, Master Kevin. How very beautifully you have made the hall!"

"Shelagh! My dear—that is—my dear Mrs. Quinn, I am delighted you could come."

The major had momentarily forgotten his other guests and gave his arm to Mrs. Quinn, which gave Nicholas the chance to claim Beth.

"It would appear that you have lost your dashing admirer!"

"How cruel of you to mock me when my heart is broken!"

He laughed, but dryly, without real humor. "You will mend. You will go back to Milford Hall in Somerset and play Lady Bountiful again, and doubtless marry the nearest neighbor whose estates run with yours. I give you credit, though. Once every year for a little while, perhaps in November, you will think about that Sydney felon and the narrow escape you had." Before she could answer or pull her arm away from his suddenly tightening grasp, he looked at her. His voice was harsh, questioning. "Well, won't you?"

Here was her chance for a pert, amusing, and very light answer. They were at a convivial dinner party, after all. A place for gaiety and flirtation. But her spirits were not equal to the usual witty badinage she indulged in with her male friends in Bath and London and Brighton. She said finally, when she got her voice fairly under control,

"I don't expect you to believe me. Why should you? You've known Arabella and you measure me by her

standards. . . . What is it like in Sydney this time of
year?"

He was shaken, but pretended a lightness he did
not feel any more than she.

"Very pleasant. Crowded, sometimes primitive. The
Outback is certainly primitive."

"Heavens! After the dazzling court life of Saltbridge, I could certainly never submit to primitive
Sydney."

"I did not say that Sydney was—" He realized belatedly that she was joking now, and smiled. "Yes. You've
fitted into Saltbridge better than I ever expected.
What a brightness you would give to my city! Not that
I am going to expose you to it."

Nevertheless, for a moment, she saw that he had
considered her in the light of a woman who might fit
wherever she was happy. It is a step toward her happiness, and his, if he would only permit himself to admit it.

"I wonder what I must do to convince you that I am
an army daughter? I have lived behind the gun, beneath the cannon, and upon the arid Iberian plains.
However . . . Mr. Hutterby! How very pleasant to
see you again!"

Austin Hutterby looked like the splendid relic of
the past century which he was. He wore the out-of-
fashion silk hose and knee breeches, the sky-blue,
watered-silk coat, and the gleam in his eye that was a
warning to all females.

"My dear Mistress Milford, you have never looked
lovelier." As he had seen her but once before, this was
less of a compliment than it seemed, but Beth accepted it in the proper spirit, wishing she could remain with Nicholas. She mentioned his name, tried to
present him to others of the neighbors from more dis-

tant estates, but by that time the crowd had enclosed her, and Nicholas was nowhere in sight.

She made up her mind to enjoy herself, but the effort of eluding Austin Hutterby's elegant hands was not part of her enjoyment. The guests were presently summoned to dinner in the long, formal, white and gold dining hall, and Beth found herself at the right hand of the host, with the senior female of the party, a lady from beyond Ballyglen, sitting at Major Wells's left. Careen was sitting halfway down the table between Nicholas and a somewhat callow lad who proved to be Shelagh Quinn's nephew from Ballyglen. Unfortunately, Austin Hutterby had been placed on Beth's other side. She stayed as far away from him as possible and was both sympathetic and amused to note that the face of the Anglo-Irish lady on his other side was a study in expressions of surprise, shock, stupefaction, and finally outrage.

Partly due to Hutterby's obvious interest in Beth moments before, Kevin had become aware of her.

"How bright and vivacious you look, Beth!" he murmured under cover of the general buzz of conversation. "May I call you by that charming name? I wanted you to know I have sent some money to that gypsy beggar. Not a great deal, I'm afraid, but the family will be glad of it. They never see more than a few farthings from one week's end to the next."

"It was very good of you," she said automatically. She was wondering what on earth Shelagh Quinn's Ballyglen sister was saying to Nicholas that made him laugh so hard. His somber face lighted with the uncommon expression she had seen in his face once or twice.

"I may as well confess, it was your influence," Kevin Wells went on, unconscious of her real interest.

"It was exactly the sort of thing my Molly would have advised. Like you, she was born to properties and affluence, but she took a serious interest in the poor and the unfortunate. Creatures like that gypsy family."

"Creatures, Major? I don't like to sound pious, but are we not all creatures? God's creatures?"

He cut a succulent slice of roast mutton and chewed it thoughtfully. Finding a way out of the small dilemma she posed, he answered her in triumph, "Molly would have said that, too. Precisely. But she was well aware of the responsibility some of us have been given to look out after those poor unfortunates without our advantages."

"I wonder who decided we are equipped to look out after them, rather than that they should look out after us."

He shook a finger at her playfully. "Now, that, my dear Beth, is something Molly would not have said."

She tried not to show her boredom with this silly talk and glanced away, catching the attention of two people: Nicholas, who had apparently been watching her for several minutes, and Shelagh Quinn, who showed Beth and Major Wells one of those calm expressions quite impossible to read. Perhaps it meant no more than it exhibited. Beth remarked, "How beautiful Mrs. Quinn is! I don't believe I had realized it before."

With genuine enthusiasm he agreed, but as though the woman were somehow in costume and would turn back into that nice, common Irish villager in the morning.

"Beautiful creature. Molly always said these villagers had a kind of primitive loveliness. Fades early with most of them. They have a hard life." He considered the woman, looking down the table as someone spoke to Mrs. Quinn, and she replied in her quiet, level voice. "Though I must say, Shelagh is exceedingly well preserved, for a female near on thirty."

As he must, himself, be near on forty, she felt this an uncalled-for comment. "She is strikingly beautiful, and I have seen princesses with manners not nearly so good as hers."

He was pleased, as though this somehow reinforced his own good opinion of her. "Have you now? Well, I confess she gave me a start when I saw her this evening. I'd no notion she could look the lady and play the part. You see?"

Beth examined the pattern of her plate with casual interest. "Someone told me recently that Mrs. Quinn reminded many people of your late wife."

He let out a quick explosion of laughter, cut off abruptly. "Not a joke in very good taste, I'm afraid."

"I was not joking." All the same, to her deepening annoyance, she became aware that his laugh had directed everyone's attention to the head of the table, including Nicholas', who looked dour again. She could guess his thoughts, that this flibbertigibbet, Beth Milford, was flirting thoughtlessly once more.

The major considered his old acquaintance, Shelagh Quinn, in a new light, but Beth's entire effort as a matchmaker was interrupted by a stifled shriek from the lady on Austin Hutterby's other side. She drew away from him with indignation, but he seemed utterly imperturbable. The interruption was compounded by the entrance of Kevin Wells's butler-footman to report the arrival of a man who was not invited to dinner but was certainly awaited by the host.

The major apologized to his guests and left the

room briefly. Beth caught a glimpse of a man in uniform, looking splendid but vaguely menacing in his red, white, and gold regimentals. What was he doing here now if he was not a part of the dinner party? Also, she suspected Major Wells had been waiting for him with some anxiety.

It seemed to Beth that he took a long time with the soldier. Where had the man come from? What was he here for? Such soldiers were the only law in this part of the world, and law suggested that he must be here about O'Beirne's death. Did he know something about it?

Or about some other criminal matter?

By the time Kevin Wells returned, everyone was ready to adjourn to Madeira whiskey, poteen, and, in the case of the women, a bit of choice gossip in the ladies' withdrawing parlor.

It was in this pleasant, well-worn, and comfortable atmosphere that Beth met Shelagh Quinn's sister from Ballyglen, and the subject of Lady Hagar came quickly to Beth's mind. Annie Fisher was very nearly as attractive as the younger Shelagh, with the same quiet competence and lack of affectation, and like Shelagh, she observed a great deal.

Beth said, "I believe you encountered Lady Hagar the other day on the streets of Ballyglen, did you not, Mrs. Fisher?"

"My oldest boy it was, ma'am. Said it was a surprise-like to see the old lady walking fast as a young one. My lad'll be knowing Her Ladyship tolerably well, but he's never seen her walk faster than he could keep up without running."

Careen, who had been whispering secrets to a giggling girl from beyond the Hutterby grounds, looked up.

"Did you say Grandmama was running, Mrs. Fisher?"

"That I did, Miss Careen, or as near as makes no matter. My boy, Padraic, worked about the stables here at Wells Hall when Miss Molly was alive. He saw a bit of Her Ladyship when she visited here, and it's his word—not mine, mind you—that Lady Hagar must be vastly improved."

"She wasn't, you know, Mrs. Fisher. She scarcely walked anywhere. Was Paddy quite certain he saw Grandmama?"

"She being swathed in a shawl and heavy cloak, it was hard to say. But she had left a message at Ballyglen Castle where the lord lieutenant is expected soon. He has lingered in Galway, so they say."

Careen turned to Beth. For the first time her deep concern was there for all to see. "It isn't like her, Cousin. Nothing about this whole affair is like Grandmama."

Shelagh Quinn said quietly, "I am persuaded my nephew told the entire truth as he saw it."

"No, no. I've known Paddy since time out of mind. But it worries me that what he saw is so unlike my real grandmother."

Several voices repeated, "Your *real* grandmother?"

Beth saw that Careen was looking upset and put in anxiously, "I believe the matter will be settled as soon as Lady Hagar has her interview with the lord lieutenant." Even as she spoke, she prayed that the matter settled would not concern Lady Hagar's suspicion of Nicholas.

Meanwhile, the men were strolling into the great hall where the big, welcome fire crackled and exploded on the huge hearth. As if by accident, the ladies wandered over to the open doors and were soon enticed to join the gentlemen.

Beth lingered, however. She had seen the uniformed soldier in the passage, moving toward the little bookroom behind the ladies' parlor. It was necessary for Major Wells to go back to his guests, thus leaving the soldier alone with a mug of the local poteen.

Beth took the train of her iridescent green skirts in one hand and followed the officer into the bookroom. He was considering the drink in his hand with such an extraordinary expression compounded of puzzlement and shock that Beth's fears were momentarily submerged in amusement at the young man.

"It is not harmless, sir, if that is what you are asking yourself. It is the local whiskey, made from potatoes."

"To be sure. I should have guessed." He took another swallow of the contents, shuddered, and then recollected himself. "But what am I thinking of, ma'am?" He saluted and bowed with a certain grace. "Captain Ian Macondrie, very much at your service, ma'am."

She sank in a curtsy. "Elspeth Milford, Captain. At your service."

He had brought her hand to his lips but stopped excitedly. "Milford! You wouldn't be Old— Pardon. General Milford's daughter?" She nodded. "But I knew you after Corunna. We shared a mule during our escape from Boney's General Soult in Spain."

She tried to see him as the frightened, curly-haired boy her own age, who had fled with her and an ill-tempered Spanish mule long ago. There was not much of that scrawny boy left in this splendid specimen of His Majesty's loyal officers. Perhaps the uniform was responsible, in part. At all events, as her old acquaintance, Ian Macondrie, he might be easier to question.

"My dear Captain, how very good to see you again!

Of course, I remember you. That was quite an adventure." Getting down to more immediate matters at once, she went on, trying to conceal her anxiety beneath a businesslike tone. "But I daresay you are not here to ride mules with the local lasses. I should think you are with the lord lieutenant for Ireland, and—let me guess—you have just seen Lady Hagar Faversham. As a result, you wonder how much truth there is in what she has told you."

"Ah, Miss Milford, you know what my business is, I see. In a manner of speaking."

Feeling her way toward an effort to discover his mission, she suggested, "Then Her Ladyship has told you. But she is a temperamental old lady with many crotchets. She might suddenly make accusations without any proofs whatever."

"I'm afraid we are at cross-purposes, ma'am. Lady Faversham has not brought an accusation. Although I make no doubt it was intended that we should think so. It's my opinion and the opinion of our host, Major Wells, that Lady Faversham never reached Ballyglen."

"No! That can't be true."

"Forgive me, Miss Beth, but that very point brought me to this place. If she did not reach Ballyglen, how far did she go? Or did she go at all?"

She found the edge of the major's big desk under her fingers and clung to it as one hard bit of reality.

"You mean she is in hiding?" She prayed that this was true, or at least that he thought so. "For what reason?"

"I'm afraid not even that could explain that person pretending to be Lady Faversham in Ballyglen."

"But, Ian, Mrs. Fisher's boy saw her."

"Did he? Or did he see another person, younger, fast on his—or her feet? Someone who left notes to be delivered from the inn but always when no one was around to see who left them."

She floundered for a challenge to that. "The writing. Careen knows her grandmother's hand very well. She had not the slightest doubt the note was in Lady Faversham's hand. But you have not seen the note, have you?"

"I am persuaded we will find an explanation for that, Miss Beth. What the explanation is, I am not prepared to say at the moment. In fact, that is precisely why I am here." He drank another swallow of the poteen, looked over the mug at her, grimaced at the taste, then smiled at his own reaction. "If I survive the local brew, that is to say."

She had never felt less like responding to his joke but managed a wavering smile, trying all the while to find some rational explanation for this strange inaccessibility of Hagar Faversham.

"Mrs. O'Beirne, the major's housekeeper, an eminently respectable woman, saw Lady Hagar in the pony cart on the afternoon she took the Ballyglen Road."

"Beg pardon. I have just talked with Mrs. O'Beirne and she tells me that, to be precise, she saw the pony cart and a heavily shrouded female, but she did not see any particulars of her face, and we are precisely where we were."

Beth saw a shadow cross in front of the candle sconces in the hall and assumed Kevin Wells was coming. She said quickly, "Can something have happened to her on Ballyglen Road, after she left Saltbridge?"

She was startled when Nicholas Cormeer walked into the room, obviously having heard what went before. "I doubt you will find your answer on the Ballyglen Road, Captain."

The officer covered his surprise at Nicholas' appearance by a quick assumption of efficient formality as Beth introduced the two men. "To get to your objection, sir, may one ask why there will be no answer on Ballyglen Road?"

"It is far more likely that Lady Faversham's disappearance is somehow connected with the death of a tower servant, a local man named O'Beirne."

"Yes. I have heard of this fellow's drowning. What makes you think the two events are connected?"

Seeing Beth's nervousness, Nicholas crossed the room and put his arm around her in a proprietary way that pleased and relieved Beth, while it warned the young captain of their close relationship. It might be a dog-in-the-manger attitude, Beth thought, but she was glad of it all the same.

Nicholas, meanwhile, explained the finding of O'Beirne's shoe and stocking just inside the woods.

"In spite of the rain and fog lately, there are stains on both articles, stains that I believe to be blood. I've no doubt whatever that the man was murdered there. His disappearance coincides with that of Lady Faversham almost to the hour."

"Coincidence?" asked the captain, but it looked as though he was considering certain possibilities while Nicholas dismissed his first sharp response.

"I do not believe in such coincidences. According to my stepdaughter, the man was intensely loyal to Lady Faversham. What more natural than that he should defend her from some fate—death, in all likelihood—and be murdered himself?"

They all heard their host, Major Wells, showing his guests various family portraits in the gallery outside. Captain Macondrie and Nicholas studied each other. Macondrie said,

"I am inclined to agree with you. Would you have any notion who might be responsible for these two murders? If murders they were?"

"Not at the moment. But I do know that my . . . my cousin here, Miss Milford, has twice been threatened, so I don't doubt there is a murderer about the premises."

Captain Macondrie exclaimed abruptly, "Beth! You mean you have been assaulted?"

Nicholas did not like this use of her first name at all, she saw with considerable pleasure. Captain Macondrie added hurriedly, "Your beautiful cousin and I have been friends from our youth in the Peninsular War. I say, can you take me to the place where you believe this O'Beirne was murdered?"

"Certainly. It might be well to go at once, or as soon as we can get lights and men."

Macondrie was taken aback. "What? Would you go dressed as you are?"

"Very likely there are already villagers who have looked at the area. They discuss nothing but the death of their fellow villager. I am convinced that if we wait very much longer we will give the murderer—or murderers—time to cover their tracks. I spent much of the morning and several hours last night looking about the area, and found no proofs beyond the objects you know of, but I'd stake my life that is the place."

Kevin Wells came into the room. He frowned at Nicholas' familiarity with Beth. "The place for what, may I ask?"

Captain Macondrie murmured, "The—ah—evidence pointing to— Well, that remains to be—"

Nicholas cut in flatly, "The place where the body of Lady Faversham may be found in the woods. You recall the spot where you shot the tinkers' boy."

While the startled Macondrie looked from one to the other of the men whose mutual antipathy was evident, Kevin said, "See here! That was an accident. I've paid the boy's parents. They agree it was an unfortunate mistake."

Beth told Macondrie, "I believe it was to protect me. Major Wells thought I was being assaulted by Sylvano." She added quickly, "It was not the case."

But the major's feelings had been wounded and he asked with a deep sense of injury, "Am I to understand you are walking out of my house in the middle of a dinner party in order to wander through my woods? I asked you here, Captain, to— But you know why I asked you here."

He had apparently expected Captain Macondrie to keep his mission secret, but Beth could have told him that her wartime friend had never kept a secret, even from the enemy French. Captain Macondrie blurted out now in all innocence, "Yes, yes. To be sure. We were to look for evidence of criminal activity at Saltbridge Tower. I believe it involved a villainous ex-convict from the Antipodes."

Major Wells was left dumbfounded and probably embarrassed, but Nicholas gave a short, sharp burst of laughter.

"I am the villainous ex-convict. And I suggest, by all means, that you examine Saltbridge Tower as well as the area where I believe O'Beirne was murdered."

Macondrie managed to get away from the awkward moment gracefully by agreeing with an ingratiating smile. "My apologies, sir. But I quite agree with you that both areas should be explored. If I might change my boots and retrieve my travel cloak, we can proceed at once. I say, Major, we can count on the honesty of the locals, can't we?"

Nothing was going as Major Wells had intended, but he was resolved not to be cheated of his prey and insisted that there must be witnesses wherever Nicholas Cormeer went.

"Really, Major!" Beth cut in impatiently, "Must you be so offensive?"

By coincidence, at this moment when he turned scarlet at her insult, Shelagh Quinn passed the doorway, stopped, and inquired in her quiet way, "Will you be joining your guests soon, Master Kevin? They appear a trifle restive."

Beth could have smiled at the abrupt transition in Kevin Wells's face and manner. His soldierly male pride had been ground underfoot by Beth's remark, but Mrs. Quinn restored his good opinion of himself. He would turn to her now as the new image of the late Molly Wells, no doubt.

"Thank you, my dear Shelagh. I will join them shortly. Then I'm afraid I must hurry away after these—gentlemen."

"Thank you." She seemed to have been about to add the dip of a curtsy and the polite "sir," but before she could so so, Major Wells excused himself coldly to Beth, took Mrs. Quinn's arm, and escorted her back to his company.

Beth argued briefly but ineffectually that she could point out the exact spot where she and Sylvano had found the shoe and stocking. Like Careen, she was forced to take her wrap and get ready to leave for the tower.

The other guests began to depart. For a few minutes there was pandemonium as the portico and steps came alive with people awaiting carriages or going off to fetch their mounts. More or less by accident, the tower carriage came by just as Nicholas and Captain Macondrie came out on their way to the woods area.

"Ladies, will you be so good as to permit us to ride with you?" the captain asked gallantly.

Beth hesitated. "I believe Mrs. Quinn—"

Shelagh Quinn had arrived on the steps with Major Wells. "Thank you, no, ma'am. Master Kevin will be good enough to drive me back to the tower."

So the captain and Nicholas took the seats opposite Beth and Careen. The team started off. No one said anything. At one moment Nicholas reached forward and took Beth's hand briefly. His smile warmed her even more than his touch.

"Why so silent, Cousin?"

"It has been a busy evening, and threatens to be even busier."

"The sooner we settle this business, the sooner you are safe." A heartbeat later he added, "Both of you."

Careen's faint grin acknowledged her inclusion in the remark, but, to Beth at least, she looked a little cynical, as if she had guessed that her own inclusion in his concern was belated.

Through the night, with the first luminous wisps of fog settling over the cold darkness, the carriage bounced and rattled behind the ancient Hutterby coach. No one said much, although Captain Macondrie tried valiantly to make small talk.

Beth could not keep her eyes off the woods, that long line of deeper darkness that paralleled the rough sheep track on which they traveled. As they came opposite the area where Sylvano had found O'Beirne's shoe, Nicholas signaled the coachman to pull up. Over his shoulder he told Captain Macondrie: "It is along here." The captain leaped off after him. Nicholas turned back, said to Careen, "You'll take good care of Cousin Beth, won't you?"

Careen's thin young back straightened. "I will. I promise."

The men had already crossed the sand and shrubs when the light of a lantern flickered within the woods and one of the villagers came rushing out toward the captain whose uniform could be seen in spite of his enveloping travel cape.

"If you'll be coming this way, sir!"

Beth ordered the coachman, "Stop here, please." She was getting down when Careen tried to dissuade her. "We should go home. He told us we would be safe there."

"I am not going to wander through the woods alone, if that is what you imagine."

Careen drew back, hurt by Beth's sharp remark. "Very well, Cousin. I'll wait."

"You need not. I want to show the captain where we found the shoe and stocking." She was already hurrying over the sand. Careen called something after her but she could not hear it. She had nearly reached Captain Macondrie who turned, waited for her, and asked,

"Can you recall the exact spot where you and the boy were? There seems to be some discrepancy."

"I will be glad to. Only let me rid myself of this stupid train." She swept it up and fastened it inside her silk waistband.

"Beth, stay out of here!"

She could not mistake that voice. Nicholas would have taken her by the shoulders and moved her firmly out onto the sand, but one of several village men and an elderly woman, badly shaken, surrounded them.

The woman cried, "Don't you be after sending her away, sirs! Ma'am, 'tis a female I'm needing now. My man is that sick—it's the reason we stumbled over the roots back there. Him being with a little too much poteen under his jacket when we crossed the stile and all. Ma'am, could you help me with him? He'd rather not be seen like this by the fine London gentlemen."

Beth hadn't the faintest notion what this was about, why everyone should be concerned over a drunken man's stumble, unless he had stumbled over something connected with O'Beirne's death.

"Of course. I'll follow you. Someone flash a lantern on the ground so that I may see my way."

"Now, look here, Beth," the captain called aimlessly while Nicholas scowled, whether at Beth's conduct or at the captain's referring to her so familiarly, it was hard to say. Beth made her way after the village woman, and instead of concentrating on the area where O'Beirne's shoe had been found, Nicholas went after Beth in an attitude clearly protective.

"Here, ma'am." The woman drew Beth to a heavy man on his knees trying to rise to his feet. The little glade beyond him looked familiar in the light of the second lantern that had apparently fallen from his hand and was now setting on a half-submerged rock. Before Beth could help the wife pull the man up on his feet, Nicholas came forward, seized him under the arms, and lifted him up.

"Thankee. Thankee." The man's voice was blurred, but the sentiments were clear.

Beth paid little more attention to him. She was moving onward, beginning to recognize the area now. The stile was beyond, and the sluggish little stream where Molly Wells had fallen and died. If, of course, she had fallen accidentally. . . . But tonight seemed a time

for every evil thought. Beth had scarcely gone the
length of the man's body when she found the roots he
had stumbled over. She had more than half expected
to find something else which would connect the
death of O'Beirne to this spot, but the roots seemed to
be the only stumbling block for the drunken man. She
walked around the roots and a rotten tree stump, her
evening sandals sinking occasionally into a pit of sand.
Through the lantern's rays she saw the stile composed
of stone blocks and the stream, clogged with debris,
wandering away into the darkness.

"What do you see?" Nicholas asked, but she thought
that the same idea had occurred to him.

"Nicholas, you said you didn't believe in coincidence."

"Very true. What is the coincidence here?"

"Molly Wells died from a fall off that stile, the stone
steps. And now . . . I had no idea O'Beirne's shoe
was found so near it. I suppose, with the path running
at a tangent to the woods, so to speak, it was obvious.
But if O'Beirne was murdered there and Mrs. Wells
died under suspicious circumstances so close by . . ."

"And we are looking for Lady Faversham." He
moved her aside, took up the lantern, and went ahead,
breaking branches in his way.

She asked, "Then you too think Molly Wells was
murdered?"

He did not answer, but the village woman, helping
her husband make a wobbly exit from the woods,
looked around, her eyes wide.

"Is it so, ma'am? Our Miss Molly was done in, like
we thought?"

"Not quite as was suspected," Beth snapped. "My
cousin was in no way responsible."

"That's as may be, ma'am." The woman tramped on noisily through the underbrush.

Nicholas reached the stone stile, examined the area, including the bed of the stream, and started back, but this time pushing his way through a thick clump of woods, carefully studying the ground. "Quite a large slab of earth has been turned here recently. Beth, call the captain!"

She moved, then stopped, moved closer behind him, and looked over his shoulder. The toe of his shoe had uncovered something. He knelt and scratched the top-soil away, then, in a sudden frenzy, dug deeper. She caught her breath, watching.

"Is it?"

"Cloth." He had found something, some stained material.

She knelt beside him. He started to pull out the cloth from its burial place, but stopped. "Do as I told you. Go along."

"Tell me, please."

"I think it is that pink, furred robe she wore in bed. She was wearing it that afternoon when I arrived and went up to see her."

"Oh, God, no!"

"The poor creature may have been murdered in the tower itself. Damn! I liked her!" He struck the ground with his fist in his impotent anger, then looked at her. "Go with those villagers. Don't let yourself be caught alone. Bring the captain."

Feeling helpless and hating it, she ran after the villagers. She kept thinking of Hagar Faversham's old bones lying here in the cold earth since the day Nicholas arrived at Saltbridge Tower.

CHAPTER SEVENTEEN

When the captain and Nicholas uncovered the bare, pitifully thin foot of the old lady from the dark woolen material in which it was wrapped, Beth found herself shaking and sickened for the first time since her girlhood in Spain when she stumbled upon a pocket of the British invasion army blown up by the French invasion army.

"No signs of a bullet that I can see," the captain said in low but businesslike tones. "Knife marks? I think not. I wonder . . . Natural death? Or perhaps smothered. What do you think?"

Major Wells had joined the men. "Undoubtedly smothered." Nicholas looked hard at him. He shrugged. "Much more likely than a natural death, in the circumstances."

It was *all* very natural to these men, Beth thought bitterly. The life of one old, brave, cantankerous female had been cut off, but they discussed it in cold indifference to her humanity. Common sense came to the fore then, and Beth knew their manner was far better than weeping, wailing, and hysterics. She recovered herself when she saw Careen's pallid face.

"Don't look, dear. Come away." She led Careen up to the stile, farther from the men who were gently gathering up the body of Hagar Faversham. Careen looked as though she might scream. Beth put both arms around her and the girl whispered against her shoulder, "I didn't cry when they told me Mama died. Oh, Beth! That was a sin. And now Grandmama is gone. I never loved anybody but Grandmama."

"I know. I know. We should go home now. She wouldn't want you to stay here."

Careen let herself follow Beth's lead. She seemed to have lost her own volition for the moment. As they passed the group gathered around the shallow grave, she stopped, her stunned expression suddenly turning to great shock.

"Careen, are you ill?"

The girl shivered. "Let's go." She began to run, thrusting her way between interlaced trees and bushes that snapped back cruelly in her face. She very nearly fell over a pile of moldy leaves before Beth caught her. Careen let herself be led out across the sand, past curious villagers to the tower carriage. The new coachman was walking team and carriage up and down but rushed back to help the ladies into their seats.

During the short ride home, Careen said nothing. Beth murmured, "It must have been very quick. She was not well, you know." She felt the stupid inanity of the remark and subsided, but when they reached the quadrangle and left the carriage, Careen put her arms around Beth, saying, "Please don't let anything happen to you, Cousin. You're all I've got in the world now. You and—" She broke off suddenly.

Following what she supposed was the thought Careen had not expressed, Beth reminded her, "You are all I have as well, dear. But you still have your stepfather. He cares a great deal about you."

Careen laughed. It was a short sound, almost a sob,

and startled Beth, who wondered if she was becoming hysterical. It would not be surprising, in the circumstances. So much had happened in the last few months since her mother's death.

"Grandma could have been murdered for several reasons. It might have been because she knew something about him, or about his past."

With this revelation that Careen could suspect Nicholas Cormeer of murdering Lady Hagar, Beth realized that she herself knew him to be innocent. Part of her own fear disappeared with that knowledge. The man she had come to know and love could not possibly commit such a monstrous crime. There was a special mystery about Lady Hagar's suspicion of Nicholas, and the thing that she had said against him the last time anyone saw her alive. The old lady had been wrong. That was all.

"Careen, you are very young. I know you have suffered many losses, and I am so very sorry. You know that. But your stepfather is a good man who has also suffered greatly. He had no reason in the world to murder your grandmother, and you must not believe such a vile thing."

Careen mumbled something, then, as Beth did not understand, she repeated while they climbed the tower steps, this time in appallingly loud, ringing tones, "That old black travel cape he wore when he arrived. He used it to—to wrap her in it. I saw it tonight when he and the captain were taking her body out of that grave."

"No!" Beth whispered, horrified. "That can't be true! Besides, there must be hundreds of capes like that in such a rainy climate."

Opposite the door of Beth's room, Careen stopped. Her dark eyes looked savage.

"But there is only one in Saltbridge with a piece of the hem torn and mended in a triangle shape. I saw that the first day. And, Beth, I never did see Grandmama again after he visited her room."

Beth was frantic. "I don't believe it! Careen, how can you say such a thing about a man who has been good to you? Someone who cares for you?"

Careen's face twisted with the pain of her own belief in this terrible thing. "Cousin, wasn't this done by someone who cared for me? Someone who knew that when Grandmama was dead Saltbridge Tower would be mine? And you were attacked for the same reason. *To give me your estate!*"

"Who told you all this? The morning after I had been given that drug, you didn't even believe it was deliberate. Who has been talking to you?"

She was evasive at once. Beth sensed it even though Careen shrugged and started up the steps to her own room, leaving behind her the flat statement, "I can think for myself. I'm not entirely stupid." Then, as Beth tried to think of something that would turn her from this horrible suspicion, Careen leaned over the balustrade. "Cousin, do be careful. Don't open your door unless several of us are here. Not, at least, until it's settled."

"Nothing is settled, Careen. A dozen people might have had access to Nicholas' travel cape. Careen?"

The girl hurried on. By the time she reached her floor she was running. As Beth heard the door slam and the bolt thrown, she had a disconsolate feeling that Careen wanted to weep alone.

She felt much inclined to do the same thing when she was locked into her own room, the damp, depressing place which made her think incessantly of Hagar

Faversham, who had been taken out of her room across the hall and murdered.

Dorothy came by shortly afterward with warm water for washing, and Beth, whose hands were extraordinarily cold, found the water as comforting as the carefully wrapped hot bricks in her great bed.

"Has Mrs. Quinn arrived?" Beth asked as Dorothy obligingly offered to brush her hair.

"Yes, mum. Just now. She said that major man was coming soon, along of the officer from the lord lieutenant's offices. And, I believe, Master Nicholas. Very odd-like."

Beth cut off speculation as quickly as possible.

"Yes. I am aware of it. They wish to look through . . . through Lady Hagar's bedchamber and perhaps other parts of the building."

"Very odd-like," Dorothy repeated, meeting Beth's eyes in the mirror. Getting no response she remarked in martyred tones that she would remain up if necessary until the gentlemen had arrived. Beth assured her that if she was wanted she would be called, and Dorothy finished Beth's hair with a snap and a quick, over-all brushstroke, and left. Beth was sorry afterward. Perhaps the girl had been overworked. It was awkward to note these things in another woman's house. At home Beth knew each of the servants by name and duties. She was able to give orders, to listen to complaints, and act on them. Until the discovery of Lady Hagar tonight, she had not felt that she had the right to give orders, even when she did so. Saltbridge Tower was the property of Lady Hagar. But that was over now. Even tonight the tower and lands belonged to Careen Faversham.

If I were to die, she thought, and perhaps if Nicholas Cormeer were found guilty of murder and hanged, how very rich Careen might be!

She did not know that Nicholas would leave his estate to Careen, but he had certainly given indications of doing so. Still, she closed her mind to this new suspicion as she had when Careen gave her reasons for thinking Nicholas was guilty.

She had undressed and prepared for bed partly because the maid had come in as usual and led her through the ritual, but she was not sleepy and sat in the one comfortable chair the room afforded, trying to reason out the events of the evening, and indeed, of the past months at Saltbridge. It was only a theory but she felt that Molly Wells's death served some purpose, that her "accident" had occurred too close to the burial place of Hagar Faversham to be one of Captain Macondrie's coincidences. Probably the same hand that struck down Molly Wells had murdered Lady Hagar, and that certainly eliminated Nicholas Cormeer.

Whose hand?

As she curled up on the chair to keep her feet warm, she ticked off the names of those with possible motive, beginning with Kevin Wells and Shelagh Quinn. Perhaps Kevin and his wife had quarreled over his attentions to Careen. Perhaps Mrs. Quinn wanted to marry Kevin. And Careen? No. Some villager with a long-standing grudge had done it. One of the gypsies, or all of them. But why?

Her thoughts went around and around until confusion blurred these painful suspicions and she closed her eyes.

She came back to consciousness abruptly when she heard heavy, booted footsteps in the passage outside. She unscrambled her body from the chair where one foot, tucked under her, had gone to sleep, and hurried to the door, listening. Almost immediately she made out Shelagh Quinn's voice, directing the men:

"Her Ladyship occupied this chamber, gentlemen." Major Wells said something indistinct and she went on, "Yes, sir. Mr. Cormeer's room is just beyond. You do not object if the gentlemen examine your room, sir?" That must be directed to Nicholas. "Dorothy and I have laid back the coverlets of the various bedrooms and put in hot bricks, but otherwise everything is as it usually appears when the beds are made up."

The hum of voices receded into Lady Hagar's room, but by this time Beth was wide awake, shaking with the cold and her anxiety. She snatched the simplest of her day gowns out of the armoire along with a petticoat and shift. Then she poured what remained of the water from the big pitcher and washed rapidly, finding the icy slap of water in the face sufficiently calming. She had just finished dressing when the men came out of Lady Hagar's room, and Mrs. Quinn led them away so that Beth could not hear them. She unbolted the door and looked out.

"And don't forget," the major put in. "Half a dozen villagers remember that cloak around Her Ladyship as having belonged to Cormeer."

No one paid any attention to Beth except Nicholas. He had stepped back so that the others might enter his room, and he looked around at her now, with a smile meant to be reassuring, but it merely reminded her of how much she loved him, how much she felt that circumstances seemed to close around him as if fate itself were determined to test him to the utmost. She touched her lips with her fingers and hoped he would understand this symbol of her love and support.

She stayed in the doorway, watching. Soon they

would come out apologizing to Nicholas and go elsewhere. Meanwhile there was the long, harrowing wait.
After some banging of armoire doors and cabinet
drawers, Mrs. Quinn's voice became audible: "Dorothy, turn back the mattress on the bed behind you. . . ."
There were sounds again, low comments, and the major's sharp question:

"What is that at the other end? No. You, girl—
Dorothy—whatever your name is—something white.
Paper, isn't it?"

"A letter, I'd say, sir."

There was a long pause, Perhaps they were all reading the letter. Beth moved away from her room toward the end of the little hall where the others were
gathered. For the first time Nicholas showed what
must have been a deep, pent-up anger at this invasion
of his own property.

"That happens to be a letter from Lady Faversham
to me, written after I informed her of my wife's
death. I used it as an introduction to the lady when I
arrived and she kept the letter. I assure you I do not
save Lady Faversham's correspondence beneath my
pillow."

"Or your mattress?" the major demanded, his voice
like the angry bark of a dog.

Mrs. Quinn put in, "Excuse me, gentlemen. I do not
see the point of the discovery." She, too, had evidently
been reading the letter which Captain Macondrie held
open in his hand.

Beth could see Dorothy on tiptoe peering at the paper.

"What's them little squiggly marks, sir?"

All heads at once bent over the letter. By this time
Beth was near enough so that Captain Macondrie offered her the letter.

"Can you see what you make of this, Beth?"

She read the letter, which said no more than she had expected it might and certainly nothing to incriminate Nicholas:

> My dear Mr. Cormeer,
>
> You express yourself very coolly in the business of my daughter-in-law's death at sea, but I daresay you have your reasons.
>
> Do not be concerned about affairs here at Saltbridge. The longer I live the more I find admirable qualities in my beloved granddaughter that are totally dissimilar to those of her mother and are, in fact, more like those ascribed—in my younger years—to me.
>
> Should you wish to address a note to your stepdaughter who has now lost mother and father and has no fortune to bless her, I suggest you write care of the Ballyglen Inn where there is always one of the local villagers or gentry who will oblige by carrying the letter to the tower. Otherwise, there are those who are not acquainted with the simple superscription of Saltbridge Tower, Galway.
>
> I wish you better luck with the next Mrs. Cormeer. Choose more carefully this time.
>
> Hagar Faversham

Beth had a dreadful desire to laugh. Not only had Lady Hagar hinted that Careen would need someone's fortune, but had been brutally frank about the dead Arabella and even advised this new widower on his choice of a second wife. It was exactly what one would expect of the indomitable old lady. Beth looked up. Everyone seemed to be watching her with suspended breath.

"I don't in the least see what this has to say to anything. Even if Mr. Cormeer had put it beneath his mattress, I see no harm in that."

Careen had come into the room in her night rail and barefooted. She looked flushed, her lovely eyes blurred as if she had been crying. She had read the letter over Beth's shoulder. "Let me see it."

Beth gave it to her. Shelagh Quinn said calmly, "Miss Careen, would you please notice the peculiar little marks of the pen below certain words? Squiggly marks, as Dorothy calls them."

Nicholas looked grim and sardonic. "There seems to be a general desire to make me some kind of monster. I am aware that my old storm cape was used to wrap Lady Faversham, but it must be obvious to you, Captain, that I would hardly use my own clothing if I had murdered her. As for this letter, I don't pretend to know how it was returned to my room. It was in Her Ladyship's possession. She took it from me when I met her. I haven't seen it since."

The captain turned to Major Wells and Mrs. Quinn. "I confess I must agree with Mr. Cormeer. I see nothing incriminating in the letter."

They were all startled by Careen's cry. "But don't you see? Most of the words in this letter that have marks under them were in the letter Grandmama wrote from Ballyglen."

Beth interrupted, "But she was never in Ballyglen, was she? So how could she have written that note to me? I mean—" Vaguely, she began to understand.

Careen said, "I'll show you," and rushed out of the room.

Most of them must have guessed what she would

bring down to them, the brief note delivered by Major Wells to Beth the day she and Mrs. Quinn were moving furniture.

"I fail to see how another letter from Lady Faversham has any more bearing on the matter."

Major Wells and Mrs. Quinn looked at each other. He appeared to be startled at an idea that had just occurred to him, but Beth was certain Shelagh Quinn had guessed the connection the first time she glanced at the letter.

Careen came running down the steps and into the room. She held a paper in either hand. She cried, "Look at them. Nearly every word the same. The words in the Ballyglen note were copied from the writing in Grandmama's letter to Nicholas." She thrust them into Captain Macondrie's hand.

Everyone except Nicholas closed in upon the captain, who read the short note presumably written by Lady Hagar in Ballyglen. Immediately, he saw the proofs. "Almost every word in the note does appear in Lady Faversham's letter to Cormeer, and as Miss Careen says, it seems to have been copied directly from this longer letter. Clearly, it was intended to fool someone like Miss Careen who knew her grandmother's hand better than the rest of you."

The major said, "Then that explains why he saved the original letter. In case he might need to copy Lady Faversham's hand again."

Beth might have ignored this, but the change in Captain Macondrie's manner seemed ominous to her. He had put the two letters into an inside pocket of his cloak and turned to Nicholas, who looked a trifle pale, though there was an angry twist to his mouth.

"Nicholas Cormeer, I hope it will not be necessary for Major Wells or myself to resort to force. I would like you to return to the offices of the lord lieutenant with me."

"This is preposterous!" Beth exclaimed. "Anyone in Ireland might have written the note, or placed that letter in Mr. Cormeer's room, or wrapped Lady Hagar's body in his old cape."

Captain Macondrie, trying to behave well in an awkward situation, ignored her. To Nicholas he merely said, "Well, sir?"

Nicholas smiled his contempt of this change in the captain's manner. "Unlike you gallant soldiers, I do not threaten to create a scene in this house. I see I had better reserve my defense for the lord lieutenant."

Captain Macondrie, looking relieved, unobtrusively took his hand off the pommel of his sword.

"Thank you, sir. Shall we leave now?"

Nicholas started to button his greatcoat. He paid no attention to any of the others in the room but looked only at Beth. She had never loved him so much. Without taking his eyes off her, he said quietly, "May I speak to Miss Milford? Alone."

Kevin Wells bestirred himself to protest, but Careen interceded suddenly, "Please let them. Perhaps he will tell her why he—did it."

"Aren't you afraid for your cousin's life?" Kevin Wells demanded. "If you aren't, I am."

Everyone waited for the girl's reply. She stared at Nicholas, blinked, and rubbed tears away impatiently. "No. He wouldn't. Not Beth. Never Beth. I think I must always have known that."

In all this time Beth could not speak. She had always thought heartbreak was a word used by players on the stage at Covent Garden, but now the pain she felt was beyond anything she had ever known, a physical thing that gripped her throat so that when Captain Macondrie ushered the others out into the passage and closed the door, leaving them alone, she could not even speak his name.

He guessed the depth of her mood and with a whimsical little smile held out his arms. She went into them and was held tightly, painfully to his body. When he kissed her, she clung to him, sensing that this passion between them was a poignant attempt to preserve the moment in their memory. Afterward, with her cheek against his, he murmured softly, "It will all be over once I've convinced His Lordship. I am known in London. Australian affairs are still talked about in England, you know."

"But if they don't take the matter to London! Nicholas, if they decide here in Ireland—"

He laughed. "Well, then, the matter will be settled overnight."

"Don't!"

He put her away from him, still holding her, and talked to her very sensibly, as if she were Careen's age. "My darling girl, I want you to listen to me. I am forty years old. I cannot live forever. I have rewritten my will since knowing you. I want my estate to go to you to administer for Careen. I owe it to her because—in a sense—I let her mother die."

"Arabella drowned." If there was worse, she did not want to know it.

He shook her gently. "What a goose you are! I believe you actually think I murdered her, and you are willing to love me in spite of it all. My darling! You are one in a million females!"

"Then, when this awful business is over, you will see that I would make you a good wife. Oh, Nicholas, I have lived on battlefields and slept in haystacks and consorted with the worst ruffians in two armies. So—"

His laugh was warm and ineffably dear to her. "So you and I would suit to perfection. Beth, I won't run from you. If you are willing to sacrifice yourself, I must be the man who claims you. No more majors and captains for my girl." He kissed her hair with a light touch, and looking over her head, seemed to see painful memories grow vague and disappear.

"I believed you were another Arabella! What a fool I was! She ran away from me, you know. I'd made a pretty settlement on her. Now she had enough money to return to this ineligible lover, whoever he was. I never knew. I followed her on board. We quarreled. There was a bit of shouting back and forth. I stormed out and she bolted her cabin door. She had been drinking a bit. No more than Madeira, but when we went aground that night and I tried to get to her, she had barricaded the door. She must have been asleep, perhaps with the help of the Madeira. When I called to her she was sleepy, sounded vague and wouldn't let me in."

Beth closed her eyes. Poor, stupid, greedy Arabella!

"I got one of the mates. We tried to break open the door. We had very nearly succeeded when the ship broached to. It was all darkness and confusion, and when I swam up and filled my lungs with night air, there was nothing around me but debris. She drowned in that barricaded cabin. Poor thing! If I hadn't followed her aboard and quarreled with her, she would have been able to escape."

Beth held him closer. "It wasn't your fault. That is nonsense. But I will take care of Careen until you return."

"The worst of it is, the old lady's real murderer is still free. I don't want you and Careen to open your doors to anyone except each other and the servants you trust. By morning, I hope to be at Ballyglen and persuade His Lordship that you are in danger. Meanwhile, trust no one."

"I can't stay here. I am going to pack and follow you as soon as I can get Careen to go with me. General Milford's name ought to carry some little weight if they try to condemn you out of hand."

"No! It may not be safe on the road."

With his usual good manners Captain Macondrie rapped on the door. "Ready, Cormeer?" He followed this with his entrance.

It seemed to Beth that dozens of eyes stared at them from the doorway. She withdrew from Nicholas' arms. He kissed her hand with exquisite politeness and went out. He did not look back.

She heard Dorothy remark to Shelagh Quinn, "Poor creature! Miss Milford looks as if there'd be no point to life without him. I hope she don't do anything foolish. I worked once for a lady whose son blew his brains out when his mistress was took off for stealing or some such thing."

"Hush! Don't chatter so," Mrs. Quinn ordered her as they went after the three men.

Roused to action, Beth ran to the door and then to the steps, but they had reached the ground floor and were on their way to the courtyard. She found Careen sitting on the top step crying, and said, "Hurry! We've no time to lose. We've got to get to Ballyglen and speak for him."

"No," Careen managed to say between sniffs while she searched for a handkerchief. "It was all just as he said it would be. That Nicholas Cormeer seemed so nice, but he's turned out just as he said."

"*As who said?*"

Careen looked up at her, gathering her wits. "I

mean, as Nicholas said. I wasn't to like him because he'd been a convict and all. He said he'd never like anyone but you. Not that it matters now. I never was in love with him. Not after seeing Sylvano. But I just meant—I meant Nicholas turned out the way he said he was."

Did she mean that? Beth tried to think back, to recall every word Careen had said. It seemed to her that there was much more to it, yet she could not make the girl talk. She felt like boxing her ears. Instead, she said, "You will have to come with me by morning, so make up your mind to it. Do you want to sleep in my room tonight? We should stay together."

"No. I'll bolt my door. And, Beth, you bolt yours. That's the important thing." Then she scrambled to her feet and rushed up the steps to her own room.

Beth stood there a minute or two, wondering what to do next, but of one thing she was certain. She did not feel safe in this passage, nor with the people in this house. She went into her room and bolted the door. Then she sat down on the bed and tried to think what was best to do, how to persuade Careen to go with her.

What had Careen really meant? Who had turned out just as *he* said?

CHAPTER EIGHTEEN

The idea of Arabella's lover lingered with Beth. Arabella had not said she was returning to Saltbridge, and there was no clear reason why her lover should be in this small, solitary district where every villager knew everyone else; yet the murder of Lady Hagar had occurred here, the attacks on Beth herself, and what was virtually an attempt to kill Nicholas Cormeer by legal means.

But to what purpose? Except for Careen, no one benefited, and Beth refused to speculate on the girl's guilt. Careen would never have struck down her grandmother, no matter how great the financial motive. Nor was Hagar Faversham's estate sufficient motive.

Arabella's lover. . . . Her lover. . . .

Major Wells? It seemed ludicrous, yet his wife had died—or been murdered—at a time most convenient to bring him together with Arabella.

"No. It isn't possible. There isn't a man in Saltbridge who could have been Arabella's lover, someone whom she wasn't permitted to marry when they were young. . . . For what reason?"

But her first duty, in spite of Nicholas' insistence, would be to persuade Careen to make the journey with her and speak for Nicholas. If not, then she must go alone, but she was determined to use all the influence of her father's name and reputation to get the case removed to London.

Someone scratched on the door, the sound bringing back the warnings of both Nicholas and Careen. She called out, "Yes? What do you want?"

Dorothy asked plaintively, "You still awake, mum?"

"That would be evident. Did you want something?"

"Mum, that Quinn female says I'm to sleep in carriage house, but that's so far from here. And it's all dark now."

Poor soul! Beth understood her problem very well after her recent experience in the courtyard at night. "You may sleep in Lady Hagar's room the rest of the night, if you wish."

Dorothy moaned. "Oh, no, mum. Me sleep in a dead person's room? Not me! But if you could lend me an extra candle, or maybe let me take the one from the newel post below?"

"I had better give you one of these. Heaven knows we don't want the tower stairs in darkness." She unbolted the door. The girl ventured in hesitantly while Beth looked around the passage and then over the balustrade. Shadows remained immobile. There were no untoward sounds. The fog had evidently kept out the usual wind and the house was very still. She came back into her room.

"I almost wish the wind would blow," she remarked, obviously to herself, since Dorothy shivered at the mere thought.

The girl was busy trying to twist one of the candles out of the candelabrum on the reading stand where Beth left her toilet articles. Beth saw that the girl's nervous hands would not complete the task without breaking the candle. She crossed the room to help her and saw an expression of great animation on the girl's usually colorless face. She wondered what had aroused this uncharacteristic excitement. At all events it was flattering to the girl's looks. She suddenly presented herself as a pretty woman. So suddenly, so unexpectedly, that Beth was chilled by a foreboding.

"You may take the entire candlestick. You had better hurry. It's quite late."

Dorothy made a demure little bob of a curtsy.

"Thank you, mum. Will that be all, mum? You wouldn't like me to brush your hair to make you sleep better?"

"No. Good night." She suspected Dorothy was dawdling. Not that she blamed the girl. It would not be pleasant walking through the courtyard alone at this hour. "Hadn't you better sleep in the tower tonight, Dorothy? There are other rooms. The little back parlor behind the great hall, for example. Someone slept in that room the night before I arrived."

She was dumbfounded to see that the girl smiled at this, a sly, twisted grimace. "You were very interested in that uninvited guest, weren't you, Miss Milford?"

The change in her voice, her language, warned Beth. She knew now she was dealing with an enemy, this wretched little, conniving creature whom she could easily best if it came to a battle royal. Was it possible the girl had a weapon?

Beth pretended to ignore the sly challenge, the betrayal of the different woman behind the bland facade.

"Good night, Dorothy."

"Good night, Dorothy. Do this, Dorothy. Do that, Dorothy. Snap, snap, snap! I've nearly broke my back making all those dutiful little curtsies to you. But I thought of this minute, and it made it all worthwhile."

Beth braced herself. She was not stupid enough to imagine the girl would so completely betray her real self if she hadn't something besides her scrawny arms to count upon. A knife, probably. Like that woman long ago in Spain who was mistress to a French general and tried to oblige his army by stabbing Beth and Ian Macondrie. Ian was surprised and received a nasty stab wound in the hand, but Beth had come up behind the woman, brought her knee hard into the woman's spine, and then slammed her against the wooden slats of the mule's stall.

Dorothy had certainly accumulated some grudges against Beth. From the capacious pocket of her gray, homespun skirt, she drew out a small gun in her right hand.

"Quite in the mode," Beth remarked coolly. "A derringer. And the handle is expensive. Pearl? Not your property, of course. Give over, girl! I've met your kind before."

The girl's face contorted. "Think you're a mighty fine toff don't you? Well, we'll see how you like having that elegant face shot away."

"You really are an unpleasant little creature." Beth moved toward her, a reaction the girl had obviously not expected.

She cried, "Suicide you'll be, my fine mistress! Didn't I say so when they were all trooping sadly away? 'She'll kill herself,' I said. 'She's that unhappy.'"

"You had better say poor little Dorothy!" Beth suited action to her taunt, throwing herself hard against the girl's left shoulder at the same time that she kicked the girl's legs. Dorothy went down in a groaning heap. The gun spun away, dropping harmlessly before the open door.

Beth got her by the throat, shook her. "Why have you done this? Why? What is this family to you?" She was frantic to find out what could be used to save Nicholas.

"N-nothing to me. But there—there'll be money . . . promised." Her once blank face was scarlet, her eyes looking bulbous under Beth's violent pressure. Beth thought . . . In another instant I'll know the truth . . . and it will save him. . . .

"You murdered Lady Hagar and O'Beirne. You tried to murder me that first night."

"No. No. Not me. Him. Smothered the old lady, and then O'Beirne saw us burying . . . But that first night I only gave you laudanum so you wouldn't find out."

"Find out what?"

"That he—slept downstairs that night."

"Who?"

Beth became conscious of a metallic, jingling sound on the stone steps. She could not identify the sound, but it was ominous. She felt her victim revive under her hands and begin to struggle again. She dared not let the girl go, but she needed that little pistol lying in the doorway. With one hand she stuffed the girl's sash into her mouth, trying to force it between her teeth. Dorothy was still wriggling and making guttural sounds when Beth swung away from her and sprawled full length, reaching for the little pistol.

Her groping fingers touched the gun, sent it just out of reach. She was getting to her knees to make another, longer plunge for it when the doorway seemed suddenly filled with glittering bangles that caught the light and flashed with a blinding sunlight. Beth looked up. So the gypsy Tzigana was in this with Dorothy!

The creature seemed enormous in all those bangles, the heavy hem of beads, the huge, looped earbobs, the layers of bead strings, and the bandeau of coppery circlets over the coarse black hair. But then, from the beginning she had feared Tzigana.

The gypsy's sandal came down hard upon the little gun. There was no hope from that weapon. Tzigana's big, toothy grin flashed in the dark face. Beth got to her feet just as the gypsy slammed the door, making Beth a prisoner between Tzigana and Dorothy. The latter fumbled with the gag, clawed, and spat it out, mumbling.

"Jude! Have done! She's tricky. We can't afford to wait."

"Jude?" Beth echoed, trying to play for time.

As the tall gypsy was illuminated by the candle flare from the candelabrum, Beth stared at the woman's face. . . . That sensual large mouth and powerful nose, the heavy cords in the neck, all might possibly have been those features of a strong peasant woman; yet she knew now what she should have suspected at their first encounter outside Saltbridge Tower. The woman's strength and height had suggested that she was, in fact, a male. Much easier to make a female disguise out of all the gewgaws of his gypsy forebears, for he certainly had some Romany blood.

"No!" Dorothy put in hoarsely. "End it. You can't trust the witch."

He waved one hand, lean and sinewy, that glistened with gaudy trinkets. "The lady has the right to know at least that, thanks to us, Careen will have both the lady's money and the convict's fortune. And Careen will be kind and generous to her dear father. Hasn't she permitted him to visit her here and even, when the weather was bad, to sleep down in her very own back parlor?"

"Careen's father! You?"

"Jude Duvayne. My Christian name, though my sympathies are with my mother's people. I am Romany-born. We met in Dublin, Arabella and I, when she was shopping for a trousseau. Marrying that poor stick of a fellow, Faversham. We fell in love. We would have married but Arabella's parents would have none of that. Then the poor girl got in the family way. Nothing for it but to marry Faversham. But we swore to be together someday, when she had the money for us. Matter of fact, she told me that in the last letter she sent me, from the Antipodes when she said she was leaving that convict!"

Dorothy whined, "You always talk about your horrible Arabella. It's me that helped you here."

"You and my little girl believed in me. That's true. Which is more than I can say of Her Precious Ladyship, Hagar Faversham. She always suspected Arabella had someone in Dublin. But she would have been suspicious of any male. When Arabella wrote me from Australia, I decided to make my little Careen aware of me. So Tzigana appeared. Much easier to explain a gypsy female to Her Ladyship."

"And me. I helped you, don't you be forgetting."

The gypsy ignored the girl. "The loyalty of my Careen! I'll wager I could tell her what we do here tonight, and she'd not take it amiss. Now, there's a female! And my own flesh! I'll not forget that soon. Arabella bequeathed her to me, in a manner of speaking. How glad my Careen was when she discovered Nick Cormeer was guilty! Anything to protect her old father." He stooped and picked up the derringer as Beth moved toward him. "Now, ma'am, you'll have done with this unpleasant business. We don't want any mess. No bruises on you, so don't make trouble."

Someone—was it that evil little Dorothy?—had mentioned the word "suicide", so it was natural that she and the monstrous Tzigana, Jude Duvayne, would not want her to be found with a bruised body. That might make the entire idea of suicide a lie. With her thoughts working more rapidly than ever, Beth decided this was her one weapon. This and the scream to arouse Careen or anyone else in the house.

She moved toward the door. The gypsy laughed. She eluded his hand as he called, "A game one, we have here."

"I told you so. Get it done, Jude!"

Beth feinted a move toward him. He reached for her. She brought up sharp against the door and sent scream after scream tearing from her throat. The gypsy belatedly understood Dorothy's warning. Beth ducked but not quickly enough to avoid the heel of his hand, which cut across her forehead, hurtling her away. Dazed, she tried to scream again as she fell, but the sounds came out garbled, breathless.

She must have been unconscious for a minute or two, and though she kept her eyes closed, when her senses returned she was enraged when she found she had been lifted and thrown upon the big, ancient bed. Here Dorothy tried to arrange her body and limbs, clearly with some idea of presenting an artistic suicide.

"The bullet must come from the right," she directed. "She is right-handed. Against the temple. It will be quicker."

"A pity," Jude Duvayne said, crossing below the foot of the bed to reach the right side. Beth watched beneath her lashes, saw that only Dorothy stood be-

tween her and the passage. There was but one bullet
in the derringer, and such guns were notoriously inac-
curate unless, as Dorothy had suggested, they were
touching their target.

No time like the present moment! Beth threw herself off the left side of the bed, against Dorothy, with
the door and her safety across the room.

Everything happened then. The door burst open.
Careen stood there with her hands behind her like a
small child. Her usually narrow eyes were wide with
the horror of what she saw.

"Father! No! It was Nicholas. Not you. You said it
was Nicholas . . ."

Beth felt her arm seized so hard it was nearly
wrenched out of its socket. The gypsy had come back
around the bed and pulled her against his body.

"Be quiet, sweetheart. Careen, you know it is all for
you, my little girl. Run along to bed now, and when
morning comes, you'll be the richest female in Ireland."

Careen swallowed repeatedly, trying to get the
words out. "I thought it was Nicholas. You said so.
But you, then it was you who left the letter in his
room! You killed Grandmama and wrapped her body
in his cape. . . . Father, why? Why?"

"For you, sweetheart. To make my little girl happy.
You wanted to be rich. You wanted to marry that idiot
major. But there was his wife in the way. I thought if
there was no wife, you'd marry him and have his estate." He must have guessed that his monstrous crimes
had repulsed his child. His voice took on a smooth,
wheedling charm. "My little girl, it was all for you."

Careen ignored this. She said, "Let her go, Papa.
Beth, can you walk?"

"Certainly." All the same, when Beth tried to move

she felt the cold butt of the little pistol pressed against her temple.

"Papa!" A little pause. Careen was acting very unlike herself. Stiff, tense, yet she remained with both arms behind her in little-girl fashion. Her mouth was not a child's mouth. It was set, pale and hard. It gave her whole face an almost frightening maturity.

"You are so clever, Papa. No wonder you wouldn't let me tell anyone about you. But if Cousin Beth is to die, it had better look natural. Dorothy, I never knew you were part of Father's plans. If you are to profit also, you had best see that Beth is in that bed. The poor suicide you were babbling about."

Jude Duvayne laughed. He was obviously relieved.

"There's my clever little daughter. And you will be generous. You will remember that your old father gave you everything. You are right. Your cousin should be found lying stiff and proper in her bed."

The little derringer dropped away from Beth's temple. With his free hand he started to maneuver Beth back onto the bed with Dorothy's help. Beth gambled upon her reading of Careen's face and her stance. She did not struggle. Seconds later she knew she had been right. Careen's right arm moved, came into sight. She pointed a musket over Beth's head at the large target of Jude Duvayne.

"Papa, please don't make me do it. . . ."

Dorothy screamed. The gypsy looked up, caught his breath.

"You damned little ingrate! It is all for you."

He raised the derringer again toward Beth. There was a deafening noise. The room was filled with powder and Dorothy's screams. As for Jude Duvayne, the musket ball carried him stumbling back against the wall. His eyes remained open, glazed, his mouth slack, but he was dead before he collapsed upon the floor in a mass of blood-spattered trinkets, beads, gaudy skirts, and bronzed feet and ankles.

The musket dropped from Careen's nerveless fingers.

Careen stood in the doorway looking at her empty fingers, her vision of them blinded by tears.

"Father . . . Father . . . I didn't mean it."

CHAPTER NINETEEN

Careen cried, "He loved me. He did. It was for me he did all those terrible things."

"Yes, dear," Beth lied, soothing her as best she could. "Don't think of it now."

Beth had closed the door, leaving Dorothy disheveled and sobbing over the dead Jude Duvayne, but this cold, dark passage was no place to console Careen, who was shivering in the thin ball gown she had worn to Wells Hall a few hours previous. Had that been this same night, or aeons ago?

Careen whispered, "But how could he kill Grandmama? And you. Oh, Beth, if you had died, there'd be nobody at all who cared."

"Yes, there would. A man who came all the way from the Antipodes to take care of you. He could be the father you never really knew."

Shelagh Quinn, who had just come in from the courtyard, called up the steps to them. "Miss Milford, is it you up there? The young gypsy, Sylvano, asks to see you. It is very late, I told him. If you wish me to call for assistance while you speak to him . . ."

Careen, who had her arm around Beth, would not let her go far. "I'm certain he knows nothing about what my—what Jude Duvayne did. Sylvano wouldn't hurt anyone." She tightened her nervous hold on Beth.

"But if anyone tries, well, I'd do it again! I'd take Grandmama's pistol from behind the clothes in her armoire and do it all again. Oh, Beth. It was awful— what I did."

"I know, dear, but it was almost an accident. He frightened you into squeezing the trigger back." She raised her voice. "Mrs. Quinn, if the boy is able to climb the steps— And, Mrs. Quinn, send the new coachman and the stableboy with some hemp to bind a prisoner. There is also a dead man here."

Just as Beth had expected, the incredible Shelagh asked no questions, said calmly, "Yes, ma'am," and a minute later the young gypsy boy was climbing the steps. He grimaced and was not at his lively best. Beth and Careen looked at each other, and with a common instinct, separated and went down a few steps to help him.

"Miss Careen," he managed to get out, breathless from what must have been a great deal of painful strain, "my mother says you must lock all your doors. Tzigana is coming here. She says he is dangerous. I am to tell you that he is a half gentile, half Romany, named Jude."

"Yes, we know," Beth put in.

"He paid to travel with our wagon, mistress, so he could see his daughter, Miss Careen. He was afraid Lady Hagar would not let him see her if she knew who he really was. But Mother says now he must be mad. He wants to kill Mistress Milford here. He says we will all be rich if he does this. But I could not let him. My mother, she says it is enough. He must be stopped. She believes he may have killed others as well."

"Thank you, Sylvano," Beth said. "You must sit down. You can scarcely stand."

Careen called, "Shelagh, will you bring a drop of poteen? It will warm him." Forgetting the horror in Beth's room, the girl knelt beside Sylvano as he dropped gratefully to the top step and leaned back against the wall. "Poor Sylvano. You have been very brave. Hasn't he, Beth?"

"Very brave, indeed. Sylvano, where are your parents now?"

"They rode off to fetch up the captain from the lord lieutenant's office. He rode away not an hour since with two other gentlemen. Mother said you would need them all here to protect you."

"Thank God!" Beth whispered, more to herself than to the boy and girl with her. Thinking of Nicholas she said, "He is out of danger at last."

Now that Careen found something constructive and pleasant to do in caring for the kindly young Sylvano, Beth felt herself undergoing a reaction of her own, a kind of palsy that only stopped when she found it necessary to instruct the coachman, the eager young stableboy, and Mrs. Quinn, who came up with them to ask if she might be of assistance.

Beth was happy to inform her, "Yes, Mrs. Quinn, it seems that Mr. Cormeer was completely innocent. Lady Hagar was murdered by one of the tinkers, a man masquerading as the gypsy, Tzigana."

"I see. Major Wells will be relieved to know that his suspicions were unfounded."

Beth said sharply, "Major Wells's conscience is of no interest to me. Will you please have the body of the dead man in my room covered? But do not remove it. And have the servingwoman's hands bound. Her feet also if she gives any trouble."

The males did their task with the aid of Mrs. Quinn. Dorothy squirmed, cried out, and begged everyone to believe she had been forced by Jude Duvayne to help carry away Lady Hagar's body. "And Jude knocked O'Beirne in the head. The silly old fool had followed us clear to the place in the woods where we were burying Her Ladyship. O'Beirne was a surly fellow at best, believe me. . . . We had to kill him. You must believe. There was no other choice. We thought it would confuse things if Lady Hagar was in Ballyglen for so long. Then, when no one could find her, it would be too late to— Well, it would seem that dreadful convict man had done it if we worked the evidence right. . . . Miss Milford, you know he made me—"

Beth turned away. There must be some sympathy for the woman, but she could find none in herself at this moment.

Beth went down to join Sylvano and Careen who had helped the boy to his now familiar couch in the back parlor. It seemed forever before the boy suddenly sat up with his hand raised.

"I hear them, mistress. The horses' hooves. The gentlemen have come back. My mother and father are with them, maybe. Mistress, you will tell them I am here, please?"

Before he finished speaking, she was out of the room and hurrying through the courtyard. The coachman opened the big gates and Nicholas, who had dismounted while the captain and Major Wells were calling "Gateman!" started on a run toward Beth.

When she managed a short breath after their crushing embrace, she assured him that she had not died at Jude Duvayne's hands. And it was absurd but delightful that he would keep asking if she was hurt. She must look quite as disheveled as the luckless Dorothy, but she did not care.

He added, "I nearly went mad, thinking we might

be too late. The gypsy tinker and his wife told us what they had discovered about their vicious friend."

She laughed. She and Nicholas had been so alike in their reaction. "And I nearly killed Dorothy. She was Duvayne's partner. I wanted her to confess to your innocence."

By the time they reached Careen, who approached Nicholas torn by panic and tears, Beth realized how well Nicholas dealt with people, even the volatile Careen. He let her apologize for her lack of faith in him, kissed her forehead in a paternal way she could not misunderstand, and told her that everyone made mistakes in judgment and someday he would tell her about his own.

She might have cried again in explaining how her actual father had died, but Beth asked her sensibly, "Had you rather he shot me?"

Careen hugged her with frantic feeling and then ran away to "look after Sylvano," when Captain Macondrie came back with the major. It was evident to Beth that, despite that night's tragedy, Saltbridge Tower and its household were in a far better way than they had been only a few hours before when they all set out for Wells Hall. Unlike the major, Captain Macondrie had no compunctions about having suspected Nicholas of the crimes.

The tinker and his wife, Ameera, had remained with their son and Careen in the back parlor, but Captain Macondrie explained to Beth: "I am persuaded the gypsies did not know about this Jude Duvayne's crimes. They seem to have believed he was merely interested in his daughter's happiness. The woman Dorothy does not implicate them in any way."

"There is no doubt Careen was his daughter?"

"Who knows? It hardly seems likely he would have

gone to these extreme ends to get the young lady a fortune if he could not later prove his connection with her."

"He mentioned love letters from Arabella."

Nicholas agreed. "It certainly fits Arabella's behavior to me. She had loved some man since before her first marriage. There seems to have been no other, and this Duvayne's position, with no money or prospects, would have made it impossible for her to marry him."

"The woman Dorothy will be of great help," the captain put in. "Major Wells and I did our best to jot down the substance of her confession, with the help of your excellent Mrs. Quinn. We began with this Dorothy's first acquaintance of Duvayne, who met her something over a year ago on the estate and set out to win her love. Her own part in the scheme to make Cormeer guilty began when she persuaded everyone that Lady Faversham had known something against Cormeer. She seemed to think that in our eyes this would give him a motive to murder the old lady."

Beth remembered something suddenly and in a fury at herself startled everyone by crying, "Of course! What a fool I was!" They all stared at her. She explained. "I accepted Dorothy's remark so easily that I came to believe a quarrel between Nicholas and Lady Hagar had actually occurred. Now that I look back, I see. It was never anyone's word but Dorothy's. My dearest, can you forgive me?" He had reached for her hand and she raised his fingers to her cheek.

In the doorway Shelagh Quinn cleared her throat; Major Wells looked up. Apparently he understood her signal. He got up, stood stiffly before Nicholas.

"Sir, I am as responsible as that blackguard was for your difficulties with Captain Macondrie. I hope you will do me the honor of forgiving me and perhaps, someday, you will forget my ungentlemanly conduct."

The major had done his duty like a good boy, and Shelagh Quinn smiled faintly, with satisfaction. Nicholas accepted his salute and apology, "With pleasure, sir," and watched him leave the big room in Mrs. Quinn's company. Then Nicholas turned to the captain with a wry grin. "All the same, I don't suppose we shall ever be what the children call bosom bows. Unfortunately, we fell in love with the same woman, and I had the incredible luck to win her."

Captain Macondrie looked from one to the other of them. Though it was clear they wanted to be alone, he remained watching them with amusement and a fine pretense of innocence.

"Good Lord! You mean Beth? As I learned long ago when I was a mere sprat of a boy, you'll find her a rare handful. I hope you are up to it."

REMEMBER IT DOESN'T GROW ON TREES

ENERGY CONSERVATION -
IT'S YOUR CHANCE TO SAVE, AMERICA

Department of Energy, Washington, D.C.